THE BUM'S RUSH

THE BUM'S RUSH is the third novel in the Leo Waterman series. G. M. Ford lives in Seattle and is also the author of the highly acclaimed Frank Corso series.

G. M. FORD

THE BUM'S RUSH

PAN BOOKS

First published 1997 by Walker & Co.

First published in paperback 1998 by Avon Books
an imprint of HarperCollins Publishers Inc., New York, USA

First published in Great Britain 2007 by Pan Books
an imprint of Pan Macmillan Ltd
Pan Macmillan, 20 New Wharf Road, London N1 9RR
Basingstoke and Oxford
Associated companies throughout the world
www.panmacmillan.com

ISBN 978-0-330-42753-1

1 3 5 7 9 8 6 4 2

A CIP catalogue record for this book is available from
the British Library.

Typeset by IntypeLibra, London
Printed and bound in Great Britain by
Mackays of Chatham Ltd, Chatham Kent

Visit **www.panmacmillan.com** to read more about all our books
and to buy them. You will also find features, author interviews and
news of any author events, and you can sign up for e-newsletters
so that you're always first to hear about our new releases.

To Arnold Jay Abrams, the friend of a lifetime.

To rock-and-roll hearts on the

long and winding road.

Go softly, my friend.

THE BUM'S RUSH

1

IN THE LOW DARKNESS OF THE ALLEY, the sole delineation of blood from blackness was a certain vibration of line where the animal movement ended and the uneven bricks began. Ahead in the gloom, a succession of shoulders moved as a single beast, ears hot and full of blood, lips mumbling encouragement to some bizarre ballet being danced down on the rough gray stones.

George lifted a stiff hand to my elbow as we closed the distance. Twenty years on the streets had filed his instincts smooth. He knew. This was trouble. Without willing it so, I found myself stopped. George's hand fell to his side. Harold wedged himself tight between my right shoulder and the wall. Inside the circle of men, white smoke from a trash fire rose up the west wall, adding further insult to the overhead ocean of airborne waste that had been hanging low over the city for the better part of two weeks. An inversion, they called it.

"That's it, git 'er." A slurred voice rolled along the alley, oddly amplifying the silence left in its wake. I could hear it now. Under the shoe noise and the grunting. First the sporadic ticking of the fire, then, down at the bottom, a continuous, rhythmic keening, at times almost a whistle, rising insistently from the ground. I willed my legs forward, but apparently they had other plans. Before I could get a grip, Norman shouldered me aside and strode out ahead.

Arriving at the circle of men, he reached in and separated the nearest pair with enough force to create a staggering chain reaction around the entire circle. On his left, the force ricocheted the heads of two loose-necked drunks. A bottle shattered on the pavement. An emaciated guy of about thirty, his blue watchcap dislodged and rolling at his feet, stumbled to one knee, clutching his ear. On the right, the old guy in the tweed overcoat was squeezed, seed-like, out into the center of the circle where he stood blinking and chewing his gums, waiting for his numbed nerves to give him some sort of hint as to what in hell had just happened. I followed Norman through the breach.

Two figures rolled and kicked amid the damp refuse. Up close, the sound I'd heard back in the mouth of the alley was less a whine of terror and more a groan of strained resistance. Sitting astride a struggling figure, blue bandana worn pirate style, was a ragged specimen—forty going on seventy-five—his leathery face a maze of booze-etched crevices, landscaped here and there by a thin beard and mustache. He tore at the clothes of the other figure, who was scrunched into a defensive posture, one hand with a death lock on the belt line of a sagging pair of trousers, the other clawing at the dangling sleeve of a green satin jacket, torn to strings at the shoulder, revealing an oblong breast, big brown nipple slightly off center, peeking from beneath a bunched flannel shirt.

With a single lengthened stride, Norman punted the pirate back to Penzance. The ungodly force of the huge boot completely separated him from his victim, propelling him airborne express to the far side of the circle of men, where he came to rest, rocking silently on his spine, face smoothed with purple blood, bug-eyed paralyzed at the feet of a pair of Indians who seemed unable to comprehend this sudden change in tonight's entertainment schedule.

The remaining figure immediately regained her feet and tottered toward the east wall, the free hand hauling her drawers back up over her hips, one eye, visible through her hair, never leaving Norman. Instinctively, I reached to help. She backed against the wall, pulled her right fist back into her sleeve, and waited for my next move.

George stepped between us. "Leave her be, Leo," he said. "Don't be such a goddamn social worker."

"She needs—" I started.

He stepped in closer. "Yeah. She needs a lotta shit, Leo, and ain't none of it gonna come from you neither. 'Less of course you wanna take her away from all this. You gonna marry her or something?"

Over George's left shoulder, I could see that she was halfway back the way we'd come, eyes welded to us, using the wall for support.

The pirate had rolled onto his side and retched up a small pool of thick liquid that struggled to spread itself upon the dirt. The eight or nine spectators began to stagger off into the darkness.

"Ally ally infree." Norman roared from behind me. He held down the center like a ragged obelisk. Bigger even than usual. Wearing everything he owned. The better part of six-seven, his massive arms spread as if in embrace, his gnarled hands beckoning. On the street they called him Nearly Normal Norman, or sometimes just Normal. It was a joke. You only had to once look into Norman's eyes to be absolutely certain that this person was not watching the same channel as the rest of us. A couple of years back, the last time he'd earned himself a state-mandated tune-up, I'd watched six cops and a couple of paramedics fail to get him into an ambulance. The third wave of reinforcements finally tracked him down over in Hing Hay Park, where he was contentedly feeding corned-beef hash to the park's feral pigeons.

As the gathering crowd jeered, they'd cornered him in the pagoda and Tasered him six times. He'd seemed to devour the voltage like some walking storage battery, his eyes glowing ever brighter after each shot of juice. It wasn't until they'd busted the third syringe off in him that he even began to slow down. I don't care what anybody says, I still contend that if he hadn't been naked, they'd never have taken him.

The pirate, resting now on his knees and forehead, groaned piteously and again began to heave, this time dry.

Normal slid a massive arm around the nearest Indian. "They call you Little Bird, don't they?"

"Some do," the guy agreed, looking straight up at Normal.

Normal inclined his head toward the other fellow. "What's your buddy's name?" he asked.

"Na-Ke-Dan-Sto-Li," the guy answered slowly, carefully wrapping his moist mouth around each syllable.

"What's that mean?" I asked.

"Dances with vodka," the guy said.

Normal embraced the pair as they yukked it up.

George approached the old guy in the overcoat.

"Hey, Monty," he said. "Your name's Monty, ain't it?"

The old guy's eyes, thick and milky with cataracts, rolled in his head like a spooked horse. A constant marination in fortified wines had begun to tenderize the old boy. Begun to separate skin from bone, leaving the impression that the slender sinews holding the face could, at any moment, give way and allow the whole mess to slide south, circle the drain of his toothless mouth, and disappear altogether down the cosmic gullet.

"I ain't done nothin'," he said, looking around, searching for the voice. "I was just watchin'."

Harold stepped around me, pulled a wad of singles out of his pocket, and hustled over to the two younger guys, who stood stock-still, eyes frozen on Norman. George approached the old guy.

"It's me, George Paris. Remember me?"

The dazed look on his face suggested that the old guy didn't remember anything more distant than his last forty-ouncer.

"Used to live in that room across the hall from you down in the Pine Tree, back in eighty-five. You remember?"

The old guy squinted, the act nearly throwing him off balance. For the first time, a glimmer of recognition crossed his face.

"Oh," he stammered. "George, yeah, you and that other guy."

George pulled a pint of peach schnapps from his coat pocket, unscrewed the top, and handed it to the old codger.

"Right, Ralph. Ralph Batista. You remember old

Ralph? That's who we're lookin' for. We're lookin' for Ralph. You—"

The old man's face closed like a leg trap. He licked his lips and handed the pint back without taking a drink.

"Don't know nothin' about none of that," he said.

He turned to leave. A low growl from Norman stopped him cold. He turned back to George. His eyes were full of water. "Come on, man. I ain't done nothin'. I don't know nothin'. Come on."

They stood, lockjawed, staring at each other for a long moment.

"Go on, get outta here," George said finally. The guy didn't need to be told twice. He started down the alley toward the woman.

"Go the other way," I said. He did.

I stood and watched as the boys alternately bribed and threatened the rest of them. Even from a distance, it was apparent that they were getting nowhere. It had been that way all night. I checked my watch. Twelve-fifteen. A sudden wind cut through the alley, carrying the smells of fryer grease and salt water, swirling the white smoke to the walls, leaving a foul-smelling landscape of muted shadows and fog.

We'd started at noon, down under the viaduct, kicking cardboard houses, rousting sleeping drunks, passing out sandwiches, singles, and booze. We'd braced every derelict in a ten-block area. We'd been by the Gospel Mission twice. We'd worked our way through the flocks of juicers and junkies congregated in Occidental Park. We'd pulled 'em out of their warm hideyholes in parking garages and vestibules. Nada. Nobody had seen Ralph. Guys he'd known for twenty years were suddenly having trouble remembering his name. My mouth was dry and smooth like ceramic. My stomach felt like it was full of scrap metal.

The pirate had pulled himself to his feet. I could hear the breath wheeze from his wet lips as he lurched off.

George appeared at my side. "Nobody knows shit," he said.

Back in the early seventies, George's banking career had fallen victim to both merger mania and an unquenchable taste for single-malt Scotch. His grim demeanor, well-defined features, and slicked-back white hair made him look like a defrocked boxing announcer. Anyone who didn't look into his eyes or down at his mismatched shoes could quite easily mistake him for a functioning member of society.

Harold and Norman pushed their way through the oily smoke to my side. Harold shook his head sadly. Harold had, for better than twenty years, managed a shoe department for the Bon, but like many of the denizens of the district, had surfed himself into the streets on a wave of cheap booze and failed marriages. He used to be taller. Every year seemed to carve more meat from his already skeletal frame. I'd always figured his huge Adam's apple and cab-door ears would surely be the last to go, found on some Pioneer Square sidewalk, mistaken by some wino for an escaped cue ball and a couple of dried apricots.

"We've been about everywhere I can think of," I said. "Any of you guys got an idea?" This led to a prolonged round of head shaking and foot shuffling.

"Maybe he left town," said George, finally.

"Oh, bullshit," shot Harold. "Other than that time Leo took us all out in the sticks, Ralph ain't been out of Seattle in thirty-five years. You just feel guilty, that's all, so shut the fuck up."

Harold's attitude was tantamount to a peasant's rebellion. Shovels, rakes, flaming torches, the whole thing. Since Buddy Knox's death, George had always served unchallenged as leader and spokesman for this little group. To my knowledge, other than some occasional bickering when they were out of booze for a protracted period of time—say, fifteen minutes—George had never been challenged.

"Guilty," he spat. "What in hell have I got to be guilty about? I wanted to hear that kinda shit, I'd call one of my exes."

"If you hadn't thrown him out—"

"He's a fucking wet-brain. He spends his whole goddamn check and then sponges off—"

"Hey, hey," I interrupted. "This isn't getting us anywhere. Are you guys sure you never seen this guy who came by for his check?"

"I told you," George said impatiently. "Some little mulatto in a fur hat said Ralph had sent him for his pension check. I told him to piss off. Ralph wanted his check, he could hustle his ass up and get it."

Norman was stomping out the remains of the fire, using both feet, turning, dancing to his own music. "Global warming," he said when he noticed I was watching. "Average world temperature is fifty-eight degrees now. Up two degrees in twenty years."

I knew better than to disagree with him.

"I need a drink," George mumbled.

Couldn't say I disagreed with that either.

2

I WAITED FOR THE ETHIOPIAN CABDRIVER to give me even the smallest hint that he understood English. No such luck.

"Let them off at the Zoo. On Eastlake." I talked slowly, emphasizing each syllable, as if time and sincerity would most certainly overcome any pesky language barrier.

He remained focused on George, Harold, and Norman, whose synchronized swaying movements gave the impression that they were ice-skating while standing still.

"You know where that is?" I asked. Nothing, "Eastlake—" I started, louder this time.

"No," he said.

"It's easy. Just take the Lakeview exit off—"

He cut me off. "I know where the Zoo is, man. Don't get your panties in a wad." He pointed. "It's them I don't know about. I don't think I want 'em in the cab."

I handed him two tens. "Here's ten for the ride and ten for you. They'll behave. I guarantee it."

"I don't ride no bums," he protested.

"They're not bums," I said. I reached in my pocket and pulled out a business card. LEO WATERMAN INVESTIGATIONS. He held the card at arm's length, using only his fingernails.

"They're undercover," I said. "We're on a case."

George belched and began to slide under the cab. Norman jerked him upright by the collar. The air was suddenly alive with the smell of mothballs and recycled beer.

The driver squinted at me. "Hell of a disguise," he commented.

"We go to great lengths," I assured him.

He boosted himself up, looked down at George's mismatched shoes, and then back at me. "It's all in the details," I tried.

He sneered and reached for the shift lever. I waved another ten at him. "Just to the Zoo."

Before he could decide, I dropped the money in his lap, reached in, opened the rear door from the inside, and pushed the boys in.

"I'll call you guys in the morning. Don't worry. We'll find him tomorrow. Get some rest."

He slammed the cab into drive. The force of the start closed the door. I watched as the cab headed up past Pioneer Park and turned right up Cherry. The lights from the oncoming traffic silhouetted the trio in the backseat. On either side of Norman's tangled mane, a head rested on his shoulder. Male bonding.

I turned and headed back down First Avenue toward my car, which was parked under the viaduct, down by the OK Hotel. The breeze from the Sound had freshened into a serious wind, bringing with it the smells of wet newsprint, day-old fish, and diesel fuel.

First Avenue was forlorn, the square's usual glitter and rattle reduced to low-wattage bulbs over locked cash registers. Melancholy, like a nobly appointed Victorian parlor, thrashed and reeking after a fraternity party. A huge sigh escaped me as I walked. It wasn't good. We should have found Ralph by now. Harold was right. Ralph was either living within ten blocks of where I was walking, or he wasn't living at all. My stomach ached.

A Graytop cab rounded the corner of Main and started toward me. My first thought was that the Ethiopian had changed his mind and was bringing the fellas back. No; this time it was a guy with an impeccable white turban and full beard. He rolled down his window and made eye contact with me. Even across the median he caught my attention. I shook him off and kept walking.

Oriental Rug Express was in the twenty-seventh year of its going-out-of-business sale. This time they meant it. Everything must go.

I turned west down South Washington, straight

into the wind, thinking about Ralph. Stifling a shudder, I pulled my canvas jacket close at the throat as I walked.

I had my head in two places; that must have been why I missed her. One was down, watching the sidewalk, cutting the breeze; the other was stuck firmly up my ass, worrying about Ralph. She must have been trailing me. Skittering through the maze of alleys, one step ahead at all times. I never saw her until she put a hand on my arm.

I believe that had video replay been available at that moment, mankind would surely have had its first documented case of human levitation. The tape would certainly have shown me losing all terrestrial traction and gliding unpowered over to the nearest car. Future TV experts could count on years of profitable debate as to whether the tape had been doctored and, if so, whether I'd acted alone. Next thing I knew I was sliding along a fender, using my ass to feel for a break in the cars where I could tumble out into the street and run.

She stood with her hand still extended at the shoulder, her long, lank hair fanned by the wind. The green satin jacket was still mangled at the shoulder, but she'd secured her pants with a doubled piece of rough red twine. "Hey," she said.

"Hey yourself," I said between gasps.

She lowered her arm, hiding her hands in her sleeves.

"Didn't mean to scare ya."

"You didn't—" I started.

She smiled, showing fleeting crow's-feet that sailed up and away from her dark eyes. Her teeth were worn and discolored.

"Actually, you scared the crap out of me," I said.

"You're a whole lot faster than you look," she said seriously.

She was a big, long-boned woman, all knobs and elbows and angles. It was hard to guess at her age. Anywhere between thirty-five and fifty was the best I could manage at the moment. Long, dark hair, streaked with gray, parted down the middle. Big features. Eyes set wide apart beneath thick black eyebrows. She gave me a kind of amused grin that reminded me of Houdon's statue of the seated Voltaire, elderly, way past any tawdry need for redemption, smiling that thin smile of reason.

"I wanted to thank you guys," she said.

I waited, listening to the sound of my pulse still raging inside, checking her out. She wasn't carrying everything she owned, which meant she had a good secure place to flop.

"For . . . you know . . . the help back there in the alley," she went on.

"No problem."

"I was doin' okay back there, you know?" she said, shifting her weight from foot to foot. "He wasn't gettin' none. No way. I was just waitin' till he got his pants down. Then I was gonna fix him up good."

She punched her right hand out of the sleeve. What looked like the business end of an old-fashioned hat pin stuck four inches out from between the knuckles of her first and second fingers.

"I was gonna fix him good," she repeated.

I didn't have a response, so I kept my mouth shut.

"He's right, ya know," she said.

"Who's right?"

"The old guy with the white hair. George, I think they call him."

"Right about what?"

"About there bein' nothin' you can do for the likes of me."

Years of keeping the wrong company had seriously eroded my patience for street-corner philosophy. I started to leave. "Listen, I gotta—"

"Maybe I could help *you*, though," she interrupted. "You ever think of that?"

I stopped. "How's that?"

She checked the street, then took two paces backward into the shadows, lowering her voice. "They say you guys are lookin' for the old guy with the one tooth in front. The goofy one always hang with George and Normal and that other guy. That so?"

"*Who* says?" I asked.

"Everybody, man. You fuckin' kiddin'? You guys been kickin' ass and taking names all day long. Don't be dumb. That Normal put the fear of God in folks. Hell, man, nobody's talkin' about anything else."

"They haven't been talking about where Ralph is," I said.

"They're scared, man. Scared shitless."

"Scared of what?"

"Sucker's dangerous. He cut a bunch of folks."

"Who's that?"

"They had to take one guy's arm. I seen him myself the other day, mister. Got him a sleeve without a damn thing in it."

"What's his name?"

She bent at the waist, leaned out, and checked the street again. A solitary bicyclist rolled past us down Washington, tires hissing on the wet pavement, his progress marked by a pedal-generated taillight, which flickered its way around the corner to the left and was gone.

"Hooker," she said.

"His name is Hooker?"

"Got him a big hooked knife too."

I hate knives. The idea of a hooked knife made my intestines churn.

"What's he got to do with Ralph?"

"That's Hooker's gig, man. He gets the oldies and the goners. The ones got monthly checks comin' in and he gets 'em a room and keeps 'em wasted. Gets 'em to start havin' their checks mailed right to the hotel so he can get his hands on the money."

"What hotel?"

"You know. Over in Chinatown. Across from the little park."

"The Alpine?"

"Yeah. That's it."

"And Ralph's over there with him?"

"That's what they say."

The Alpine was a regular stop for anybody working scumbags and skip traces. If your quarry was the dregs of the earth, broke and on the run, the Alpine was always a good place to start looking. It would have been kind to say that the Alpine Hotel had seen better days. It would have been kind, but it wouldn't have been true. The Alpine was not a grand old lady gone to seed. She had sprung to life as a boil on the ass of humanity. An afterthought, a corn crib for people, raised from the mismatched, vagrant bricks of nearby projects, the Alpine had originally provided temporary haven for starry-eyed miners heading for the Klondike. Two weeks of being stacked in the Alpine like cordwood among the wretched refuse did wonders for alleviating the trepidations of a hazardous Arctic journey. By the time the ship arrived, most men were more than ready to go. Most were willing to swim along behind the ship.

Only the lobby showed a concession to time. Originally occupying the entire ground floor, the lobby had long ago been converted into seven extra rooms and now gave the impression that one had mistakenly walked from the street into a broom closet.

"You know what floor, what room, anything like that?"

"That's all I know."

"I guess it's my turn to thank you," I said.

"Except—" She hesitated. "—they say that after he starts gettin' your checks—" She let it hang.

"Yeah, what?"

"They say . . . they say you go out with the garbage. That him and that little nigger wrap you up in plastic real good and put you out with the trash for the trucks to pick up."

My mouth filled with a taste that could only be stomach lining. I reached in my pocket and pulled out what money I had left. Looked like forty-three bucks. I held it out to her. She met my gaze. She took the money and slipped it into her jacket pocket. "George is right about you, you know."

"I know," I said.

I turned and began to jog toward my car.

3

I JERKED THE SPARE TIRE OUT AND THREW IT to the ground, where it bounced twice and then began to waffle, each rotation smaller than the one before, torn between the dictates of gravity and centrifugal force. I rummaged down in the damp well where it had rested and found the metal box just where I'd stashed it. I took it around to the passenger side, where the light from the hotel sign was brightest.

A painted and embossed picture of a mission building, backed by brown, naked mountains. "The Mesilla Valley in Southern New Mexico," it read. In a spasm of holiday zeal, somebody in the family, Aunt Hildi as I remembered, had once sent me cookies, fudge, or some such shit in it. I'd canned the cookies but kept the box.

I pried off the lid and let it drop. The rags, stiff on top, got more pliable as I approached the center and found the little Colt .32 and half a box of shells that had been packed in there for at least five years.

At the bottom I came across what felt like a leather stick. I pulled it out. It was a spring-loaded sap that had been given to me by a pimp called Baby G. G had assured me that this honey and a simple flick of the wrist would surely render even the most recalcitrant opponent helpless and drooling at my feet. The bulbous knob wobbled obscenely in the limited light. It consisted of a leather loop that tightened around the wrist, an eight-inch braided handle, and a leather-covered knob of lead about the size of a small hen's egg. Between the handle and the lead were two inches of heavy-duty spring, which, according to its former owner, exponentially increased its operational effectiveness. I dropped the sap into my pants' pocket, knob down, where it weighed heavy and secure like a massive extra ball.

I dry-fired the .32 a couple of times, checking the action, then popped open the cylinder and filled it up. After dropping the extra shells into my jacket pocket, I raised the gun to shoulder height and sighted south down Alaskan Way.

She stood there in front of the gun. I dropped my hand, pointing the gun at the pavement. "You gotta stop sneakin' up on me," I said.

"I wanna help."

"You already did."

"I mean like really help, man."

I thought it over for about four seconds. No

denying it, I could use all the help I could get. "What's your name?" I asked.

"Selena."

"You know that hotel at all, Selena?"

"Scumbag chinks run it," she said.

Wildly politically incorrect, but essentially accurate.

"Right. So usually there's an old Asian woman at the desk."

"Same old squinter all the time."

"You think you can whip her in a pinch? 'Cause I can't have her getting on the phone warning anybody while I'm upstairs looking for Ralph."

"I'll kick her ass," she said without hesitation.

"Get in."

I threw the tire and the metal box back into the trunk, slammed the lid, and ran around to the driver's side. I backed the car out of the spot, turning as I backed, until I had it pointed south, the wrong way down Alaskan Way. I jammed her in gear and went bouncing up the street. Within the limited confines of the tiny car Selena smelled remarkably like a freshly opened can of Campbell's vegetable soup.

"What the hell's wrong with this car, anyway?" she asked as we turned left up Jackson.

"It's a long story. The frame isn't quite straight with the car."

"Cool." She sounded relieved. "I thought it was me."

"It takes a little getting used to."

"You ain't shittin'. If we was goin' very far, I think I'd puke."

Last year, while running for my life, I had, in a moment of drug-induced euphoria, driven the Fiat through the family room of Ester and Rudy Oatfield's lovely new modular home. The old girl had been pronounced a total wreck. Dead. A goner. Scrap metal on wheels.

In one of those defining moments when any man smarter than a crocus, regardless of his ability to rationalize, is forced to confront at least momentarily his own endemic stupidity, I decided I wouldn't hear of it. Against the heated insistence of my insurance agent, the best advice of three body-and-frame specialists, and the general laws of physics, I'd insisted that she be rebuilt. Despite the best efforts of modern unibody technology and a couple of thousand out of my own pocket, she now crabbed down the road at a horribly oblique angle, giving the impression that she was constantly driving directly perpendicular to hurricane-force winds, which forced her to tack her way from place to place like a sailboat. Selena's reaction was not unique. While I had over time become accustomed to driving at a thirty-degree angle, passengers uniformly found the experience to be quite unsettling. Their loss, I figured.

I gave the little car all she had. Disregarding the lights, leaning on the adenoidal horn, I bounced roughshod over the intersections, hoping I would attract a cop. I figured that if I could get them to chase me inside the hotel, they'd have no choice but to roust the place, thus keeping me away from that goddamn hooked knife. No such luck. Every espresso bar in the city was safe tonight.

I took a right on Fifth Avenue South, then slid the car around left in front of the Red Front Tavern, abandoning the horn, shifting up King now toward the Alpine, a block and a half up the street. I slowed to a crawl as we cruised past.

"There she is," said Selena as we eased by the entrance. The blue light of a TV, mounted down under the counter, illuminated the old woman's face behind the battered kiosk.

I pulled the car to a stop at the corner, fished a red key-chain flashlight out of the glove compartment, and got out.

"So listen—" I started. "You and I are going to go stumbling in there like we want a room. Then I'm going to get the old woman out from behind the desk, and you're going to keep her out of trouble while I go upstairs. Right?"

"I got it," she said.

"What are you gonna do if she gives you a hard time?" I pressed.

"I'll knock her scrawny ass out," she replied.

You had to admire the woman's confidence.

"Take my arm," I said as we approached the door.

We stumbled in through the door, arm in arm, leaning on one another, heads together, giggling like a couple of horny drunks. The old woman rose from the stool behind the counter, lacing her long fingers together on the desk as we shuffled across the room.

Her nearly lipless mouth formed a perfect circle as she began to speak. Since it was open, I stuck the barrel of the gun in it. Using only the slightest pressure to the left, I sidestepped her out from behind the desk and sat her down on the tattered red couch. I stepped back.

"Hooker and his friends," I said. "What room?"

"You're not police," she said, her eyes as hard as gravel.

I put the little gun on her forehead and cocked the hammer.

"You're right," I said. "We're not the police. The police would need a warrant. The police would respect your rights. Unlike me, they might even give a shit whether you lived or died. Now"—I tapped her on the forehead with the barrel—"one more time," I said in a whisper. "I'm not going to ask you nice again."

For the first time her shark eyes flickered. "Four," she said.

"What room?"

She shrugged. I started to move the gun.

"I don't go there," she protested. "He rents the whole floor."

I turned to Selena. "Keep her on the couch and away from that damn phone."

The carpet in the stairwell was stained in the center and slippery with wear. I took the stairs one section at a time, covering the spaces like a swat team, satisfying myself that all was secure before moving up. Each floor was protected by a metal fire door, its deep burgundy paint chipped and peeling, the once brass handles soiled and green.

The fire door to the fourth floor was tied open; a black nylon rope connected the doorknob to the handrail. The narrow corridor was lit by a single light fixture a third of the way down, the finger-like fluorescent bulb glowing like a welding rod. Four doors lined each side of the hall. Even numbers on the left, odd numbers on the right.

Holding the gun low, down by my right hip, I walked to the far end and turned back to face the hall from the other direction. I rested my back on the far wall and waited to see if my entrance had attracted any unwanted attention.

Somewhere in the building something electrical turned on, creating a deep underlying hum that swallowed all ambient noise. The atmosphere smelled of old sweat and new urine. I waited in the semidarkness. A fluttering sound escaped from under the door on my left. Breathing deeply, I worked on slowing my heartbeat. A siren rolled up King Street. The hum stopped as suddenly as it began. Someone snored loudly, coughed twice, and then was quiet again.

Using my left hand, I tried the knob on room 400. In spite of my care, the worn mechanism rattled as I eased it around. With my back pressed to the wall, I reached over, eased the door open a foot, and went back to waiting. The sound of congested breathing worked its way into my consciousness. I shifted the gun to my left hand and pulled out the mini-flash. In two quick strides I stepped across the threshold and around the corner, now occupying the same spot on the inside of the wall that I had just occupied on the outside.

The muted light from the hall showed a single bed wedged against the right-hand wall. The floor was awash with old newspapers, junk food wrappers, and aluminum cans. Somewhere out in front of me, along the bottom of the rear wall, the sound of scurrying feet made my skin crawl.

I took three long steps to the side of the bed. She slept on her back, wrapped in a shiny plastic shower curtain that was covered with black-and-white pictures of movie stars. George Raft smiled out from under her chin. Her scalp, nearly white, showed from beneath her thinning hair. Her teeth, uppers and lowers, grimaced from a glass of cloudy water on the floor next to the bed. The only other object in the room was a particleboard dresser, missing two drawers, on the wall opposite the bed. The proverbial dresser of deal.

Retracing my steps, I backed out into the corridor and eased open the door across the hall. I ran my pathetic yellow light around 401. It was empty and being used as a garbage dump. On the west wall an embroidered missive, GOD BLESS OUR HOME, hung badly askew. A galaxy of small red eyes dared me to enter. I decided to pass.

I moved up the hall to 403. He sat straight up in bed the minute I opened the door. Under thirty, balding fast, a face as bland and open as a cabbage, with that vaguely Asiatic quality of Down's syndrome. He blinked and squinted into the light.

"Easy, partner," I said. "Wrong room."

"I don' wanna go," he said.

"You don't have to," I said as I reclosed the door.

I stepped across the hall and waited to see if he was going to make any trouble. I gave it what I figured was a full three minutes and then tried 404. The ancient hinges groaned for the whole swing of the door. Same arrangement as the first room. Trashed dresser, double bed against the right-hand wall. If liquor bottles were returnable for refund, this person could clean up. The bed seemed to be covered with a pile of old towels and rags. I was about to back out into the hall when the pile sighed and then moved.

Pocketing both the gun and the flashlight, I began to rummage through the pile on top of the bed. I found his feet first. He was upside down on the bed. I stepped down to the footboard. Like the old woman, what was left of Ralph lay on his back. His skin lay in pools against the striped mattress as if he had partially melted in the sun. His normally portly frame had withered to little more than half its normal size. In the half-light of the room, I could clearly see the shadow of the corpse he carried.

I clamped one hand over his mouth and shook him. Nothing. His warm breath whistled through his nose onto the back of my hand. I shook him again. Still nothing.

I hauled him up out of the bed by the arms, bent at the waist, stuck my left shoulder under his chest, and stood up. He felt like he was made of balsa wood. I balanced him on my shoulder and headed back for the door. The kid from across the hall stood in the doorway.

"Where you goin' with Ralph?" he asked. "Ralph's my friend. He hasn't been feelin' too good. Ralph—"

I ignored him, brushing him aside, double-timing it up the hall with Ralph on my shoulder. I almost made it. As I took the first tentative step onto the stairs, I was pushed hard from behind, sending me headfirst down the stairwell, turning twice, bouncing hard on my side, driving the wind from my lungs.

Ralph saved me. His unconscious body got between me and the final concrete wall where we came to rest. Even with Ralph as a buffer, the blow rattled my teeth and swam my vision. Ralph licked his lips and snored quietly.

The voice came from the top of the stairs. "Where the fuck you think you're goin'?"

He was short. Some sort of Pacific Islander. Coffee, no cream, complexion. Dark. From Fiji, someplace like that. Maybe five-three, no more, his hair grown out into an ill-tended 'Fro that blocked the hall light from his face. He held a bent tire iron with both hands.

I reached into my jacket pocket. Quickly I patted the other. My throat tightened, and I began to sweat. I rolled off Ralph. Keeping my eyes on the tire iron, I felt around the area immediately around where we had come to rest. Must have bounced out during the fall.

He came skittering down the stairs diagonally in a series of small, mincing steps, the tool held out in front of him like a lance. I was still pulling the sap from my pocket when he was on me. As the iron descended, I stood upright and stepped inside, taking his forearm on the top of my head, jamming my neck down into my torso. Grabbing the arm with my left hand, I pinned his elbow on my shoulder while I pistoned my knee at his groin three times.

He was quick, getting one leg in front of the other and taking my knee harmlessly on the side of his thigh. With a grunt, he wrenched his arm free and stepped back. This time I was ready.

In a panic, I forgot all the simple-flick-of-the-wrist stuff Baby G had taught me. I hauled off and smacked him squarely between his eyes with the leather-covered egg. Gave it all I had. The sound was reminiscent of the time my aunt Sonja lost control of a standing rib roast back when I was fourteen or fifteen. The hollow, sickeningly wet smack, followed by the absolute silence. The old man had risen, spread his downturned palms dramatically to the sides, and pronounced the beef to be SAFE. Sonja, as I recall, had been significantly less than amused.

The little guy never even twitched. He lay there as if he'd been poured into the spot and allowed to dry. I started to reach for Ralph, but stopped short as the light at the top of the stairs blinked.

This one was no midget. A wiry six-two in a pair of soiled boxer shorts. He held a glass crack pipe in his right hand. His thinning hair stood out in all directions. Even shadowed, the face had that corrugated quality so often found in smallpox victims. An angry red scar ran diagonally across his chest from just under his left nipple to just above his right hip. All that interested me, however, was the hand at the end of his long left arm.

He stood the way knife freaks often do, with his knife arm totally relaxed, his hip canted to that side. This both gave the impression of street-corner nonchalance and allowed the hand to dangle out of sight behind the knee. If you weren't paying attention, it was a deadly combination.

I'd just caught a glimpse of it before it disappeared. An oversize linoleum knife, its curved blade worn bright from constant honing, resting out of sight now behind his leg. My insides moved in upon themselves, converging toward a single spot like a dying star.

"Ralph and I are leaving," I said, as much to myself as to him.

"You think so?"

He dropped the pipe to the floor and spread his arms for balance. I could see the knife's wooden handle between his fingers.

I let go of Ralph's collar, slipped the loop over my wrist, and pulled it tight. Despite the knife, I liked my chances. I outweighed him by at least thirty pounds. Anything I hit with the sap I was going to shatter. "Come on," I said up the stairs. "You anxious, buddy? You want some like your little friend here? I wobbled the sap up and down. "Come and get it, fuckface."

I couldn't see his eyes, but his body language said he wanted no part of anybody who was going to fight. I grabbed Ralph's collar again, making sure I had a hold on everything he was wearing, and began to drag him toward the next flight of stairs.

Hooker started down the stairs toward me. I let go of Ralph and stepped around to face him again. He stopped on the first step. Uncertain. His scar seemed to glow in the dark.

"Where's he goin' with Ralph?"

The voice took us both by surprise. It was a moment before I realized that the thin voice had come from behind Hooker. From the fourth-floor hall. Hooker wasn't so dim. In one swift motion, he turned, grabbed the kid by the hair, and hauled him down onto the stairs. The kid squealed, whooping in and out like a siren as he fought for breath. I could hear movement within the hotel. We were beginning to wake the two-legged rodents.

Hooker had the kid by the hair, pulling his head back at an ungodly angle. From below, I was looking directly up the kid's widely distended nostrils. His high-pitched wail filled the stairwell. I grabbed Ralph again.

Hooker reached all the way across and put the tip of the blade at the corner of the kid's eye. "You toss that head-knocker up here or I'll take his eye."

"Take it," I said. "Ralph and I are leaving."

I told myself not to look back, but as usual myself

was a poor listener. When Hooker dug the tip of the blade into the far corner of the kid's eye, the screaming went up three octaves. A single stream of blood flowed down the side of the kid's face.

"Stop. Stop," I screamed.

Hooker sneered at me through widely spaced teeth.

"Toss it up here."

I unwound the sap from my arm and underhanded it past him down the hall. Before it ever hit the floor Hooker had tossed the kid aside and launched himself toward me like Superman taking off.

I saw a small red poppy bloom in his armpit before I ever heard the flat crack of the little revolver. The bullet took him just under the left arm. He landed face first on Ralph, then, groaning, rolled on his back to the floor. I stepped forward and pinned his wrist with my foot. He was still strong enough to resist a bit as I pried the knife from his spasming fingers.

Selena stood at the bottom of the flight of stairs in the combat position, feet spread, the gun held in both hands before her.

"Where's the nigger?" she asked.

"Upstairs. I think I busted his head."

"One apiece," she noted.

"I thought you were watching the old lady," I said.

"You didn't sound like you was doing too good."

She had a point. "We better get the hell out of here," she said.

"There's no running on this one. They'll have us both in the county lockup by noon."

She set the gun on the carpet and turned to leave. "Not me. I ain't talkin' to no cops."

"We'll not only walk," I said, "we might get a medal."

She eyed me suspiciously. "A medal?"

"All you got to do is two things."

"Like what?"

"First, you have to clam up when the cops get here. Tell them I'm arranging an attorney for you and that you want to speak to your attorney before speaking to them. Can you do that? They're going to try to scare the shit out of you, but you can't let them."

"Like what are they gonna scare me with, man?" she said. "What are they gonna do, put a roof over my head? Give me three meals a day? What's the other thing I need to do?"

"Go call nine-one-one. Tell 'em we need multiple ambulances and the cops."

"You want *me* to call the cops?"

"It's what good citizens—innocent citizens," I added, "do at a time like this."

She favored me with a second of that lopsided grin and then backed down the stairs.

4

DETECTIVE SERGEANT GOGOLAC AND I got off on the wrong foot. They left me cuffed to a bolted-down chair in a fifth-floor interrogation room, hoping I'd soak up some of the fear embedded in the pale green walls. About a half hour later, he showed up. Calm. Officer Friendly. We were just going to have a little relaxed chat. Nothing to get excited about. Just a couple of good old boys shooting the breeze. Not to worry.

He was short for his weight. A grown-out gray crew cut, combed straight up, gave him the appearance of being constantly startled. The pockets of his soiled blue plaid jacket sagged like mail pouches. From the right pocket he produced a small black Hitachi tape recorder.

"You don't mind if we record our conversation, do you?"

"Go for it."

He set the recorder between us on the table. In a

low, paternal voice, he assured me that this was a mere formality, foisted upon us by a sincere but somewhat overzealous legal system. When I seemed to agree, he pushed the recorder's red button, recited the time, the location, and the date, and then read me my rights from a small blue card he kept in the case with his shield.

"Do you understand your rights as they've been read to you?"

"Yes, I do," I said. "And thank you for reading them to me, Detective Gogolac. I'd like to call my attorney now, please."

"Just a sec. I want to—"

I interrupted him. "Perhaps you didn't hear me," I said louder, scooting closer to the recorder. "I want to call my attorney now. I have nothing to say until my attorney arrives."

"Come on now, don't be an—"

I half rose, moving as far as the cuff would allow, and put my mouth directly above the recorder. "Are you telling me, Detective Gogolac," I shouted, "that you are not going to let me call my attorney? Maybe you ought to read me that part again about my right to an attorney. I'm not the brightest guy in the world. Maybe I misunderstood."

Detective Gogolac took his toy and went home. A uniform showed up about five minutes later with a phone, which he plugged into the wall and banged down in front of me. He backed to the door and stood there with his hands crossed over his fly, like he was holding himself up by the balls. I called Jed at home.

Forty-five minutes later, Gogolac made another appearance. He strolled in, hands on hips, seemingly amused.

"We don't need anything from you, Waterman," he trumpeted.

"We're on our third box of Kleenex next door. We know what went down back there. Your girlfriend's giving them everything but a blow job."

He might have made me a bit edgy without the Kleenex part. The Kleenex was definitely overkill. I grinned right back at him.

"My girlfriend? What the hell are you talking about? I thought she was your mom."

He strolled around behind me. He leaned in and spoke over my shoulder. "They told me downstairs you think you're pretty funny."

"You sure they didn't just tell you I was pretty?"

He stepped around to the front, resting his big hands on the arms of the chair. He pushed his face into mine. He had pores the size of dimes and enough nose grease to lube a locomotive. I held his gaze.

"Hell of a crop of nose hairs you got going there, Detective. You ever think about maybe training them into something decorative?"

"Don't fuck with me, Waterman."

"Jeez, Sarge, I never even realized that was an option."

He levered himself back up to perpendicular. "You want to make this hard, don't you? That what you've got in mind?"

"What I have in mind is conferring with my attorney."

There are few more pathetic sights than a grown man flouncing from a room in a full snit. It was another twenty minutes before the door opened again and Selena came shuffling in. A beetle-browed matron with an Elvis hairdo and a stiff brown shirt cuffed her to the chair directly across from me and then waddled out. Selena gave me a wink and a smile. I could hear Jed's voice through the wavy frosted glass.

"Perhaps I haven't made myself clear, Officer Gogolac. I will confer with my clients in any goddamn way I see fit."

"Detective Gogolac," the cop corrected.

"That fearsomely unfortunate fact merely validates my longstanding contention that this department needs a complete standards and promotion criteria review."

"I don't have to take that," Gogolac declared.

"What you *have* to do, Detective, is provide me access to private consultation with my clients. Singly—together—balls-ass naked, if we feel like it. Am I making myself clear, or should we mayhaps get a supervisor down here? Why don't you call the great Sanders himself? Tell him I'm down here and you refuse to let me speak with my clients. Trust me, Sparky, he'll come down here and strangle you with your own sac. If any," he added as an afterthought.

The Seattle law enforcement community viewed Jed James as a worst-case scenario come true. It was rumored that Norm Sanders, the DA, had expressly forbidden the utterance of Jed's name within the confines of his departmental offices and had decreed that Jed be referred to as simply "that man." Jed's ten years as the ACLU's chief litigator in New York had given him a political stance only slightly to the right of Ho Chi Minh and an exaggerated, abusive oratory style seldom seen this far west. No cause was too unpopular. No infringement too slight. To my knowledge, if you counted appeals, he was undefeated.

He strode into the room and closed the door. The overhead lights were reflected on his freckled pate. He wore a blue blazer and gray slacks, no tie, no socks. He nodded at Selena.

"Evening, Leo," he said amiably, sitting on the table next to me. "You want to tell me about it?"

I kept it short and sweet. When I'd finished, he left without a word. Twenty minutes and he was back. This time he addressed Selena.

"You're going to have to give them a name."

"You didn't even tell them your name?" I asked.

"You told me not to tell 'em nothin'. I told 'em nothin'. 'Sides that, they're a bunch of assholes. 'Specially that bull dyke they kept leavin' me with. Kept tellin' me about how you was spillin' your guts over here. How nobody cared about what happened to an old drunk like me. How I was gonna take the whole fall 'cause you was a guy with connections."

"Where has this woman been all our lives?" Jed asked.

"Kind of makes you wonder, don't it?" I agreed.

"What's your name?" Jed asked.

She scowled and folded her arms.

Jed persisted. "No matter what I do, they won't turn you loose until you give them a name they can link to a social security number."

"Social security my ass," she muttered.

She folded her arms tighter and looked from Jed to me and back.

"Selena Dunlap," she said finally. "Selena Dunlap. Five-four-one, eight-two, six-three-six-seven."

Jed headed for the door. "An hour," he said over his shoulder.

Twenty minutes later, the uniform who'd brought me the phone came in and took the cuffs off both of us. He was back in another five with two Styrofoam cups of industrial-waste coffee, which we left untouched on the table. Selena had wandered over to the bench at the far end of the room and was shuffling and smoothing the remnants of yesterday's

Seattle Times. When I got sick of watching the steam rise off the coffee, I wandered over and sat down next to her. Her prominent cheekbones were flushed, seemingly about to break through the skin.

"We'll be out of here soon," I said.

"Good," she said. "This place is gettin' me down, man. I'm no good cooped up. I get all goofy if I don't got some room to get around in. Makes me feel . . . weird . . . you know . . . weird."

"When Jed says an hour, he means an hour. Maybe a half hour to go now."

"They treat ya like shit in here," she announced out of the blue. "Like I'm not even a person or somethin'. Just because I'm on the streets like I got no rights or nothin'. Like I'm some kinda goddamn animal." She was moving like she was knitting in a rocker.

I tried to calm her. "Soon," I said. "We'll be out of here soon."

Her eyes were full of water. She picked up the Arts section of an old *Sunday Times* and held it in front of my face. A color picture of the late Lukkas Terry filled the center of the page, the boy next door with purple hair. "That's my boy, you know," she said, rattling the paper in my face. "Even if I ain't done nothin' else, I done that."

The door opened. Jed came in.

"You're sprung," he announced as the uniform uncuffed us both.

"Me too?" Selena asked.

"For you, I'm pushing for a city whistle-blower commendation."

"Goddamn right," she said.

"What about Ralph?" I asked.

"He's up at Providence. They took him to Harborview, but I had him sent up to Providence on my employee account."

"Thanks," I said.

"No word on his condition except that he had regained consciousness about twenty minutes ago. I've got Harriet in the office early, keeping track of his condition. If anything changes, she'll page me."

"And the hotel?" I inquired.

"They've got three full squads down there. I guess it's a hell of a mess. A whole collection of ambulatory stoners. Some handicapped kid threw himself out a window. It's a tragedy. Every camera and every elected official in town are down there."

Before I could speak, he went on. "That's how come you two are walking. I agreed that your names weren't going to come up as part of this ongoing investigation."

"What ongoing investigation is that?" I asked.

"The one where SPD, through diligent, dedicated, dogged police work, has sniffed out and subsequently smashed a virtual den of drugs and degradation down in Chinatown, thus preventing further tragedies like the one we face this evening and ensuring the continued dominance of the ruling class. To Protect and Serve, you know."

"Oh, that investigation."

"That's the one."

"What next?"

"As your attorney, I advise you to buy this woman breakfast. As you and I know only too well, my friend"—he patted my shoulder—"women of this mettle are few and far between. I recommend the standard introductory patter, followed by a whirl-wind courtship."

I turned to Selena. "You heard him," I said. "Only a fool disregards the advice of his attorney."

Selena Dunlap did not require further prompting. Jed and I followed her vapor trail to the street.

5

SHE ATE LIKE MY EX-WIFE USED TO PACK A SUITCASE.
Methodically, almost ceremoniously, stuffing every
obscure compartment with its ordained freight.
Over the past forty-five minutes she'd gone through
two eggs up, two eggs scrambled, a short stack, an
order of bacon, four link sausages, and now two
orders of toast. She'd washed it all down with five
Rainier Lites. Watching her weight, I supposed. Her
recent call for hash browns and another beer suggested that she had a few compartments to fill.

"Ya know," she said between bites, "we busted a
couple of guys, saved another guy's ass, got thrown
in the can together, and I don't even know your
damn name."

"Leo."

"How come you know those guys?" she asked
while she chewed.

"What guys?"

"George and Normal and such."

"George and Harold were friends of my old man."

"Your father?"

"Yeah. He was kind of like a local celebrity."

"That's what the dyke meant when she said you had connections?"

"Probably."

"What was his name?"

"Bill Waterman. Folks called him Wild Bill."

"The politics guy?"

"That's the one," I confirmed.

She chewed this news along with her toast.

My father had turned an early career as a labor organizer into eleven terms on the Seattle City Council. He'd run for mayor four times, each time suffering a narrow defeat. While it was great fun to have Wild Bill Waterman sitting on the council, making ridiculous proposals, campaigning in costume from the back of a beer wagon, the good people of Seattle had instinctively known that Wild Bill Waterman was by no means the kind of guy to be left running the store. As more than one of his opponents had suggested, Wild Bill's sense of humor was simply too far advanced for any office with wide discretionary powers. This was, after all, the guy who had on numerous occasions suggested that budgetary problems could be surmounted by simply giving the city back to the several bands of Indians from whom it had been stolen.

"The one who used to lead that goat around on a leash?"

"Only in election years," I countered.

"And gave away all the free beer."

"For purely medicinal purposes."

I'd heard all the stories more times than I could bear. The line between the historical character and the man I remembered was forever fuzzy, leaving me with a makeshift image of the old man that was, I suspected, an apocryphal mélange of the mythic and the mundane. I changed the subject as quickly as possible.

"These days they work for me sometimes."

She bobbed her head up and down and shook the toast.

"You're the detective guy, huh? The one George and them always braggin' about workin' for."

"I'm the one."

"I always thought they was full of shit."

"They are full of shit. Just not about that."

She nodded again and went back to work on a newly arrived plate of hash browns. I leaned back against the cold vinyl of the booth.

"What did you mean back there in the jail when you said that was your boy in the paper?"

She kept her eyes on her plate. "Didn't mean nothing," she said, pushing potatoes around the rim with a triangle of toast.

She read my eyes. "You think I'm lyin'?"

"I didn't say that," I protested.

"But that's what you're thinkin'. It is, huh?"

"Don't put words in—"

"You ain't the only one allowed to be related to somebody famous, ya know, Mr. Connections. I wasn't born no damn bum. I had me a life like anybody else. I—" She waved the toast at me. "Never mind."

Lukkas Terry had been a dominant light on the Seattle music scene. Not grunge. Not punk. Not alternative. No particular label except his own. He was a technical wizard of a one-man band whose laboriously layered studio renderings successfully crossed all generational and genre lines. God knows, I'd tried not to like his music. I'm a dinosaur. For the most part, except for jazz, I make it a point not to like anything recorded after 1979. There are few infringements so tyrannical as being forced to listen to some other generation's music. Terry's music, however, had been an exception.

His anguished, angry lyrics screamed the fears and disappointments of an entire generation, while awesome sequencer rhythm sections drove the music forward like a runaway train.

Several hundred million other souls agreed. His work regularly went multiple platinum prior to release. Lukkas Terry had truly been gifted by the muse. Unfortunately, Lukkas Terry was also dead.

Both daily papers had kept strict track of the legal

wrangling surrounding his estate. According to the last article I'd read, a bit over fifty million dollars was being held in escrow as the state waited the obligatory ninety days for familial claims. If I remembered correctly, if no family appeared, both the present estate and future royalties would fall to his manager and business partner, Gregory Conover, and his record company, Sub-Rosa Records. And none of that was the real prize. The big bucks lay in Crotch Cannibals, Lukkas Terry's as-yet-unreleased final CD. The music trade magazines claimed that advance orders for Crotch Cannibals would make it, upon the first day of its release, the largest-selling CD of all time.

I don't listen to his CDs anymore. My hand quivers as I pass over them in the racks, but I leave them where they lie. The circumstances of his passing somehow negated whatever joy they might still impart. A heroin overdose, for chrissakes. Found blue-faced on the floor of his Belltown condo with his pants full of shit. What a shame. What a cliché. Cue the Righteous Brothers. The heavenly band just got bigger and better.

Selena poured the rest of the beer down her throat, wiped her lips with the rumpled paper napkin, and slid out of the booth.

"I'm outta here," she announced, heading for the door.

"Wait," I said. "Can I—"

She stopped, turned, and gave me a rueful smile. "You can't nothin', Leo. How many times I got to tell you? You keep this up, I'm gonna have to get you a bell and a tambourine."

"Well, then, thanks for the help back there in the hotel."

"Makes us even," she said. She turned and opened the door.

"'Sides," she said over her shoulder, "you got bigger problems than that."

"Like what?" I shot back.

She reached into her pocket. Her big red-knuckled hands squeezed a familiar wad of bills.

"Like payin' the bill, sport. Remember, last time you had one of these Mother Teresa attacks, you gave me all your cash."

6

"JAMES, JUNKIN, ROSE AND SMITH."

"Hi, Charlotte. It's Leo."

"Leo?" She feigned confusion. "Not the Leo who used to work as a gumshoe hereabouts?"

"The very same."

"How's the ass?"

"It was a hamstring wound," I said. I heard her giggle.

"What, pray tell, brings your wealthy self out into the tawdry world of commerce?"

The friendly abuse was to be expected. I hadn't worked in quite a while. Back in early September, I'd picked up a major finder's fee when I'd located a homegrown bail jumper named Adrian Jolley. Adrian and I had played Pop Warner football together during the rainy fall of my tenth year. He was big for his age but never really had the stomach for it. While the rest of us were testing our testosteronic mettle on assorted fields of dreams, Adrian was selling dime bags over at the grammar school. Few find a calling so early.

A couple times, when my old man was faced with something or other so serious he couldn't even send his driver to get me, Mrs. Jolley had found me standing in the rain, the last one after practice, waiting for my ride. She'd taken me home with her, let me use the phone, and fed me incredibly dry peanut butter sandwiches and mercifully cold milk until the old man could make the proper arrangements.

Faced with a second major drug trafficking charge and a forty-year stretch of hard time, Adrian Jolley had liquidated his resources and successfully fled the country. Or so it was rumored, anyway. Every skip tracer in town had used every connection he'd owned to try to get a line on the good Mr. Jolley. No go.

As for me, I couldn't see any point in reinventing the wheel. Lots of good men were already doing all the obvious things and getting nowhere. Besides that, I had this little intuition tweaking my frontal lobes. I kept seeing the three of us in her kitchen, washing down those sandwiches, watching the looks that passed between them. Seeing their entwined arms and braided hands. Sensing their palpable need for physical contact with each other. Wondering what it would be like to be that close to either of my parents. Once in a while, I still wonder. A couple of weeks of replaying that little maternal matinee and I started calling contractors.

In the middle of the third day, I had a spasm of lucidity and called my aunt Karen in the city license department. A building permit issued to Marlene Jolley? Sure enough. A two-man general contracting operation up in Lynnwood. Dave and Donnie. Double D Contracting. Hell, yeah. A complete renovation. Turned a dank basement into a regular pleasure palace. The old girl spent the better part of forty grand on the job. Paid in cash too. Probably would have done better to just sell the place and get something else, but she didn't want to hear about it. What can we say? Ya gotta do what the customer wants.

I took what I had to the King County prosecutor's office.

It took them all of forty minutes to muster a search party, coax a warrant out of old Pterodactyl Turner, and get on the road.

I knocked on the back door, waited, and then knocked again. Only the smallest movement of the tangerine-colored café curtains suggested habitation.

"It's Leo Waterman, Mrs. Jolley," I said to the door.

The three Tac Squad cops pressed harder against the house as the door began to rattle and move. By the time the door was open a full inch, the first cop was up the four concrete stairs and through.

Unfortunately for Officer McNaughton, despite the orthopedic shoes, the support hose, and the cherubic countenance, Marlene Jolley was fast on her feet. Overcome by maternal zeal, she went absolutely batshit, lofting a boiling pot of egg noodles at the officer, whose Kevlar vest merely served to funnel the steaming mess inexorably south. While Officer McNaughton was occupied with his steaming briefs, Marlene wound up and skulled him with the pot, shattering his plastic face mask and sending him spiraling to the floor. Suddenly the room was full of cops. I stood on the brown lawn and waited until things calmed down in the house.

When I walked into the kitchen she was on the floor, Maced and manacled, allowed to snuffle about on the worn linoleum while the EMTs administered to the fallen cop. She gazed up at me through swollen eyes. "You dirty bastard," she shrieked. "I put food in your mouth. I fed you peanut butter and jelly, you ungrateful son of a bitch."

"Just peanut butter," I'd corrected. "No jelly."

They'd found Adrian reclining in his BarcaLounger, wearing a pained expression and a freshly pressed pair of baby blue boxer shorts. The months of momma's cooking had ballooned him up somewhere around two-seventy. As a pair of burly cops stuffed him into a gray SPD sweatsuit and pushed him before them up the stairs, into the hall, Adrian neither helped nor resisted. He merely stared out over our heads as if focused on some distant beacon.

Marlene Jolley was now seated at the dinette, leaning forward out into the room, away from her cuffed hands. The sight of her swollen eyes triggered some primal force deep within Adrian Jolley. With the roar of a bull, he sent cops spinning from him in all directions. "Momma!" he bellowed, lumbering across the room toward his manacled mater.

In the ensuing melee I was jammed hard against the wall, nearly upsetting Marlene in her chair as I was forced back into her. Perhaps, even in that moment of chaos, she knew it was me. I'd prefer to think that it was merely a random act of violence. Either way, when Marlene Jolley found herself confronted at close range with the very stuff of one of her tormentors, she opted for one last angry gesture. She bit me hard in the upper leg, fastening herself onto the back of me like a mastiff, grunting and shaking her head, as if determined to tear off a pound of flesh. I screamed and tried to push my way to the center of the room. She held fast. I screamed again, flailing at her.

A blow from a metal baton loosened her jaws. Still yelling, I shouldered my way out the door into the backyard, where I walked in tight circles, flapping my arms, waiting for the pain to subside.

"Son of a bitch," I chanted. "Son of a bitch."

An EMT appeared at my side. "Better let me have a look at that. Human bites are incredibly septic. Drop your pants."

It was then that I heard it for the first, but most unfortunately not the last, time. Standing out there on the lawn with my drawers around my ankles. A low rumble of laughter from inside the house. "She bit him in the ass," a voice said. Somebody snorted.

"Hold on, now. This is gonna smart a bit," said the EMT.

"It's in the upper leg, right?" I said through gritted teeth.

He grinned up at me. "Whatever you say, buddy."

After taxes, my 5 percent of the half-a-million-dollar bond had amounted to a little under nineteen thousand bucks. Color me irresponsible, but the combination of a sore leg and having nineteen grand in my bank account pretty much made honest toil out of the question.

Not only was it the most money I'd ever had at one time in my life, but the sudden riches also served to prove, once again, that my old man had been right to leave the family fortune in trust until I turned the ripe old age of forty-five. Whatever his other failings, the old boy was universally renowned as an astute judge of character. He'd sensed in me something less than a wild-eyed commitment to the puritan ethic and had arranged to protect me from my own worst instincts. The result was a trust fund of truly Florentine complexity. For nearly twenty years the trust had rebuffed all attempts to break it. A succession of greedy relatives, annoyed creditors, and one incredibly determined ex-wife had squandered bales of cash, only to be left on the outside looking in.

"I hear you had a busy night, Leo."

"Too busy for old farts."

"I'll say. Hisself came staggering in about a half hour ago with steamer trunks under his eyes and your name fresh on his lips. I was just going to call you."

"Really?" I checked the clock over the sink. Twelve-fifteen.

"He wants to talk to you."

"What about?"

"I've got no idea. He insists on discussing it with you personally."

"Must be a doozie."

"Hang on. I'll put you through."

I sat through a lovely orchestral rendition of "Raindrops Keep Fallin' on My Head" before Jed hit the line.

"Leo. I need you."

"Oh, Jed. I've waited years to hear you say that."

"I've got a job for you."

"Okay," I said.

"Strictly confidential."

"Aren't they all?"

"No. I'm serious. This isn't something I could use one of the other agencies for. Even if I hadn't saved your miserable ass last night, you'd have been hearing from me this morning."

"Hold the guilt. I'm yours. What's the deal?"

"I need you to get down to the city library and see—" I could hear papers shuffling. "Lynn Fortner. The deputy director and chief operating officer of the library system."

"What for?"

"We've got a problem."

"We who?"

"Me, the city, your uncle Pat, the universe. Pat's on the library board, you know."

"Pat's on every board."

"I gather you two aren't close."

"You gather correctly."

Actually, my father's youngest brother, Patrick William Waterman, and I had been out of touch since the early seventies, when during a family Easter dinner at my parents' house, he'd caught me getting his youngest daughter Nancyjean stoned in the potting shed. We'd have been okay if the sight of his purple face hadn't given both of us an incurable case of the giggles and if I hadn't been wearing her drawers on my head at the time.

"What's the problem?"

"One of the librarians is missing."

"A lost librarian? Oh dear me, whatever shall we do?"

"It's not funny, Leo. She's not all that's missing."

I wasn't in the mood to guess.

"Some money."

"Purloined overdue charges. What's the world coming to?"

"Just a bit under two hundred thou."

"No shit."

"No shit."

"How is it that a librarian makes off with two hundred grand?"

"It's a long story. Fortner will fill you in."

"Why the hush-hush routine?"

"Use your imagination, Leo. The Commons, man. I know you're not in favor of the project, but the voting public doesn't need this crap. They're surly enough as it is. We're already into their pockets for the new Mariners stadium and the Kingdome renovations. I don't know whether you've been reading the papers, but we're less than two weeks from another vote on the Commons project. It's gonna be close again. Something like this could tilt the balance. The city can't take this kind of foolishness right now. The press will have a field day with it."

He had a point. The plan to replace the blue-collar commercial squalor at the south end of Lake Union with an urban-renewed yuppie paradise had been contentious from the beginning, pitting the forces of tradition against the omnipresent army of drooling developers and provoking political dissension among those who usually agreed. The measure had narrowly gone down to defeat at the last general election. Jed, forsaking his usually egalitarian stance, was a major supporter. Being rather fond of squalor, I'd voted against it, knowing full well that the forces in favor would surely keep sticking it on the ballot until it passed. While it was certainly true that one couldn't fight city hall, one did what one could.

"Fortner is expecting you at two. And Leo—"

"What?"

"No paperwork. Just report to me, okay?"

"You're starting to sound like my old man, Jed."

"Scary, isn't it?"

"Flat rate. A percentage? What?"

"Regular daily rate after we're even. You owe me six hours at my rate. Which is"—I could hear the wheels turning—"a couple of days, give or take, at yours. Let's call it two days even." Before I could object, he added, "And that's not to mention the shit I'm taking from my insurance company about this newly hired employee of mine who's up in Swedish."

"There is no justice."

"Amen, brother." The line clicked, and I was back with Charlotte.

"Does this mean I should add you to the active file?" she asked.

"Might as well."

"The mean streets feel safer already."

"Thanks. Nice talkin' to ya, Charlotte."

"Harriet wanted me to tell you that Mr. Batista's condition has been upgraded all the way to stable. He seems to have staged a somewhat miraculous recovery."

Why wasn't I surprised? "Thanks again."

"She said Mr. Batista seems to be quite lucid except that he doesn't seem to be aware that he's free to leave. He wanted Harriet to post bond for him or to call you and get you to do it."

"Ralph's used to being in jail, not the hospital," I said.

"What say, for the time being, we don't dissuade him of that little notion?"

"Whatever you say."

"Thanks for the help."

"Good to have you back, Leo."

Next, I tried the pay phone at George and Harold's flop. I let it ring about forty times. Nothing. No chance everybody was up and out by ten-thirty A.M. There were people in that building who weren't finished throwing up by this time of day. Somebody must have torn the phone from the wall again. I swilled the rest of my coffee and headed for the shower.

The night wind had churned the overhead blanket of sludge, mixing it, breaking it in places, sliding it east out over the Cascades like a cavalcade of dirty elephants joined trunk to tail.

I parked the Fiat on Eastlake and walked the half block to the Zoo. I stood inside the battered brown door and waited for my eyes to adjust. An ornate, carved bar ran the length of the front room and around the corner toward the johns. The tables on the left were deserted. The next room back contained a green acre of snooker table and, farther back yet and around the corner, more tables, the dollar pool tables, and the little stage.

George, Harold, and the rest of the gang were at the far end of the bar, suckin' 'em down. The place was filled with shouts and laughter. The boys were the very models of consistency. They faced both triumph and tragedy in precisely the same fashion. While others worked in oils or stone, they had elevated to an art form the process of perpetual swillage. It was after eleven, so you could make book that they'd already had three, four beers just to tune the system—a little smidgen to get them vertical, as it were. And since they'd ventured outdoors at such an ungodly hour, it was also safe to assume that they'd all had a couple of stiff midmorning bracers— usually a peppermint schnapps or two would do the trick here. Something to keep the gaze steady and the chin firm on their way to the Zoo. After lunch and its obligatory cocktails, they would recharge their batteries with an afternoon pick-me-up or four around the snooker table, which, all things being equal, would melt right into happy hour, where, as luck would have it, all semblance of moderation could safely be jettisoned. On their way out at closing time, they'd snag a half-rack of beer and split it up among them, everyone pushing three or four deep into his pockets. That way they were primed and ready for morning. You had to admire the fearful symmetry of it all.

Harold saw me first. "Leo!" he shouted. All heads turned my way. The gang was all here. George, Norman, and Harold held down their deeded stools while Earlene and Mary leaned on the far end of the bar, blocking the gate. Billy Bob Fung was engaged in a spirited game of snooker with the Speaker, whose omnipresent sandwich board made leaning over the table nearly impossible. He played exclusively with the bridge. Today's missive read:

"You'd Probably Drive Better with That Cellular Phone up Your Ass."

"You guys heard?" I asked. It was a dumb question. The bum telegraph worked a whole lot better than any telephone, cellular or otherwise. They'd known for hours.

"We just got off the phone with old Ralphie boy," Mary said.

George ordered me a drink. I shook it off.

"The whitecoats have got him. They'll stretch his brain," Norman intoned solemnly.

"They'll have to find the fucker first," said George.

They yukked it up. Billy Bob banged the butt of his cue on the floor and hopped about like a demented elf. The rest of them dissolved in a wild backslapping frenzy.

"They'll mount him on a board and label his parts," Norman said as the din receded.

"They better get a big label," Earlene slurred.

This, once again, sent the crew into gales of laughter and, of course, called for another round. Among the fairer of the homeless species, Ralph was renowned for being, how shall we say, nobly appointed. I heaved a sigh. I wasn't sure I could sit through that discussion again. Harold, however, saved the day. "Tell us the story, Leo," he said.

I tried to beg off but didn't stand a chance. Earlene strolled over, her long face resolute. She took me by the arm and, with great pageantry, led me over and offered me Ralph's stool. This was the highest compliment a man could be afforded in these parts, the alcoholic equivalent of being named a Peer of the Realm. I leaned one cheek on the royal roost and laid out the whole story for them. They listened, spellbound, interrupting only to call for subsequent rounds at each turn of the action.

Certainly a story of this magnitude had to be properly washed down.

"We're goin' down to see him," said Mary when I'd finished.

"They won't let us in till one," said George.

"They're waiting for me in there," said Norman.

George reached out and put a hand on his arm. "You don't gotta go, Normal. Ralph'll understand. He knows how you are with hospitals. You stay here with Billy Bob. Play some snooker. Before you know it, we'll be back with Ralph."

I tried to squash this idea about them returning with Ralph.

"I think maybe the cops are holding him for a few days as a material witness," I lied.

"Then you better come with us," George said. "Help us get past the bulls."

"I'd like to," I said. "But I've got an appointment this afternoon."

"You workin' again?" asked Harold.

"Yeah. A little something for Jed."

George leaned in close. "Anything for us?"

"I doubt it. I'm gonna be looking for a lost librarian."

"You're shittin' me," George said.

"I wish."

"Breakin' yourself back in slow, eh? It's a good idea, Leo. Don't wanna be hasty about anything," George said with a straight face.

"Especially for a guy with a bad ass," added Harold.

George wasn't finished. "Yep, that's it. One little step at a time on the road to recovery. First the case of the larcenous librarian. Next week, who knows, maybe you can find you a florist or something."

This one reduced them to jelly. The Speaker scratched. Mary choked half a Seven and Seven out through her nose and out onto the bar.

"Gonna find a florist," Billy Bob Fung shrieked, hopping about. "Gonna find a florist."

They were still whooping it up when I reached the door.

7

"I DON'T LIKE IT," HE SAID. WITH A FLICK OF HIS FINGERS, he sailed my card back across the desk, where it skipped once on the black glass surface and settled neatly between my thighs. Picturing what I was going to look like retrieving it, I left it there.

T. J. Fortner, deputy director and CEO of the city library system, looked more like a high school basketball coach than a librarian. His thick white hair was cropped military-short. A pair of woolly black eyebrows accentuated his even features and suggested a youthful strength and vigor belied by the color of his hair.

"That's understandable, Mr. Fortner. Private detectives are usually part of most everybody's worst-case scenario."

"If we've got a crime here, we've got a crime here. What can I say? It's unfortunate, but it happens. I'll take the responsibility. That's part of what they pay me for. But now that we know . . . let's do the right thing, for God's sake. Let's cut our losses. Let's get the police involved. Anything else, no matter how well intentioned, just smacks of cover-up as far as I'm concerned. Makes me feel like Nixon."

"As I understand it, there are political concerns at work here."

He dismissed me with a wave. "Political concerns are not within the scope of my charge, Mr. Waterman. I'm an administrator. If I do my job properly, nobody even knows I'm here. If not—" He let it ride.

"If you don't mind the advice, Mr. Fortner, don't be in any hurry to volunteer for the blame. Trust me. I have some experience in these matters and with these people. If this whole thing can't be put to rest cleanly and privately, the people who called me into this will see to it that you and the blame will be on a first-name basis."

He thought this over. "Your background would lend itself to knowing about that, now, wouldn't it?"

"Been checking into my background?"

"I made a few calls."

"And?"

He considered his reply. "A mixed bag."

"Such is life," I said.

"On one hand, I'm told you have a real knack for finding people who don't want to be found. They also say you can keep your mouth shut. They say your family connections in the city give you a big edge."

I waited.

"On the other hand—" He let it hang. From under the desk blotter he produced an eight-by-ten glossy. I didn't even have to look. I knew what it was. "—there's this," he finished.

He held the famous picture of me and a couple of local ladies of the evening cavorting in the fountain of the Olympic Four Seasons Hotel.

"A friend of mine over at the *Times* sent this to me."

I didn't bother looking at it. "It's a long story," I said.

"Undoubtedly."

He turned the picture his way and studied it closely. I began to count the ceiling tiles.

"Now," he said. "I can understand the getups on the girls here. Tools of the trade, I suppose. But what in hell are you doing with those . . . those . . ."

"Accoutrements," I offered.

He gave me a thin smile. "Ah, accoutrements. Well?" he pressed.

"You had to be there."

He held my eyes as he slipped the picture back under the blotter.

"And what do these political types imagine that you can do by yourself that the whole police department can't?"

"All I'm going to do, Mr. Fortner, is poke around a little."

"Poke what?"

"Well, first I want to talk to the people she worked for and with. See if there was any hint that maybe something in her life had changed recently. Like maybe there was some sort of a crisis in her life. That kind of thing."

"Then?"

"Then I'm going to see if I can get into her apartment."

He shook his head slightly. "I think a couple of the women in her department already tried that."

"Did they get in?"

"I'm not sure. I don't think so."

"How well did you know Karen Mendolson?" I asked.

"I wouldn't know her if I passed her on the street." He sensed my surprise. "If you count part-timers and volunteers, this library employs the better part of six hundred people."

Again I was surprised. "Six hundred librarians?"

"Oh, no. Of the full-time staff—"

"How many is that?" I interrupted.

"Three-hundred fifty, give or take. Of that number, no more than a hundred or so are actually librarians. You know, people with degrees in library science."

"Karen Mendolson?"

"No." He tapped a green file on the left side of his desk. "U Dub. Business administration, nineteen seventy-five."

I held out my hand.

He placed his palm on the file. "Mrs. Franchini has one for you. Mrs.—Donna is Karen's direct supervisor. She can tell you a great deal more about Karen." He checked his watch. "She's expecting us now."

I took this to mean I was supposed to move. You learn to make those kinds of inferences when you're a detective. Fortner followed me out the door and down the blue-carpeted hall toward the elevators. Here on the fifth floor of the library, any vestiges of a public building had been left below. Up here, we could have been striding down any corporate corridor anywhere in the world. None of that smeared quality, the greasy residue of too many grubby hands, that one finds in public buildings. Up here all was shiny and clean.

Donna Franchini was waiting outside the elevator as the door slid open. As promised, she was holding a manila file folder. She was a tall woman, nearly my height, in a crisp white blouse and ankle-length denim jumper and a pair of sturdy black shoes the size of cinder blocks. She was impatiently tapping her right foot. Her long gray hair was twisted on top of her head in some sort of tight braid.

As she looked me over through a pair of oval

glasses, her expression suggested acute gastrointesti-
nal distress. Without either fanfare or introduction,
she said, "Follow me," turned on her rubber heel,
and started down the long hall. I stood still.

Halfway down, she realized I wasn't in tow and
turned back.

"Are you coming or not?"

"Not," I said.

"What?"

I stood my ground. "You heard me. Not."

She put her hands on her ample hips. "What's the
matter with you?"

"Depends on who you ask."

Reluctantly, she stiff-legged it back my way. "Do
you have a problem?" I kept my mouth shut.

When she got close enough, I said, "Why don't we
start over?" I stuck my hand out. "Leo Waterman.
Pleased to meet you."

She looked at me like I was a tax assessor covered
with shit.

"Don't be infantile," she said.

"Just polite," I corrected.

"And why should I be polite to you, Mr.
Waterman?" she sneered.

"Because I don't work for you, and I don't have to
put up with your crap, and maybe because we're also
not married and I'm not trading you occasional bad
sex for putting up with your lousy attitude." She
opened her mouth. I talked louder. "Or, even better,

I know this is weird, but maybe just because that's just how human beings ought to treat each other." At least she'd stopped tapping her damn foot.

"Are you finished?"

"For the time being."

"My office is—"

"I don't want to go to your office. I want to see Karen Mendolson's coworkers. The people she spent her day with."

She tapped the folder. "I am Ms. Mendolson's direct supervisor. Any and all relevant information—"

"Let's call Mr. Fortner," I suggested.

Gazing deep into each other's eyes, we shared a long Maalox moment. She took a deep breath. "I assure you, Mr. Waterman—"

"How did she manage to siphon that much money from what is supposed to be a well-organized public institution?"

She stood straighter, as if she'd rehearsed this in front of the mirror. She checked the hall for ears. None. She lowered her voice.

"She was extremely lucky. We were in the midst of a Transitional Administrative Realignment. Duties and responsibilities were being shuffled so the normal system of checks and balances was somewhat askew. Were that not the case, it would have been impossible."

"And?"

"We operate from a computerized system with an

acquisitions module. She set up a phony vendor with a post office box number. Then she ordered books from that vendor. The books, of course, never came, but she told the system they had, and the system then wrote a check to the vendor. Once the check arrived, she would delete the order record from the system."

"How could that be possible?"

"It was possible because during our Transitional Administrative Realignment the same person had control of both the vendor files and the payment files. Under normal circumstances, those duties are quite separate and distinct."

"How long did this go on?"

"Nearly nine months."

"Long realignment," I commented.

"We are a very complex institution," she responded.

I held out my hand. "Fortner said you had a folder for me?"

She wanted to refuse, but changed her mind, reluctantly handing it over after an intense inner debate.

"Her coworkers," I said. "Could I see them now, please?"

She pushed out a gust of a sigh that mussed my hair and again strode off down the hall. This time, I tagged along.

She turned left at the end, and then quickly left

again into a large office area consisting of perhaps eight separate work areas. Her heels beat time down the narrow aisle to the windows on the north side of the building. Two young women were working in the area, both in their thirties. One was blond running toward red. Svelte, athletic looking, in a black knit dress. The other had dark hair worn to the shoulder, black bangs cut straight across her forehead. Both visibly stiffened as Franchini blustered into the room.

"Mr. Waterman is looking into the Mendolson affair," Franchini whispered. "He wishes to speak with you." With that, she folded her arms across her chest and sidled over toward the corner.

"Would you mind if I spoke to them alone?" I asked.

Minded wasn't the half of it. "I am the super—"

I kept saying, "I know. I know," as she sputtered her way through another public self-assessment. We shared another touching moment before she shouldered me aside and marched out the door. We all watched her go.

"You guys on work release?" I asked.

"What?" said the brunette. She wore a blue sweater over a full-length flowered skirt.

"From jail," I said. "You know, where they, like, let you out so you can work. I figured a body'd have to be sentenced by a judge to work for that woman."

Both women hid smiles. We introduced ourselves.

The athlete was Gina Alleman. The brunette was DeeAnn Williams.

"I think if I tell you what I'm supposed to do, it might make it easier for us to talk." They seemed agreeable, so I told them the whole thing. The politics. How going to the police was our last option. That the best thing that could happen to Karen was for us to find her.

Finally I asked, "Can somebody define Transitional Administrative Alignment for me?" This time they didn't bother to hide the smiles.

Alleman jumped in. "It means that Barb Watson had a baby last—what?" She looked over at Williams. "May?"

"End of April."

"A very difficult birth," Alleman went on. "For a while it didn't look like either of them were going to make it."

"She's still not back," Williams explained.

"What were her duties?"

"She did payment files and order records."

"And Karen?"

"She ordered books and kept the vendor records."

I applied my vast knowledge of public agencies. "So, let me guess. Because this Barb Watson is still on leave, they never rehired the position. That would seriously screw up the budget. What they did was palm her work off on Karen. Am I getting warm here?"

"Sizzling," Alleman confirmed.

"So, what should have been a system of checks and balances was suddenly useless."

They nodded in unison and then both checked the hall. "They always fudge," said Williams. "They're always trying to get around the state hiring guidelines. They delay all rehires for as long as possible."

"Karen was working sixty, seventy hours a week," Alleman said.

"And you guys had no idea she was—" I let it hang.

"Well, we all knew how unhappy she was."

"Karen and—" Williams jerked a thumb over her shoulder—"were always at one another's throats. And, you know, since the thing with Earl—"

"I expected her to quit every day."

"Or burn the building down."

"What thing with Earl?"

They glanced at each other. Williams took the lead.

"You remember back right after the first of the year, when we had that real cold weather, when those three homeless people froze to death, right outside here?"

I said I did. Anchormen had agonized. Pols had

pontificated. Hearts had bled. And life had gone remorselessly on.

"You know how down on the first floor, the building has a big overhang and the homeless like to get in there right up against the building, you know, to keep warm?"

Williams took up the thread. "There was a group of regulars who had been sleeping there for years. One of them was an old guy named Earl. He carried this sawed-off broom with him all the time. Used to sweep the curbs." She made a two-handed sweeping gesture.

I knew just who she meant. The old guy had been a fixture in the city's homeless population for as long as I could remember. Sweeping imaginary refuse from the sidewalk down into the gutter with a broom so old and worn it looked more like a mustache on a stick.

"Looked like Popeye's father," I said.

"Yeah, that's him." Williams smiled. "Anyway, Karen and Earl were good friends. She sort of adopted him. Every morning she'd bring him coffee and a muffin, and sometimes if he was around she'd even buy him lunch."

"Until—" Gina said ominously.

"Until?"

"Until the higher-ups decided that these people were bad for the shrubbery. That was their excuse. That they were hard on the landscaping. They put up that fence that's there now. They got the cops to keep them out."

"They stopped letting them use the bathrooms, too."

"Then we got that cold weather."

"They found three of them huddled up to the fence, dead."

"One of them was Earl."

"Karen was devastated," Alleman said.

The sound of a bus five stories below in the street intruded upon the silence. Williams folded her arms and said, "Karen bought him a little funeral out of her own money."

"Really?"

Alleman shook her head sadly. "Karen copied up a bunch of posters about the funeral and hung them all over the square."

"All the street people came. All of them."

"Must have been a hundred of them," Alleman finished.

"You guys went," I said, more a statement than a question.

They nodded in unison. "She hardly talked after that," said Williams.

"I still think she was clinically depressed."

I kept at it. Heard the whole story of Karen's estrangement from Franchini, up until that one day when she just didn't show up at work. About how they'd been so worried they'd gone to Karen's apartment.

"What about her social life?" I asked. They both shrugged.

"Boyfriends?" A shrug, Not that they knew of.

"Girlfriends?" Again, a no.

"I think she'd just given up," said Williams. "I mean, dating—"

"You'd have to be single to understand," Alleman said.

"I am," I confessed. "I know what you're talking about. After a certain age, dates are like four-hour job interviews." We all agreed on that one. I tried again. "No social life at all?"

"She worked almost all the time," Williams said.

"Sometimes she did volunteer work at an AIDS hospice."

"And she read," DeeAnn added. "Incessantly."

"Mysteries."

"She'd read all the mysteries before they ever got to the shelves."

I pecked away at them for another fifteen minutes. The picture wasn't good. The girl seemed to be one of those urban animals who fill city apartment buildings, surrounded by their fellow travelers and yet isolated amid the clamor, reduced to routinized replays of previous days and consuming personal interests. These disconnected refugees from hope are always the toughest to find.

When it became apparent that I'd gotten everything I was going to, I thanked them for the time and took the elevator to the street.

A breeze had freshened the air, pushing the pedestrians along with their collars up. I headed downhill toward the Fiat. Three blocks down, the King County Office Building's honeycombed face caught my attention. Selena Dunlap. Five-four-one, eight-two, six-three-six-seven.

8

THE OVERNIGHT WIND HAD DRIVEN THE REMNANTS of the inversion deep into Idaho, leaving the city rubbing its eyes, blinking like a mole at the dry clarity of a Northwest winter morning. Relieved of the blanket of sludge, Puget Sound, the sky, and the Olympics now competed for the eye in complementary shades of acrylic blue, animated here and there by fast-moving patches of shade, as railroad car clouds, still deep gray at the edges, rolled east across the sun.

I parked the Fiat at the top of South Washington, next to the Nippon Kan Theater, and limped across the street. My body felt like a knuckle that needed to be cracked. I could feel every stair I'd rolled down Sunday night. My aching shoulder blades were grateful for the heat of the sun on the back of my jacket. The last of the season's leaves, curled tight about themselves on the ground, were now unfurling, coming loose and beginning to tumble about haphazardly in the swirling breeze.

I think the official name of the place is the Danny Woo International District Community Garden. Danny Woo had been a major mover and shaker in the Chinese community. He was sort of the Asian equivalent of my old man. Whatever you wanted in Chinatown went through Danny Woo. President of Gee How Oak Tin Family Society, board member of the Chinese Alliance Society and the Hop Sing Tong. The list went on and on. The guy had clout.

Back in the mid-seventies, faced with a sticky bribery rap, Danny had practiced a little image enhancement. With a great deal of fanfare and media hoopla, he'd donated this little shard of earth to the Asian community, which in turn had taken the incredibly steep piece of dirt and terraced and planted it into a model intensive community garden, whose carefully tended plots seemed almost to grow directly from the nearby skyscrapers. On a fine summer day, with the city lost behind you and the slope of the land blotting out all but the sky, it was easy to imagine yourself momentarily transported to some rural Chinese province.

I always come by once in the spring and again in late summer, when the ancient gardeners, speaking in their exotic singsong tongues, smile beneath their straw hats as they turn and smooth their allotted spaces. The smell of the loam and the incongruity of a place so pastoral existing within the very gullet of the city somehow always sends me home with a smile.

The city had been less amused. Not to be out-done by any Chinese restaurant owner, it took the remaining sliver of land between the garden and the freeway and developed the Kobe Terrace Park. They placed an enormous stone lantern at the uphill entrance. No matter that it was Japanese. Asian was Asian, wasn't it? So what if these were the same people who had packed the entire Japanese commu-nity off to desert concentration camps just thirty years before? They could damn well build a park too.

The garden was deserted now. The homeless stay out of it. They seem to know intuitively that to lie down in such a place would be to return from whence they came, voluntarily to become mulch. They prefer the park, with its paved walks and com-fortable benches snuggled beneath imported cherry trees.

I stopped at the first fork in the path, where Danny's gravel met the city's hardtop, and ran my eyes down over the terraced hillside. Out in the middle, by the toolshed, old bok choy leaves, strung between poles on heavy twine, flapped like stiff brown flags. At the extreme left, all the way down by the front wall of the garden, a remnant rhubarb grew resplendent candy-apple red. Here and there among the empty plots and the white five-gallon buckets, tall yellow chrysanthemums stood nodding, stalks shattered and bent, leaves and petals brown at the edges, but still finding sustenance somewhere deep in the ground. In the distance, out over the top of the Panama Hotel, the Kingdome squatted like a segmented cement shiitake.

I found her right where George said she'd be, camped out on a green bench at the top of Kobe Terrace Park, grinning into the morning sun, picking her teeth with a matchbook. She must have started early. At ten-forty-five in the morning, already she was seriously shitfaced.

"I knew I hadn't seen the last of you," she said when she blinked herself into focus and figured out who was on the bench next to her.

"Oh, really? How'd you know that?"

"'Cause you remind me of a dog I had years ago."

"A dog. I can't believe it. I'm crushed. After all we've meant to each other, you say I remind you of a damn dog?"

"Nice little black Lab. Lucky was his name. Good dog, friendly like Labs are, you know. 'Cept this fool just couldn't keep his nose outta things. Nothin' he liked better than a fresh cat box or a live porkypine. The cat box wasn't so bad. You know, if a dog wants to eat cat shit, long as he don't spread it around the floor or breathe in my face, I guess that's his business. You know what I mean." She leaned against the back of the bench, smoothing the sun on her round cheeks.

"A rule to live by," I offered.

She sat back up. "But now porkypines, that's a whole 'nother matter. Every time that dumbass dog would get outside, he'd find him a porkypine and then come back whinin' on the porch with a nose full of quills. We'd hold him down and yank 'em out and he'd walk around with his muzzle all swole up for the next week, and then the dumb shit would just go off and do it again."

"Must have been in his blood," I said.

"Once in a while, he'd get 'em so bad we had to take him to the vet. Get 'em through his tongue and all, you know. Vet would charge us forty bucks to get 'em out and 'fore they was even healed the dumb shit would go and do it again. Well, Bobby—that was my husband—about the third time he had to come up with the forty bucks, he took that old Lucky dog out behind the woodshed and put one in his ear." She shrugged. "To Bobby's way of thinkin', havin' a good dog was one thing, but making monthly payments on one was another."

"You're not going to take me out behind the woodshed, are you?"

She laughed. "Not me, Leo. I myself am startin' to get fond of you, but my guess is that you keep stickin' your nose in where it ain't wanted, sooner or later somebody gonna put you down."

"It's been tried before."

She grinned again. "I just bet it has, Leo. I just bet it has." She reached under the bench and retrieved a bag-shrouded bottle. I watched her throat work as she made a serious dent in it. Finished, she motioned toward me with the bottle. I declined.

"I ain't got cooties," she said.

"I'm getting old, Selena. I drink in the morning, I need a nap."

She slapped her knee. "Me too, Leo." This sent her into spasms of laughter.

I waited until she calmed down. "So listen—" I started.

She shook her head. The movement seemed to make her dizzy. She grabbed the bench with her free hand, closed her eyes, and composed herself. "No, you listen, Leo. Don't think I don't 'preciate what you're trying to do. But—"

"I only—"

She waved me off. "Button it, will ya," she said. "I'm makin' a speech here." She took a deep breath and a big dry swallow. "Nothing's gonna change anything. Maybe if—" She closed her eyes again. "Who knows," she said when she reopened them. "Who knows. If—ah, shit—" She broke into hearty laughter. "If my grandmother had wheels, she'd be a bus. It's done. Over. That's it." This time she waved herself off. "Let it go, Leo. Just let the damn thing go."

"It's in my blood," I confessed.

She groped around for her bottle, found it, and stood. "Time for that little nap," she said.

"I just wanted to know how you felt about being dead, that's all."

Her eyes narrowed as she weaved over me. "Ain't no reason to get nasty. Don't be gettin' nasty, Leo; it don't suit you. I'll have to smack you with this here bottle, you get nasty," she said with a smile.

"I'm not being nasty. I'm trying to tell you that according to King County and the State of Washington, you've been dead for years." I reached in my pocket and pulled out a copy of her death certificate.

She looked at my hand like I was trying to pass her some of the aforementioned cat shit.

"What's that?" she asked, making no move to take it.

"That's your death certificate. Cost me eleven dollars, too."

"Eleven bucks just to say I'm dead?"

"Yep."

"I coulda tol' 'em that for nothing." Again, she collapsed in great whoops of laughter. Selena's mirth was beginning to attract attention. A black man of about forty had spotted her bottle. He wore a dirty blue athletic jacket and an elongated yellow stocking cap tipped at an angle. At the sound of the laughter, he began to stumble over in our direction. When he got within ten feet or so, I turned to face him. "Need something, buddy?" I asked.

His eyes were nearly solid red, littered about the rims with some sort of seepage that looked like coarse yellow sand; his knees quivered in the breeze. He licked his cracked lips and opened his mouth.

I moved closer and said, "Take a hike. This is a private party."

"Heh, heh, my man—" he started.

"Beat it," I said.

Selena stood at my elbow. "I'll talk to ya later, Rodney. Here. Take the rest of this." She extended the bag containing the bottle. He groped for it until Selena grabbed his wrist, put it in his palm, and closed his shiny black fingers around it. Satisfied, he lisped his thanks and tottered back up the hill. Two steps forward, one gravity step back, but at least he was making progress.

Selena pulled the paper from her pocket and appeared to study it. I watched her eyes. They didn't move from left to right and back, but instead seemed to attack the words at random.

"Can you read?" I asked.

She punched me hard in the chest with the paper.

"I'm not ignorant," she said, her eyes suddenly hard and focused.

"I didn't say you were," I said. "I just asked if you could read."

She turned her back on me, smoothed the paper out on her leg, and mumbled something into the breeze.

"What?" I asked.

"I read a little," she said without turning. "Where'd you get that thing, anyway?" she added.

"I was doing a little work downtown yesterday. Paying off our bill to Jed. I figured that, you know, as long as I was there, so I walked down to the County Office Building, punched five-four-one, eight-two, six-three-six-seven and your name into the computer, and lo and behold you came up dead as a plug herring."

"It ain't right."

"No, it's not," I agreed.

"I never made no trouble. I dinna want nothin'. I just—"

She turned to leave. She took three steps and stopped. Rodney, having now mojo'd his way up to the steep part of the path, managed two mincing steps forward before falling backward for three. The old boy was losing ground. I calculated that, at his present rate, in three months he'd run out of terra firma and shuffle backward into the Sound.

Her wide shoulders again shook with laughter.

"What you call that dance, Rodney?" she hollered, starting after him. "That the cha-cha you doin'?"

Rodney turned his feet in a series of small ski

turns. When he was satisfied with his purchase, he took a hefty pull from the bottle.

"Na. Ain't no cha-cha, Lena. Heh. Heh. What it is, girl. That there's the pigeon shit shuffle, is what it is."

9

THE STEERING WHEEL PRESSED INTO MY CHEST; I hung suspended from my seat belt harness as I eased the squealing Fiat down the face of South Washington. Reaching flat ground, I huffed a sigh of relief, turned right on Fourth Avenue, and headed uptown. As I wiggled myself back into the seat, I pulled my notebook from my jacket pocket and flipped it open. Karen Mendolson lived at 905 Union. First Hill. No problem.

I climbed Pike all the way to Minor, hooked a right, drove one block, and turned right again on Union. Nice apartment buildings, mostly tilt-ups from the late sixties, on both sides of the street. Numbers in the eleven hundreds. I moved slowly down the block checking the numbers. One thousand and six was the last number before Union dead-ended on Terry. Dude.

Figuring 905 must be on the other side of the interstate, I backtracked, crossing the freeway at

Pine, then cut over to park by the Eagles Auditorium at the head of Union. I got out and walked to the corner. Across the street, the first building on the other side was the Union Square Grill, number 621. Double dude.

The way I saw it, there were only two possibilities. Either three blocks of downtown Seattle had been vaporized by aliens, or 905 Union must be buried somewhere down under the Washington State Convention Center. I headed back toward Pike Street, keeping a sharp eye peeled for anyone sporting an antenna.

About ten years ago, faced with a desperate need for a showplace convention center, but lacking any downtown property whatsoever upon which to build one, the city and the state had hit upon a novel solution. They closed two of the overpasses that crossed the freeway, bridged the space between with steel and concrete, and built a massive, green-glassed temple of commerce directly on top of the busy interstate. Creative government at its finest.

This time, as soon as I recrossed the highway, I took a hard right on Hubbell, driving down, seemingly into the basement of the city. Hubbell Street was virtually buried now, the rerouted freeway roaring in its front yard, the thirty-foot, ivy-covered retaining walls keeping it in perpetual shade, giving it a nearly medieval quality. Two blocks down, I found it, a splintered little thirty-yard section of

Union running nearly straight uphill, wedged hard between the interstate and the Convention Center parking garage.

I parked the Fiat in a wide turnout facing the northbound interstate traffic and walked diagonally back across Hubbell to 905, a five-story blond brick block of a building, dwarfed by the surrounding jungle of steel and concrete, as dated and out of place as a flapper at fetish night. The leaded-glass transom read, "The Ivy. 1927."

The door security system told me that Karen Mendolson lived in 505 and that the manager, Gladys Skeffington, was in 166. I rang 166 and was instantly greeted with a harsh buzzer and the sound of the automatic lock snapping back. I stepped inside onto the wild purple floral carpet and followed the signs around the corner to the left.

Gladys Skeffington was waiting for me in her apartment door. She was about seventy, wearing a mumu in a bright orange floral print. Her rolled and segmented arms and legs seemed to be sewn to the edges of the garment, allowing the rest of her to remain completely at large, moving apparently at random beneath the three acres of bright fabric like an overheated Lava Lamp.

Either she had considerably overestimated the surface area of her lips, or she considered the application of lipstick to be a far more creative enterprise than most. Horizontally it reached nearly around to her ears; vertically it ended just beneath her nose. Under other circumstances, the abundance of makeup could have lent a festive effect. Her facial expression suggested otherwise.

"Wadda you want?" Her voice was an octave lower than mine. I found myself totally at a loss for words. She stood there slowly chewing on her gums, looking up at me. Strings like little brown rubber bands connected her lips as she worked them up and down.

"I'm looking into the disappearance of Karen Mendolson."

"Who says she's disappeared?"

"The people down where she works are concerned. She hasn't—"

"What would those two yo-yos know?" She went back to her chewing.

"I was hoping that maybe you could—"

"Why should I?" More chewing. I looked away.

"Why not?" Two could play at this game.

"I already told those other two idiots."

"How about making it three?"

She looked me up and down twice.

"Well, you're a bit on the beat-up side, but you're still better-looking than those other two," she said finally.

I gave her my best Boy Scout posture. "At your service."

She waved a ridged finger in my face. "Don't be

gettin' smarmy with me neither, Buster. Like I'm some old fart. Just because I've got some wear on my tires don't mean I'm ready for the junkyard."

I hunched my shoulders and silently denied all.

Unconvinced, she tapped me twice with the finger. "I could still leave the likes of you for dead. Wadda you think of that?"

"I think maybe you overestimate both of us," I said.

She managed a small smile. "We'll see." She pulled the door open, turned her back, and shuffled into the room. I took this as an invitation and followed her in. She stopped, turned, and looked at me.

"Wait here. I'll make some tea," she said, massaging her gums. She moved me aside and headed back the way we'd come toward what I presumed to be the kitchen.

Hermetically sealed. The place smelled of fresh cabbage and dead skin. Narrow paths were worn into the minuscule areas not covered by furniture. The furniture and lamp shades were covered in plastic. The plastic gave me the impression that maybe the likes of me wasn't allowed up on the furniture, so I stood and waited.

Turned out I wasn't. She reappeared five minutes later with a tray. After surveying the room, she reluctantly waved me toward a plastic-wrapped wing chair and without further ado began serving me something green in a blue bucket. Actually, it was a huge blue cup. The matching saucer was half the size of a hubcap. I felt like Alice.

She settled herself on the couch. She smelled of dust and potted violets. "What's your interest in this, Bosco? You're sure as hell no librarian like those other two."

I produced a business card from my pocket and handed it to her.

"A private dick, huh?"

"On my better days."

"Why would a private dick be looking for Karen Mendolson?"

"I can't really say. But I assure you—"

She slurped a mouthful of tea with such force that it sounded like she was gargling. "Don't matter," she said when she'd swallowed. "I know just about nothin' about her except she had good references and she paid her rent on time. Quiet girl. Kept to herself. Never had any trouble with her. Wish to God they were all like that girl."

"Nothing?" I probed.

"Nope," she said. "Nobody knows anything about anybody else anymore. They're all strangers to each other. They live here, all huddled up together, but alone. They nod at each other in the halls. That's it."

"How long has she lived here?"

"Since eighty-six, when they buried us alive."

"She moved in after the construction?"

"We—my husband Jack was still alive then—we had to come way down on the rents. Lost most of our long-term tenants. There used to be a nice little peekaboo view of the Sound from four and five." She narrowed her eyes. "Now it's like being in Sing Sing."

"So she was a good tenant?"

"Oh yeah." She nodded. "Still is. Real unusual these days. Back before we was buried alive, people used to stay in one place for a while. Most of the folks we had then had been here the better part of ten years. Can't replace tenants like that, you know. Not all this running from place to place you got now." She waved her pleated arms. "Going here. Transferred there. Moving in with my boyfriend. You name it. Seems like nobody grows roots anymore. I should have more of them like the Mendolson girl. Settled. Steady."

"That's the problem," I said.

She stopped the cup halfway to her mouth. "What?"

"I get the same story from the people she works with."

"What story is that?" she asked.

"That she's a real reliable person. That it's not at all like her to be missing for a week or so without telling anybody."

"So?"

"So, they're worried about her."

"So what do you want from me?"

"I'd like to have a look at her apartment."

She shook her head. "Can't do that. She's paid up." She put her cup on the table. "Hell, she's paid up through the end of next month."

"Next month?"

"Last time she paid, she paid for two months."

"Did she usually do that?"

"Hell, no. First time. I was—" A cloud of confusion darkened her face. "I thought maybe she was going on vacation or something."

I waited. She retrieved her cup and inhaled another quart of tea.

"You think something might have happened to her?"

"I have no way of knowing. I just started on this, but I think missing ten days of work without telling anybody is way outside this woman's usual behavior pattern."

"Like paying advance rent."

"That just makes it worse."

She mulled it over. Again, she wagged a meaty finger in my direction. "You're smoother than you look," she said. "You're trying to scare me, aren't you? That's what you're trying to do."

"I'm being straight with you."

"I don't like the idea of busting up somebody's privacy. It's bad for business. This is a real quiet building. That's what these people want."

"I don't like the idea much either," I said. "But I'm thinking that I'd rather make a mistake by being too damn concerned and pushing my nose in where it's not needed than by sticking my head in the sand and pretending nothing's wrong. That's the attitude gets people killed in full view of thirty of their fellow citizens. I think I can live with being a busybody a whole lot easier than I can live with any of the other possibilities."

She swirled the tea in her cup. First one way, then the other. Then back the other way. "I wish you hadn't said that," she said finally.

"Why's that?"

"'Cause that's just what I've been thinking about ever since those two gals came here." She banged her cup back into the saucer. "Matter of fact, I haven't slept a wink all week thinking about it."

She stood and snatched both cups from the table. Mine, still full, sloshed over into the saucer and onto her thumb. She looked me in the eye. "You won't touch anything. You'll just look around?"

I gave her Scout's honor. She nearly threw the tray at me.

"I'll get the key," she said. "You wait right here."

KAREN MENDOLSON'S LIVING ROOM FURNITURE was arranged in the middle of the room, facing in at itself. White couch, matching chairs and ottoman. If you looked closely, they had a subtly embossed pattern in blue and burgundy. Glass-topped coffee and end tables. Just beginning to collect noticeable dust. Brass lamps. A peach and baby blue imitation oriental rug covered most of the oak plank floor. Matching little rug in front of the slider. Antique oak sideboard on the left-hand wall. Entertainment center on the right. Several old Bumbershoot posters were framed on the walls.

I tilted the chairs back and looked underneath for a stray magazine or a slipper. I looked down in the cushions. Not even crumbs. I walked softly over to the entertainment center and opened the double doors beneath the television. About forty CDs were arranged alphabetically in an oak carousel. Heavy on the Neil Diamond and James Taylor. Ten or twelve classical cassette tapes, also alphabetized. A videotape of *The Jane Fonda Workout*. A boxed set of *Gone with the Wind*. Fonda before *Gone*.

I went over to the sideboard and opened the drawers on top. The family silver was neatly arranged in the little compartments. A little off-color, but still silver. Napkin rings, lace tablecloths, place mats, finger bowls. Underneath, the family china was arranged according to height. Little hooks for the little cups.

After rummaging my way through the kitchen, I headed down the hall toward the bedroom. Small, feminine bathroom on the right. I stepped in. Little

ornate soaps in a crystal dish on the counter.
Matching pink toilet cover and throw rug.
Flamingos cavorted on the glass shower door.
Beneath their watchful red eyes, I went through the
room carefully. Nothing in the drawers of the vanity
except used over-the-counter medicines. The only
toothbrush was still sealed in its plastic case. No
toothpaste. No makeup case. No Q-Tips. No cotton
balls. No deodorant. Having already answered my
first question, I headed down the hall.

The bedroom was all the way down on the left. All
yellow and white. The yellow bedspread looked
Mexican and matched the drapes. The carpet was
off-white. More framed posters of Seattle events.
There were three dressers, a makeup table, and a
rustic cedar chest at the foot of the bed.

The first dresser was for underwear and stockings. I hate going through women's drawers. It
never fails to make me feel shabby. I did it anyway.
When I finished, I walked over and checked the
laundry hamper in the corner of the room. Empty.
Either Karen Mendolson managed to get by with
only three pair of frayed cotton panties, or her
underwear stash was elsewhere.

The next dresser was for accessories. Purses,
belts, scarves, and a number of esoteric items I
couldn't identify. I took my time. Nothing in any of
the purses except a wadded-up tissue and a tampon
applicator. I mentally added tampons to my list of

things that were conspicuously missing from the bathroom.

The third dresser wasn't a dresser at all, but slid apart on silent rollers to reveal a cleverly designed computer workstation. A gray Hewlett-Packard printer sat forlornly on the lower shelf. Everything else even vaguely electronic was gone. To the left, where the dust outline of the computer was still visible on the desk, a black-and-white plastic box held about twenty diskettes. To the right, a black wrought-iron gizmo kept bills neat and tidy with a series of metal clothespins. I riffled through the bills. Heat, electric, the Bon, Nordstrom, a Seafirst Bankcard, a credit account at Computer City. All paid in full. I pocketed them. As an afterthought, I popped open the plastic case, stuffed the diskettes into the inside pocket of my jacket, and started for the door.

10

"MR. JAMES IS WITH A CLIENT, MR. WATERMAN. But we have instructions to put you through no matter what. So, if you'll hold, it may be a minute or so."

"Thanks," I said.

I gritted my teeth through three minutes of Bobby Vinton singing "Roses Are Red, My Love."

Jed rescued me. "Yeah, Leo."

"A quick report. Let's start with the fact that the girl definitely left town on her own."

"You sure?"

"Trust me, my man. She took her computer and her phones with her, and I'm not talking laptops and cellulars here. I'm talking full-size computers and hardwired phones. She's moved in someplace."

"Shit."

"Her personal things are missing, too. She's neat. She took out the garbage. She emptied the refrigerator. She's gone."

"What now?"

"We're going to need to spend a little money."

"Oh?"

"I've spent all last evening going through her personnel file and her personal correspondence. She's got a father and a brother living on the Upper Peninsula of Michigan. We're going to need to send somebody up there to see if she's showed up."

"You know somebody?"

"I did a little contract work last year for a PI in Detroit named Tim Miller. I was thinking I'd contact him."

"What do you figure for cost?"

"Depending on traveling time, it's no more than a couple of days' work for a good man. Just long enough to talk to the neighbors and tradesmen. You know. Has either of them upped his egg order from a dozen a week to two, that sort of thing. Out in the country, it won't take very long. Everybody knows everybody else's business."

"Do it. Anything else?"

"I gave my cousin Paul her credit card information. He's gonna run it through the bank's system to see if she's been using them. Maybe get us a lead that way."

"What do we do while this is going on?"

"We wait."

"I hate it," Jed groused.

"I understand. This is the kind of thing for which the cops are best qualified. Our little private search is either going to play itself out in the next week or so, or it's not going to play itself out at all."

"Okay. Okay. Listen, I gotta go."

"Later," I said.

I returned the phone to its cradle and massaged my neck with both hands. Last night, after watching the Sonics whip the Portland Trailwhiners, I'd fallen asleep at the kitchen table with the Mendolson and Terry lives spread out beneath me. It was like a bad horror movie. I'd dreamed of being pursued. I'd dreamed of my father. I was being chased through an enormous old house, a mansion really. The place was thick with cobwebs and oily gray dust. The furniture was covered with smudged white sheets. I don't know who was chasing me, but the house was riddled with secret passages and hiding places, stairs and chutes to nowhere, moving walls. I was looking for a door to the outside. No matter how many times I went up and down the stairs, I never entered the same room twice. Every door led to a new room. All the while, my old man was on the sidelines exhorting me, pushing me on. "Don't let 'em get you, Leo!" he'd yell as I raced by. "They're gaining on you, kid. Pick it up! Pick it up!" I could outrun my pursuers, but I couldn't stay ahead of the old man. No matter where I went, he was there on the sidelines, a small American flag stuffed in his big fist, shoving me onward. "Pump those arms, my boy; pump those arms," he chanted.

I was still running when I jerked myself perpendicular at six-thirty this morning to find my entire body tied in a throbbing knot. Why wasn't I surprised when the twisted form in the bathroom mirror bore a striking resemblance to Quasimodo. Arrrrrrgh. For want of either a peasant girl or a bell rope, I shuffled in to bed.

By eleven-thirty, I'd staged a minor recovery. Five hours supine, a full pot of coffee, and a half-hour shower had loosened me sufficiently to facilitate sitting upright and dialing the telephone. I would, however, never play the piccolo again.

My first call had been to Ron Tubbs. Ron was in the third year of a five-year plan to put his twin daughters Kathy and Katie through Whitworth College, a plan of sufficient fiduciary magnitude to hasten lesser Kuwaiti princes to the welfare line and, it goes without saying, definitely a bit much for a guy who works for the Department of Licensing. That's why I and every other freelance, skip trace, bail jump, no-account operative who needs any official information connected even vaguely with motor vehicles immediately calls old Ron. A mind is a terrible thing to waste. Or vice versa.

He had one of those stubby drawls indigenous to northwestern Florida. "Wadda ya need?"

"I need a driver's license picture."

"Current?"

"Old. Ten, fifteen years."

"That there is iffy and a full unit, my friend."

I figured that my current financial status could weather a hundred bucks for idle curiosity. "All right," I said.

"Tell me, podna."

I read him what I'd copied from the presumptive death certificate.

"Raymond, Washington. Where in holy hell is that?" he asked.

"It's down there on the way to Astoria, isn't it? You know, like when you go down to Seaside, Oregon. Like that."

"I do believe you're right, old buddy. Now, what would that be? Grays Harbor or Pacific County?"

"Pacific, I think."

"That's even more iffy, then. Those rednecks are fresh outta the twelfth century. Paper clips are high tech to those old boys."

"Do what you can," I said. "Put anything you get in a FedEx envelope and next-day it to me. I'll next-day back and pay both ways."

"It's a done deal, champ," he said before hanging up.

On a lark, I called information and asked for Raymond, Washington. "Have they got a newspaper?" I asked.

I could hear the tick-tick of buttons being pushed.

"There's a *Willapa Harbor Herald*."

"Could you connect me?"

"Certainly, sir."

She answered on the second ring. "*Herald.*"

I was only halfway through telling her what I wanted when she interrupted me. "Oh," she said. "That's way before my time. You'd need Mr. Bastyens to help you with that. He's our editor. He's been here since the ice receded. He knows absolutely everything about Raymond and the Willapa Valley. You couldn't possibly find a better source than Mr. Bastyens."

"Well, thanks a lot. Could I speak to Mr. Bastyens?"

"He's not in right now."

Arrrrgh. I left my name and number and then hung up.

I limped into the office and riffled the Rolodex until I came up with Tim Miller's E-mail address: sleuth@znet.com. My old LCIII gave a soft *eep* as it hummed to life, sending a familiar series of colored icons dancing merrily across the bottom of the screen. I had, during these past months of inactivity, become addicted to surfing the World Wide Web, spending entire days exploring odd topics, decoding pictures of dubious moral merit, and conversing about absolutely nothing with other similarly disposed idlers from all over the globe. I was a hopeless case now. A shambling ruin of a man. The Internet and I were stuck with each other in perpetuity.

I clicked open my mail software, pasted in the

address, and typed Tim everything I had on Karen Mendolson. Send. I watched, mesmerized, as the bar filled the little box and the message went through. Good thing I'd discovered the Web a long way past my five-joints-a-day period, or I would surely have been found in some dank cellar, gaunt and wasted, staring moronically at some particularly galling dialogue box.

That little task completed, I shut down and dialed Rebecca at the King County medical examiner's office, where she toiled as a forensic pathologist.

"Howzabout lunch?" I said when she hit the line.

"Do I know you?"

Strife was to be expected. I hadn't called in a couple of days. Somewhere along the way it had been decided, by a process to which I had for some reason not been privy, that anytime the lines of communication failed in any way and for any reason, I would unfailingly be to blame. We had, after all, if you deducted the three-plus years I'd been married to Annette, only been dating regularly for nineteen years.

We've known each other since grammar school. She is the sole issue of a shore-leave relationship between her mom, Letha, and an alcoholic merchant marine who to this day remains nameless. Throughout grammar school, Rebecca Duvall had always been the tall girl who knew the answers to everything. Her mother had worked three jobs to get Rebecca through medical school. As if in penance, Rebecca had pledged to see her mother through old age. We had long ago forged an unspoken understanding that whenever Letha went to her eternal reward, we would sit down and decide what to do next about our relationship. Letha, for her part, was taking full advantage of the fealty. Current indications suggested that, like certain heavy water isotopes, she could be expected to have a half-life of slightly over twelve thousand years.

"Someplace nice," I offered.

"Now I'm sure I don't know you."

"Swear to God I'll change."

"Ah," she said. "It must be that Leo."

"I called last evening and made us a res at Palomino," I said, naming her favorite room.

"You are the sly one, aren't you?"

"I know the way to your heart."

"Straight through the sternum with a number-seven saw." I could actually hear her smiling.

"By the by," I said, "who did the autopsy on Lukkas Terry?"

"Tommy. Why?"

"Something I've been working on," I mumbled.

"Working. You mean Mr. Moneybags has been working again? Your ass is officially healed, then?"

I quickly changed the subject. "Could you ask Tommy—"

"No way," she said firmly.

"Come on," I wailed.

"No way," she repeated. "I will not be duplicitous with a colleague. There's no way I can ask him anything like that without him knowing I'm asking for you. I won't do that. If you want information from Tommy, you'll have to ask him yourself. Besides that, you know how he likes to torture you, Leo. It's one of his few remaining joys in life."

No shit. Nothing old Tommy Matsukawa liked better than getting me locked in a room full of heaped, piled, burned, bullet-riddled, head-through-the-windshield, eye-balls-hangin'-down dead bodies. I'm no more squeamish than the next guy; hell, I've seen considerably more than my share of gore, and don't for a minute think I don't understand that people who work with the dead can pretty much be expected to develop a sense of humor that's a tad out of the mainstream. Even with all of that, though, old Tommy was a bit much. No sooner did I set foot in the building than he would go out of his way to share with me the choice parts of whatever grisly carcass he was working on at the moment. At first I thought he was just being friendly in a macabre sort of way. Like he wanted to share his work and all that. After all, truth be told, it does take a certain savoir faire to fully appreciate the finer points of a good abscess. Later, I came to realize that what he really had always wanted was to bowl in Rebecca's pagoda, and he quite rightly saw me as a serious impediment to that end. Rebecca, for her part, remained wildly amused.

"I'll be down in half an hour," I said sourly. "Meet me out at the corner. I'd rather talk to Tommy on a full stomach."

"Chicken," she sang.

11

"DON'T FORGET THERE'S NO PARKING IN THE LOT because of the construction," Rebecca said as we crested Ninth Avenue.

"Still?"

"It's so bad I've been taking the bus."

"That's bad," I sympathized.

"It's even worse over in my neighborhood. The whole north side off of Fifty-fifth is closed. Some big gas company project. If you live there you have to park out on Fifty-fifth and walk in. They've dug a trench all the way across the top of the hill. I have to drive all the way up to Thirty-fifth Avenue and then come around the back."

Harborview Hospital loomed ahead. The King County medical examiner's office occupies the southernmost dungeon in the Harborview Medical Center complex on lower Ninth Avenue, hard by what in Seattle passes for the ghetto, a hodgepodge of apartments and duplexes rolling down the south and west faces of the hill toward Pioneer Square and South Seattle. They're all named Something Terrace. Yesler Terrace. Harborview Terrace. In Seattlese "terrace" means "projects," as in the public housing variety. The medical examiner's office was the last outpost on the frontier of justice. Fort Hematoma.

I turned the Fiat east on Alder and back again to the left on Terry.

"There, in front of the apartment building," Rebecca said, pointing with a long, manicured finger.

I sprinted past, U-turned in a driveway, and slipped the Fiat to the curb on the west side of the street. Neat as could be.

"Thank goodness," Rebecca said as I helped her from the car. "I can't believe you still haven't had this car fixed."

"It *is* fixed."

"I must be overly sensitive. Traveling at a thirty-degree angle was beginning to unsettle that wonderful lunch we had."

She took my arm as we marched our way down to Jefferson and turned left back toward Ninth Avenue, where we emerged from the shadows into brilliant sunshine. To the south, Mount Rainier stuck up like a salacious silver tongue. To the north, the green dome of Saint James Cathedral rose above the utility lines.

"Did you tell Tommy I was coming?" I asked as we strolled along.

"Of course."

"Thanks a bunch."

"Anytime."

"He's probably been rummaging through the freezers thawing out particularly luscious tidbits for me."

"Probably," she agreed.

"You just feel guilty."

"Who?"

"You."

"Guilty about what?"

"For kicking his ass in the sixth grade." Tommy Matsukawa, Rebecca, and I had all served our middle school sentences together at Denny Middle School.

She released my arm and inspected the treetops. "I'm sure I don't know what you're talking about."

"I can still see you sitting on his chest, holding him by the ears, banging his head off the blacktop."

"You do truly have a fevered imagination, Leo." She wagged a finger at me. "Sixties flashbacks, I suspect. That's probably why you've come to no good." When I didn't object, she continued. "Besides, if any such thing had actually happened, it could only have been because he made fun of my height."

"Ah—" I started.

"Hypothetically speaking, of course," she added.

"You still feel bad; that's how come you tolerate him. That's also how come you recommended him for the job."

"I don't know what you're talking about. Tommy's a first-class pathologist. You must be—"

"That and the fact that he's warm for your form."

She punched me hard in the arm. "Really, Leo, you're supposed to have outgrown your genital stage by now."

"He's had a boner for you since grammar school."

She started to object. I blustered her off. "And that's not even the scary part."

"Pray tell."

"The scary thing is, I think he liked you kicking his ass."

"You are such a pervert."

"Thank you," I said.

She reannexed my arm. "Speaking of that—"

"Do tell."

"Mom and Rhetta left on their cruise yesterday," she said.

"How long?"

"Two weeks bobbing about among the icebergs."

"Really," I said. "Two weeks? Aren't they usually at one another's throats on about the fourth day?"

"They're getting better. I think old age is mellowing them."

"That's a frightening thought," I said.

"Oh no. For a frightening thought, consider the

fact that lately they've been talking about moving in together."

I mulled this over as we walked. "Where does that leave you?" I asked casually.

"I think that would leave *us* about at that discussion we've always been promising to have."

"I suppose a full-fledged sprint back to my car would be considered poor form about now."

"Extremely," she confirmed. "Not only that, but I've always been faster than you."

I kept my chin high and my step steady. "I should probably start acting more agreeable, then."

"Probably," she agreed.

We strolled on, turning down the little fractured femur of Alder Street that ran along the south side of Harborview. Dug in like a bad toenail, 850 Alder was nearly buried by a latticed superstructure of steel scaffolding, wooden catwalks, and concrete forms. I'd asked everyone, but nobody knew what it was they were building. We went down the stairs. The reception desk was empty. A little red clock. Smiley face. Be back at 1:00. It was 1:20.

Rebecca removed her coat and looked up at the assignment board.

"Tommy's working in three. Second door on the left."

"I don't suppose—"

"I've got a meeting and then a logjam of lab work. Call me later. Or"—she started down the hall, smil-

ing back over her shoulder—"you can neglect me for
another couple of days and then just make another
reservation at Palomino. Ta-ta."

I watched until she turned right into her office
and then took a deep breath. I was a man with a
plan. I was ready. I'd been training for a moment
such as this, and now the moment was at hand.
During my recent sabbatical, I had filled some of the
time when I wasn't surfing the Net with movies.
Three or four a week. Sometimes more. I'd seen
everything. The Academy Awards committee should
be so wise as to seek my counsel. Somewhere along
the way, after the zillionth frame of Hollywood
gore, I'd developed the ability to see the carnage as
merely interestingly constructed plastic creations. I
no longer averted my eyes at the sight of mock internal organs. Instead, I now tried to figure out how
they had gone about constructing this thing that
looked so convincingly like a recently severed arm,
its veins and arteries still quivering, fingers easing
open for the last time. I had willfully suspended my
willful suspension of disbelief. That's what I was
going to do today. *It's just a plastic model. Just a plastic
model. Just . . .*

Three was what I presumed to be a typical autopsy
room. On the right, a series of large stainless steel
drawers provided temporary shelter for the stiffs.
Except for massive overhead lights and the big drain

in the middle of the floor, the rest of the room could have passed for a high school science lab.

I pulled open the door. Tommy Matsukawa's head popped up from behind the green-covered atrocity that lay heaped on the table in front of him.

"Hey, Tommy," I said.

"Good to see you, Leo." His eyes crinkled above the surgical mask. "Come on in. Take a look at this."

As I started across the room, I began my internal dialogue. *It's just a plastic model. Just a plastic model. Must have taken them weeks to get the feet that purple color. Interesting. I wonder how they—*

"Rebecca says you did the postmortem on that Lukkas Terry kid."

"That was my unfortunate honor," he confirmed.

I stopped on the near side of the table, with the stiff between us. Huge. A floater. Looked like somebody put an air hose up his ass. All puffed up and ready to burst like a bad soufflé. *Oh, Jesus, it's got no face. No. No. Deep breath. They just haven't put the face on yet. That's it. Amazing how they just left the holes so the artist could work out the face itself later. A lot of different people probably work on a big model like this. Specialization is the key.*

"Just your run-of-the-mill drug overdose?" I asked.

"Had enough pure smack in his system to kill a rhino. Come over on this side. Take a look at this."

I kept smiling as I walked around. *It's amazing*

what they can do with these new plastics. Look how lifelike those sawed-off rib ends are where he's cut that big window in the thing's chest cavity. Got him a little door now, like an old-time speakeasy. Just needs a knob. Joe sent me.

"Pure smack. You mean, like, untouched, nobody had stepped on it at all?"

"Pure as the driven snow. Best stuff I've analyzed in years. China White. Stopped his clock in two seconds flat."

"Where the hell does a body get uncut drugs these days?" I wondered out loud.

He winked and leered. "When you're a big-time rock star, I imagine you can pretty much get whatever you want."

Tommy pulled open the trapdoor in the model's chest to reveal a morass of internal organs, all blown up like a mottled rainbow of balloons, all fighting for space within the torso.

"Did you ever see a spleen that big?" he asked, poking a quivering purple balloon with his gloved index finger.

"Not since breakfast," I offered cheerfully. "Was there other evidence of him being an IV drug user?"

Amazing realism. They've even included aroma. I wonder if the individual organs are all scratch-and-sniff?

"That's the sad part," Tommy said, dropping the trapdoor with a wet plop. "Cops found a set of works there in the house. He had three or four fresh puncture marks. He was either a moderate user or he'd just started. Either way, he was no way ready for anything that strong."

"How much energy did the SPD put into it?"

I could see the consternation in his eyes. I should have been puking down the drain by now. I had him going.

"What was there for them to do? He's found locked in his own house, in his own bathroom, needle still in his arm. This wasn't like Beaver Cleaver suddenly went wrong or anything either. This kid had a psychiatric history you wouldn't believe. Foster homes. Been remanded to the state twice. I mean, I'm sure, you know, him being famous and all, I'm sure SPD dotted their *i*'s and such, but this was strictly a no-brainer."

"Nothing at all?" I pressed.

He ruminated. "An elderly neighbor thought she heard loud voices coming from the place on the night he died."

"Did they investigate?"

I could sense that he was smiling behind the mask. "You know what she wanted the crime lab techs to do?"

"What?"

"She wanted them to check and see if her locks had been picked. You know why?"

"I'll bite. Why?"

"Because she was sure that people had been breaking into the place and moving her stuff. Her keys and glasses. Not stealing them or anything. Just moving around so she couldn't find them. She figured it was the Lebanese couple at the end of the hall."

I took another tack. "And, from your end, you gave him the whole nine yards?"

"Hey, man, it's a big case. I've got every second on film and enough tissue samples in the freezer for a barbecue. The steel plate from his arm. You name it, I got it. My Peking ducks are in a row."

"I didn't mean to imply—" I started.

"You ever seen a pancreas?"

I took a deep breath. "No," I said. "But I've been meaning to."

He began rooting around, up to his elbow in the torso. I took another tack. "Who found him?"

"Anonymous phone tip. A woman, as I understand it. Probably one of his groupies. Didn't want to get involved. That sort of thing. Probably a user herself. They want nothing to do with the heat, but I don't have to tell you that."

"No question about any of it at all?" I pressed.

"Nada. Cut and dried . . . Ahhhh," he said, snaking his arm out of the model. In his hand was an oblong object the size of a sweet potato. He waved it under my nose. "The pancreas," he announced.

That's what it is—a sweet potato or a yam covered in guava jelly. Amazing what they'll think of—and they are scratch-and-sniff. Wow. Wonder how in God's name they did that.

Nonplussed, I ambled back around to the far side of the model.

"Well, Tommy, my man, thanks for the info and the anatomy lesson," I said.

His eyes narrowed. His cheek twitched madly beneath the mask.

"You know how come everything blows up like this, Leo?" he asked as he again pulled back the trapdoor.

"How come?"

"Because it's a closed system. Once the gas buildup begins, it has no external outlet. Once rigor closes the anus, the gas just moves from organ to organ, blowing them up like a bunch of circus balloons linked in series."

Balloons. I knew it! That's precisely what they are. They must have painted them all those ghastly earth tones. Surely they don't come in those hues.

"Until—" He let it hang.

"Until what?"

"Until they find some outlet."

With the swipe of a scalpel, he sliced away the corner of the uppermost purple balloon. A great wet whoosh burst from the corpse. The air was suddenly filled with the smell of primordial swamp gas, of putrefying organic matter, of human compost and dark, rank water. The corpse began slowly to deflate and flatten on the table. *It's just—just—*Arrrrgh. I began to backpedal.

I reeled back, slapping at the air around me as if it were alive with bees. I could feel the spores boring into my skin. The ginger chicken I'd had for lunch was packing its bags for the trip north. Clamping both hands over my mouth, I stumbled to the door, out of the room, and out into the reception area.

Tyann Cummings, the college girl who personed the reception desk, opened her mouth as if to greet me and then closed it again. A pair of white-frocked interns pulled their heads apart and looked my way. I kept jogging, right out the door and up the steps. Arrrrrgh.

The cold air washed over me like a welcome shower. I scrubbed myself in it. Brushing my clothes, tousling my hair. I must have looked autistic. So what? *Breathe. Breathe. Breathe.* I pressed my forehead to the cool corrugated metal of the construction shed, closed my eyes, and stood still. After a while, a massive orange frontloader, its scoop dripping pea gravel, came roaring by in a cloud of cleansing dust. The driver eyed me hard. I managed a small wave. He rolled on by. I stood and listened to the sounds of fading hydraulics.

Reluctantly I pushed myself off the shed and headed out toward Ninth Avenue. I was walking on rented legs. My knees were asleep. I crossed Ninth and started up Alder on the shady side, keeping the concrete retaining wall hard by my left shoulder just in case these foreign legs should turn out to be defective. Halfway up, satisfied that I was up to the task, I slipped between cars and started across the street.

Had it been one of those new Japanese models so popular with PTA members, one of those silent-gliding, rear-engined, thirty-thousand-dollar mini-vans, I would surely have been road pizza. As it was, I heard it long before I was otherwise aware of its presence.

The throaty roar of an American engine turned my head to the left. A windowless, primer-gray Chevy van, its windshield tinted impossibly dark, was roaring up the street in my direction. Leaving the pedal to the metal, the driver speed-shifted into second gear. "Kids," I thought, and hustled to get out of the way.

I was two-thirds of the way across the street when the van began to veer from the right-hand lane, angling toward me. Very funny.

Just a few years ago I might have stood my ground and given the asshole the one-finger salute. No more. Nowadays the cretin probably had a rocket launcher or something, so I began to move along the line of cars, looking for a break where I could slip up onto the sidewalk and end this silly game. The van was so close now that I could hear the squealing of a worn fan belt. The sound of water moving through the system. Any second now, I expected the stupid son of a bitch to turn away and have a good laugh at my expense.

When the driver held his line and jammed it into third gear, my central nervous system suddenly knew that he was past the point of no return. The crazy bastard was going to hit me. I took three long strides, pushed off on my left foot, and dove up onto the hood of the nearest car. My ears filled with the sound of a roaring engine. My chest felt the initial impact and then the tearing of metal as the van ripped along the side of the car.

I slid across the slick hood and disappeared headfirst over the far edge, somersaulting, coming down hard on my left shoulder, half on, half off the grass strip separating the sidewalk from the street. Using the door handle for leverage, I pulled myself up in time to see the van disappear over the rise on Alder. The Acura's alarm system had been triggered. The car's horn bleated insistently. I stood, shaking.

I tuned out the horn and took inventory. Everything was more or less where I remembered, except for the left knee of my trousers, which now hung down like the trapdoor in Tommy's floater. A flap of skin half the size of a dollar bill had been torn loose from my shin. Twin rivulets of blood ran down into my sock. I tried to return both flaps to their original locations, but they had other ideas. Urged on by the rhythmic horn, I reversed course and limped back the way I had come.

Rebecca, Tommy, the two interns, and Tyann were gathered in a clump next to the reception desk. Having a good chuckle, I figured. All heads turned my way as I burst through the door.

Tommy had untied the top of his surgical mask, which now hung down on his chest. He grinned and waved me off. "Oh no, buddy, I'm not going for it. I got you, man. I got you. I wasn't born yesterday. I'm not going for this crap."

"Really, Leo," Rebecca chided.

I pulled up my pant leg, revealing the carnage. "Really what?" I demanded. "I'm standing here bleeding like Teddy Kennedy's liver, and you jerkoffs are making fun of me."

Rebecca instantly knew I wasn't kidding. She detached herself from the others and came to my side.

"What happened?" she asked.

"Some asshole tried to run me down."

She knelt and pushed up my pant leg.

"Jesus," breathed Tommy.

"Tyann, get my bag from my office," Rebecca said. She looked up at me. "Are you hurt anywhere else?"

"I don't think so," I said.

She turned toward the interns. "Wilson, call the police."

I wagged my head. "Never mind," I said. "It all happened too fast. I didn't get the plate number or anything. There's nothing the cops can do now but take up a lot of my time."

Tommy wandered over to inspect the wound for himself.

"That's going to be real sore in the morning," he announced gleefully.

Tyann returned with Rebecca's medical bag.

"Not as sore as the owner of that new black Acura out there is going to be," I said, as Duvall led me over to the nearest chair and began to dab at the wound with a clean piece of gauze.

Rebecca stopped dabbing. Tommy stood in the middle of the room, hands on hips. He pointed at Rebecca. "This is despicable. You told him, didn't you? You told him about the car."

Before she could respond, he went on. "This is sick, you know. A grown man mutilating himself just because he can't take a joke."

I looked to Rebecca for confirmation. "He bought a new car?" She nodded. "A black Acura?" She suppressed a small smile.

"No way," Tommy trumpeted. "No way. I'm not going for it."

I looked down at Rebecca, who had resumed her dabbing. "Remind me to go to church more often," I said.

"Forget it, Leo. Just forget it," Tommy sneered. "This time you lose. That's all there is to it. End of story."

"Tyann, open the door, would you, please?"

The girl looked confused but moved across the room and pulled the door open. Above the construction melee and the sounds of passing traffic, the insistent nasal note of the alarm horn rolled in.

12

YESTERDAY'S GAIETY WAS GONE. THE ZOO WAS SILENT.
George, Harold, and Normal sat low at the far end
of the bar, nursing flat beers. Their expressions
suggested that prohibition had suddenly been
reinstated. I nodded at Terry, who kept polishing
glasses, and limped down the length of the bar.

"How's Ralph?" I asked.

"Parched," answered George, without looking up.

"Arid," Harold added.

Norman met my gaze. "The whitecoats have
freeze-dried his brain."

"What's the problem?" Nothing. I tried again.
"You gonna see him today?" Their heads turned
away like synchronized swimmers. I waited. One by
one they went back to studying their beers.

I tried again. "How's he feeling?"

"How would we know?" asked Harold.

"You didn't see him?"

Harold wagged his head. George broke the silence.

"Nazi bastards threw us out."

"Fascists is what they are," corrected Harold.

"He'll be digital when he comes out," said Norman.

"Thrown out for what?" I asked.

"It's what they do," said Norman. "They throw people out."

I ignored him. "For what? Thrown out for what?"

They muttered but kept their mouths clamped tight. I wasn't in the mood. Despite my best efforts, the cops had gotten an hour and a half of my time. By the time they got through busting my chops and Tommy got through bouncing around on his head like Yosemite Sam, I didn't get out of there until just before four. Maybe it was because my leg hurt. Maybe I was feeling guilty for not getting down to see Ralph. More likely, I subconsciously wanted a drink. No matter. I decided to stop at the Zoo on my way home.

"Let me take a wild guess," I started. "Let me see, I know this is off the wall, but—" I put a finger on my temple. "It couldn't be that one of you geniuses tried to slip old Ralph a little nip, now, could it?"

They huddled closer to one another. Again I waited.

Finally, George unknotted his jaw muscles and swung around on the stool. "We wanna talk to Mr.

James. Ralph's got rights, don't he? They can't just hold him there, can they? Poor bastard ain't had a drink in the better part of three days. Mr. James has gotta help us get him outta there."

"What are you, crazy? Mr. James is picking up the tab for this, fellas. He's got Ralph in there on his employee account. No way he's gonna help you guys." George started to speak, but I didn't give him the chance. "What the hell is the matter with you guys, anyway? A couple of days ago Ralph was damn near dead, and now you guys are down there trying to sneak booze to him."

"It'll kill him, Leo," Harold said seriously. "He ain't been sober a day in thirty-five years. He's too old to start now. They dry him out, he'll blow away."

"The snakes are comin' soon," said George. "You're mister hooty tooty now, but you know what I'm talkin' about. I seen you when you was dryin' out, Mr. Leo Waterman. I remember what you was like."

"Who knows—" I started, "maybe, you know, Ralph stays sober for a while, you never can tell, maybe he'll like it."

George curled his lip at me. "What is it with you, Leo? You sound like you oughta have a TV show."

Before I could object, he went on. "Wadda you think, none of us ever tried to dry out before? You think you're the only one who ever went through that fucking rigmarole? Shit. If I had a dollar for every goddamn twelve-step meeting I been to, I wouldn't be drinkin' this shitty beer."

Harold piped in. "Buddy used to say that if you counted me and him and George and Ralph, we been through recovery so many times we probably bought Betty Ford her first clinic."

"It don't work for everybody. You got to get that in your head, Leo. Some people find a higher power; some just find the power to get higher," George mused. "Wadda you think, I never thought about any of this? You think I never asked myself how come I ended up like I did? Like I didn't notice I'm on the street or somethin'? Christ. The life I lead, you get to think about where you are every hour of the goddamn day, so if you wanna do your impression of Mr. and Mrs. Clean White America, you take it the fuck up the road, whydoncha?"

I should have known better. Who was I kidding, anyway? There was no arguing with these guys. These were master rationalizers. They were, after all, the same guys who had invented the concept of having been "over-served," wherein one could rise from near death, mottled and shaking, and declare that one's present ghastly condition could be directly traced to having been grossly "over-served" by some irresponsible barkeep or other.

"He's in good hands," I countered. "They'll do what's best for him. He'll be back here before you know it." They were not swayed. "Tell you what," I said. "I'll stop in and see him myself. Just to make sure he's all right. Okay?" Nothing. "I wouldn't let anything bad happen to Ralph, and neither would the hospital. Right?" Silence.

They studied their beer and grumbled at my back as I limped back out the door into the last of the winter sunshine. Long shafts of peach light scattered across the ground now, east to west. Bright triangular remnants glowing amber among the square, dark buildings and gathering shadows. I groaned slightly as I eased myself back in the Fiat and continued north on Eastlake, crossing the university bridge and then hanging a nosebleed right down to Northeast Forty-second, keeping the wheel crimped as I rolled all the way around the ramp, back down under the bridge deck, spiraling down toward the ship canal and then east toward home.

I could hear my phone ringing through the door. I fumbled the key into the lock, banged open the door, and sprinted to the phone on the kitchen wall. The recording had already started.

You've reached 329–6480. Waterman Investigations.

"Hello!" I screamed over the recorded message.

Sorry I couldn't be here to take your call personally.

"That's not right," came from the other end.

Your call is important to us. So if you'll please—

"You there, or what?" the voice shouted.

At the tone, please leave a detailed message.

"I'm here. Just hang on for a second."

I'll get back to you as soon as possible. Thanks.

"Sorry about that," I said when the line went silent.

"That message isn't right," the voice said.

"It's not?"

"You mean 'in person,' not 'personally,'" he said. It was an old voice. Sounded like Jonathan Winters doing Maudie Frickert.

"Huh?"

"On your message. You say you're sorry you're not here to take my message personally. That's not right. You've confused the phrase 'in person,' which means physically present, with the word 'personally,' which means to take something to heart. Personally is the opposite of impersonally, which means detached. Your message ought to say that you're sorry that you're not there to take my message 'in person,' not that you wish you could take my message 'personally.' Got it?"

"Got it. Thanks," I said. "Who is this, anyway?"

"You called me. I ought to be asking you that."

"This is Leo Waterman of Waterman Investigations."

"Oh, a man with a title, eh? Well, then, this here is Chuck Bastyens of the *Willapa Harbor Herald*. How's that?"

"Oh, sorry, Mr. Bastyens. Thanks for calling."

"What can I do for you, son?"

"I was trying to get some information about a

woman who used to live out there in the Raymond area."

"What woman?"

"A woman named Selena Dunlap."

"How old?"

"I'd guess somewhere between thirty-five and forty-five."

A long silence ensued. "A big, rawboned girl?"

"I don't know about the girl part, but the big, rawboned part is about right."

"Son," he said, "don't be getting politically correct on me now. I'm eighty-one. You're all kids to me."

"Sorry."

"Sounds to me like you're talking about one of the younger Graves girls. But that can't be."

"Why's that?"

"Because, boy, I ran her obit a while back, and it's generally considered poor journalism to do that for anybody but the dead."

"Rumors of her death may have been grossly exaggerated."

"Sounds like you read a book once."

"General studies major," I confirmed.

"A Renaissance man, eh?"

"Specialization is for insects," I said.

"So you should have known better than that message, now shouldn't you?"

"Yes, sir."

Semantically satisfied, he went on. "State sent an

investigator down. Talked to lots of local folks. Sent me a copy of her death certificate a couple of months later."

"I know. I've got a copy. I showed it to her, too." He was quiet for so long, I was afraid he'd hung up. "What can you tell me about her?" I prompted.

"If this is the same girl, just about everything, up until she was twenty-two or so." I waited until he got around to it. "You know anything about this part of the state, Mr. Waterman?"

"I've driven through a few times."

"Well," he started, "this part of Pacific County is sort of out of joint with the rest of the state. We've got a wild and woolly past. Used to be more whorehouses in Raymond than there were churches, if that gives you any idea. We're not near anything. We're not even on the way to anything. Just about anyplace you can get to by going through Raymond can be gotten to easier by going some other way. You hear what I'm saying?"

"Yes, sir. I do."

"We got little pockets of people living out in the mountains who haven't changed much since the turn of the century. We was down south, they'd call the pockets hollers and the folks hillbillies. You understand what I'm telling you?"

"I do."

"Well, one of those little pockets of folks is a little valley over east of town, before you come down the hill into the city. I'm sure it's got some official name on the maps, but around here folks call it Crow Valley because a family named Crow was the first one there. Matter of fact, there's still quite a few Crows around here. Some of 'em still down in that little valley too. Anywho—another of the families down in that particular little pocket of plurality was the Graveses. Third-generation loggers. For years, they had a whole herd of bare-ass children running all over the woods out there. Some they sent to school. Some they didn't. Those that went, most of them never made it through high school. Just married somebody from one of the other families in the valley and started the whole thing over again."

"I get the picture," I said.

"Selena Graves was one of the younger ones. Maybe the youngest. I don't remember anymore. Hell, I'm not sure the parents could have told you either." He chuckled. "It was that sort of deal. Anyway, Selena married a boy from out of the valley called Bobby Dunlap. One of the first to marry outside. She couldn't have been more than sixteen or seventeen at the time. He worked for Weyerhaeuser setting choker. Just another kid with a chain saw and a pickup truck. Liked to party. Liked to drink a lot of beer and smoke a lot of weed, but otherwise a nice pair of kids. I used to see them together at the Raymond Café once in a while. Seemed like a nice young couple. Always had their heads together, grinning like they had secrets they were keeping from the rest of the world."

He reminisced for a minute and then continued. "Anyway, about in . . . seventy-three, somewhere in there, they'd been married a year or so when she had a baby boy over at the hospital in South Bend. It's a matter of public record. Christened him Lukkas Dunlap, Lukkas with two *k*'s, which was how Bobby's daddy spelled it. A real piece of work, that one."

He slipped into his thoughts again and then snapped back. "Well, life goes on, you know. They settle in and start raising their own generation of barefoot children. There was a lot of work in the woods in those days. Not like today. Those two kids were doing pretty darn good. Cops had to come out once in a while to tell them to turn the Lynyrd Skynyrd down on a Friday night, and there was some talk that they were selling a little weed to their friends, but other than that, they were pretty much living the redneck version of the American dream."

I waited for him to regroup.

"That went on for about five years. Maybe a little longer. Wouldn't you know it? Talk about bad luck. The kid survived five years of setting choker, the most dangerous job in the civilized world, and a week after he gets promoted to faller, a freak wind blows one back at him. Poor kid was cold and stiff before they cut him out and got him to the hospital in South Bend. I guess, from what they tell me, the girl just came apart. The family had written her off for moving outside the valley, so there was no help there."

"So she's about twenty-one and alone," I said. "And the boy's five or six. Is that right?"

"Yeah," he said. "But don't get me wrong. The girl was a long way from destitute. I mean she damn well should have been able to make it. She had Weyerhaeuser benefits, state benefits, the whole thing. Heck, she was probably making more money than half the folks in town." He stopped.

"But?"

"But she just couldn't stay away from the sauce," he said sadly. "She already had bad habits, and it was like losing Bobby Dunlap just set some animal loose inside her. I'd see her coming out of the liquor store at eleven in the morning, juiced to the ears, always holding that little boy by the hand. It was a damn shame," he said. He was nearing the end of his tale now, the lines coming more quickly. "She lost it all. The house. Sold the furniture. Everything. Drank it all up. Put it up her nose. I don't know. There's a lot of stories; I can't say for sure. Either way, she and the boy end up living at the old Raymond Hotel, which, believe you me, has never been any place to be raising a kid." He hesitated. "There was some talk about things she was doing to raise extra drinking money, but I don't want to go into that." Silence. The rest of it came out in a rush. "Well, one Saturday afternoon, the boy falls down the stairs at the hotel. Breaks his arm so bad they've got to screw it back together with a steel plate. Ambulance comes, carts him off. Nobody can find the mother. Cops go through the hotel, find her shacked up and shitfaced with some Chinaman on the fourth floor." I heard him breathe. "Well, that's when the state stepped in and took the boy from her. Said she was an unfit mother. Which I suppose she was."

"And?"

"Well, the boy went to a couple of foster families here in the county. That's a paper trail that's easy enough to follow. But then, about six months later he gets adopted, and the story ends."

"Sealed records?"

"Even more sealed than usual. No sooner would the county find the boy a foster home than Selena would find out about it and start showing up, making herself obnoxious to the families. Showing up drunk, demanding the boy back, threatening folks. That sort of thing. Ended up having a couple of restraining orders against her before she was through. Spent more than a few nights in the can over it, too. So, when the adoption came around, they made damned sure nobody was going to follow that trail."

"And Selena?"

"Left town," he said. "I can speak to that one

personally. Saw her go with my own eyes. Blind drunk. Everything she owned wrapped in a bedroll on the back of a Harley-Davidson. Sittin' up there, if you can believe it, behind some yahoo with MOM tattooed across his forehead."

"I believe it. And that's the last you heard of her?"

"Until that state investigator showed up saying they were thinking about declaring her dead."

"He say why?"

"Said it was confidential."

Thin ticks of plastic static could be heard above the silence of the line.

"Thanks," I said.

"Wish it was a happier tale," he said.

"Me, too."

"Excuse the old newspaperman in me, son, but I've got to know. Is there a story for me in here somewhere?"

"Could be," I said. I didn't make him ask. "If there is, I'll do the best I can to see to it that you get it first."

He made sure I had his home number, reminded me to fix my phone message, and said good-bye.

I shivered as I rose. I was stiff and sore from sitting in one place too long. In a spasm of optimism, I'd left the shades up and all the windows open when I'd left this afternoon. The apartment smelled cleaner than it had in months. The same dust seemed better, now that it had migrated to different places. The sheaf of papers I'd collected at the library and at Karen Mendolson's apartment had blown all over the floor, lending a festive air to the place. I stepped over them as I went around closing the windows and turning on the heat. As I passed the desk, I punched the button on the surge protector. I waited as the computer eeped to life, then set the modem about dialing my Internet carrier. Busy, as usual. I left it on perpetual redial and left the room.

I pulled a Beck's from the refrigerator and, using my free hand, scooped all the papers into a messy pile. I spent the next ten minutes at the kitchen table sipping beer and separating the research I'd done on Lukkas Terry from the stuff I'd taken from the girl's apartment.

I was still rearranging the material when I heard the unmistakable sound of a couple of modems swapping electronic spit. By the time I got to the desk, I was already on-line. I checked my E-mail. *Doo tee dee doo.* You have mail! One message:

Date: Sat 17 Feb 1996 00:00:18-0500
To: LeoxxW@eskimo.com
Sender: sleuth@znet.com
Subject: Mendolson Job

Leo, old buddy, nice to hear from you. Can always use a little work. Will drive up to the peninsula this

weekend. Will have something for you by Mon. pm.
Two days @ 250 per. + expen. Ok? Flash me back
if anything about this is no good. Over and out.

Ron Miller
sleuth@znet.com

I quit the mail program and was about to shut
down altogether when I noticed the little pile of
disks I'd liberated from Karen Mendolson's apartment. Plain black, double-sided, double-density
disks with no labels. I picked up the top disk and
slipped it into the machine. Because she had a Mac
at work, I figured she probably had one at home too.
Not many people mess around with both. Sure
enough, after a quick check for viruses, the little icon
appeared on the screen: "Digest" was all it said. I
double-clicked it open. It read:

Date: Thu, 14 Dec 1995 00:00:1-0500
Reply-To: Mystery Literature E-conference
<DOROTHYL@KENTVM.KENT.EDU>
Sender: Mystery Literature E-conference
<DOROTHYL@KENTVM.KENT.EDU>
From: Automatic digest processor
<LISTSERV@KENTVM.KENT.EDU>
Subject: DOROTHYL Digest-12 Dec 1995 to 15
Feb 1995
To: Recipients of DOROTHYL digests

\<DOROTHYL@KENTVM.KENT.EDU\>

There are 25 messages totaling 1003 lines in this issue.

Topics of the day:
1. Sayers' anti-semitism
2. J. A. Jance
3. comment on Valentines mysterys
4. Cleveland Pi's
5. Hindsight and DLS
6. A REAL Cyber-Mystery
7. MacLean's Wisdom
8. Help needed re Ellis Peters
9. Sayers attitudes
10. Edgars
11. Hardboiled vrs cozy debate
12. Richard Barre's new book
13. Twelve Monkeys
14. Dropshot
15. D. L. Sayers
16. Think of England
17. Quaker Mysteries
18. Lie Back and Think of England
19. WONDER BREAD
20. That Phrase Again
21. Howlers in Favorite Mysteries
22. Harlan Coben
23. Dotty L-anti-semitism

24. Edgars/12 Monkies/Howlers
25. <Nosubject given> (2)

I scrolled down to the first message:

DATE: Tues, 12 Dec 1995 18:29:42-0500
FROM: 7603168@mtimail.com
SUBJECT: Sayers' anti-semitism

Flame me if you must, but I completely fail to see
how one can be excused anti-semitic views merely
because they were prevalent at the time. Some
things do not change, and an abiding regard for the
universal value of one's fellow human beings is most
certainly one.

Lilly Rowan (Archie Goodwin's friend)
aka Barbara Reynolds
http://www.apox.com
br@apOx.com

Hmm. I kept on. A review of a new mystery book
by Seattle writer J. A. Jance. A request for anybody
who knew of mysteries centering around Valentine's
Day. Somebody inquiring about fictional PIs from
Cleveland. It went on and on. And on and on.

Four cups of coffee and four hours later, I'd
waded through all six disks. One through five had
all been the same. A chronological record of some

sort of compiled digest dedicated to discussing mystery fiction. The digest appeared to be called Dorothy L, apparently named after a famed writer named Dorothy L. Sayers, whose somewhat antiquated attitudes regarding Jews were, at least in the period between December 1995 and March 1995, engendering quite a heated debate as to whether current late-century standards should be grandmothered backward in time to include prewar dowagers. I was staying out of it.

I learned that Victorian mothers used to advise their soon-to-be-married daughters to "Lie back and think of England," that the movie *12 Monkeys* had confused a hell of a lot of people, that somewhere out there there were probably mysteries that featured Chilean CPAs, that Dorothy L represented the cozy end of the cozy versus hardboiled debate, that the digest apparently originated at Kent State University, that an inordinate number of the subscribers were located either at universities or at libraries, that most of the participants seemed to be quite well educated and fairly articulate, and that many subscribers adopted what they called noms, using the name of one of their favorite fictional characters instead of their own. Finally, I learned that if someone got off the subject of mysteries or got too nasty with other subscribers, somebody using the nom Danger Mouse would step in and gently but firmly threaten to jettison the miscreant into blackest cyberspace.

The sixth disk was different. They were all messages to Dorothy L like the others, but these were all from the same person and all on the subject of Sayers's anti-Semitism. The first one read:

DATE: Tue, 19 Dec 1995 18:21: 42-0600
FROM: J. P. Beau@aol.com
SUBJECT: anti-semitism

Pleeeese. Spare me! How can you possibly think to transpose a modern set of values on a time fifty years distant? It's absurd. Ms. Sayers professes a set of values which were totally appropriate for a woman of her station in that time period. How dare you dismiss her work with a wave of your politically correct hand.
Sorry if I sound a little strident, but this particular thread seems to bring out the worst in me.

J. P. Beaumont (J. A. Jance's Seattle Detective.)
Karen Mendolson:)
J. P. Beau@aol.com
KMen@KingLib.net.com

Bingo. I'd seen these same messages as I'd worked my way through the journals. I scrolled my way to the end. All from either the library address or the America Online address that I now presumed to be Karen's apartment. All part of the great Sayers debate. The more of them I read, the more I liked Karen Mendolson. Any enemy of PC is a friend of mine. I returned the slide to the top, ejected the disk, and reinserted one of the others.

It took me two tries, but I found it. The E-mail address of this person called Danger Mouse. Seemed as good a place as any to start. I copied the address from the message, clicked open a new message of my own, and pasted in the address.

Date: Sat, 17 Feb 96 09:12:13 EST
From: LeoxxW@eskimo.com
Subject: This Digest
To: KROBINSO@KENTVM.KENT.EDU

Hello. I came across Dorothy L while surfing the web. Could you tell me more about it please.

Thanks,
Leo Waterman

Send. I stood and stretched. My shin throbbed. I could still feel the touch of those stairs I'd rolled down the other night. As I reached for the mouse to shut down the computer, someone began banging on my apartment door. Had to be Hector. Nobody else could get in. Hector Guiterrez was the superintendent of my apartment building, a banished Cuban whose negative attitude toward Castro's regime had earned him seven years in prison, fourteen days in a leaking boat, and another two years behind barbed wire in south Florida. Even after all these years in the land of the free and the home of the brave, Hector still harbored a deep, abiding distrust of authority figures. Hector was an ardent subscriber to the conspiratorial view of history. Everything was a plot. A new postman was a potential CIA agent. If he lost a sock in the dryer, he figured it was being microanalyzed in some underground laboratory.

Years ago, for reasons I'd never fully understood, Hector had unilaterally adopted me as a coconspirator. I'd never been totally clear as to whom we were conspiring against or to what ends, but it seemed to make Hector happy, which was good enough for me. Off the pig. Subvert the dominant paradigm. It was us against the world.

Sure enough. There he was, his boiled-egg head gleaming, his thick mustache, just beginning to show traces of gray, twitching furiously. He blustered past me into the room, waving a Federal Express envelope, taking laps around the coffee table, cutting the air with the envelope.

"Leo, jew chit. I got better tings to do dan chase abter you."

"Sorry, Hector. You should have called, man, I would have—"

"Called? I chould hab called? Who de fock jew kidding? I been trying all damn day. You on that focking Web all de time. Not eeven da pope can call you, Leo. You out dere focking around all de time." He passed the envelope under my nose. "Dat's how dey get your brain. Dat's how dey control you. Dat's what dey gonna make happen. Gonna control your brain tru de wires."

I knew better than to ask exactly who "dey" was. Ask him that, and you could be here till dawn.

He stopped waving the envelope and pressed it against my chest with two hands. "Eeet come about one o'clock," he said. "I gotta run. Just got a call. My broder Rueben, you remember Rueben—"

I said I did. Rueben and I had once spent eighteen hours handcuffed to one another, but Hector seemed to feel that a mundane moment such as that was insufficient to engender recall.

"Hees daughter Elena, she just go into labor up at Providence. Rueben gonna be a grandpapa." He started for the door and then turned to wag a finger at me. "Jew see, dey could call me and tell me of dis, so I could be part of de joyous event. I'm not out dere on dat focking Web all de time. *Si?* Gotta go."

I stood with my back to the door, listening to Hector whistle his way down the hall. When the tweeting faded, I walked into the office and punched

the button on the surge protector. The screen went
black. The room fell silent. I wandered back into the
kitchen, leaned my elbows on the counter, and
pulled the strip on the envelope.

13

IT WAS THERE WHEN I FIRED THE MACHINE UP in the morning. The little musical tone announced that I had mail. I checked my electronic mailbox. One message.

> Date: Sun, 18 Feb 96 14:45:42 EST
> From: "Kara L. Robinson"
> <KROBINSO@KENTVM.KENT.EDU>
> Subject: Re: Your query
> To: Leo Waterman <LeoxxW@eskimo.com>

Hi Leo,

DorothyL is an e-conference for the discussion of mystery literature, films and television. It is high traffic, enthusiastic and often overwhelming. The subscribers are extremely knowledgeable about mysteries and tend to welcome "newbies" with open arms. Just remember though, off-topic postings are

severely frowned upon, as are flaming and general
rudeness.
Let me know if you want to know more.

Danger Mouse AKA
Kara L. Robinson

I went into the kitchen, started a pot of coffee,
and returned to the office. I cracked my knuckles,
stretched my back, and began to type.

Date: Sun, 18 Feb 96 08:17:56 EST
From: Leo Waterman <LeoxxW@eskimo.com>
Subject: Re: Subscribing to DorothyL
To: "Kara L. Robinson"
<KROBINSO@KENTVM.KENT.EDU>

Kara:
Thanks for the quick response. How do I get connected to DorothyL?

Best,
Leo Waterman

Short and sweet. Send. Shutdown. When I heard
the modem click off, I picked up the phone and
dialed Jed. He picked up on the third ring. His voice
sounded as if he had hooks caught in his throat.

"Jesus, Leo, what time is it?"

I looked back over my shoulder at the clock on the stove. Oops. Eight-twenty in the A.M. "Just a little before nine," I lied.

"Isn't this Sunday?" he asked.

"Some places," I hedged.

I could hear him sitting up in bed. "You found the Mendolson girl."

"Not exactly."

"How not exactly?"

"Exactly not at all."

"Then what in holy hell are you calling me before eight-thirty on a Sunday morning for?"

"This library thing—" I started. "This is a straight deal, right? You're not holding anything back from me, are you?"

"Like what?"

"Like something that would give somebody an uncontrollable urge to run my miserable ass over."

I had his attention now. "Really? Like with a car?"

"A van, actually. But yeah, a lot like that."

"You okay?"

"A scrape here and there, but otherwise I'm okay."

"I swear. The job is just what it seems to be," Jed said. "When?"

"Yesterday afternoon."

"Must be about something else. Can't be the library."

"That's what I figured. I just wanted to be sure."

"Oh?"

"I've been doing a little poking around in something else. It seems to be making somebody real nervous."

"So it would seem," Jed said. "You want to tell me about it?"

I did. He stopped me right away. "Whoa," he said. "Listen, man, I liked her too, but that doesn't make her Lukkas Terry's mother. We have no way of knowing that this woman is even who she claims to be."

"Oh, she's Selena Dunlap all right. I got her one and only driver's license picture last night. It's her, Jed. Younger. Happier. But it's sure as hell her."

"That doesn't make her anybody's mom," he pointed out.

I told him about old Chuck Bastyens's story and the stainless steel plate Tommy Matsukawa had in the jar.

"We'll need documentation," he said.

I agreed and went on with my story. He stopped me again halfway through. "How in hell did anybody find out you were poking around in her paperwork?"

"Damn good question. Whoever it was knew, like, instantly. Hell, my old man couldn't have found it out that fast on his best day. I only bought the death certificate day before yesterday. Whoever this is must have serious connections."

"All the more reason to be careful," he said.

I finished my story. I knew he was with me when he said, "I am, after all, the woman's attorney of record."

"You most certainly are," I agreed.

"It's my duty as an officer of the court to see to it that her rights are represented as vigorously as possible."

"Yes, it is."

"We wouldn't, after all, want to be participants in yet another example of corporate greed run amok at the expense of the rapidly disappearing middle class."

"We certainly wouldn't."

"Okay, then," he said. "As *your* attorney, I advise you to watch your ass at all times. There's gonna be some noses seriously out of joint when I stick the monkey wrench in the works tomorrow morning."

"Trust me, I shall pay the utmost attention," I said, gently massaging my shin.

"I'll file a restraining order first thing on Monday, which by the way, Leo, in this part of the globe, is tomorrow. So if you don't mind—"

I said I didn't. Before I could hang up, he said, "And, uh, Leo, you don't suppose you could put in a little time on this case I'm paying you for, do you? Just in your free time, say." *Click. Hmmm.*

I cleaned up my breakfast mess, grabbed my keys off the hook, and headed for the garage. The newspaper articles I'd collected on Lukkas Terry said he'd recorded the much-anticipated *Crotch Cannibals* in a state-of-the-art recording studio attached to his manager's house. What better way to spend this glorious Sunday morning than meeting Mr. Seattle Rock and Roll himself, Gregory Conover?

Everybody knew the story. Wangled a late-night DJ job on KXR when he was only twenty. Back in about fifty-nine, Top 40 format. Separated himself from the pack when he began to promote rock-and-roll shows at the Spanish Castle, an old roadhouse about halfway between Seattle and Tacoma. My personal connection to Gregory Conover was the summer of sixty-seven. The summer of love, when he got the city to let him use the old band shell in Volunteer Park for a series of concerts. He combined local acts like Crome Syrcus and Magic Fern with California acts like Moby Grape and the Quicksilver Messenger Service and set the town on its ear. What I remember of it was great.

He'd had his ups and downs, disappearing from the public eye for most of the seventies, unfortunately surfacing only long enough to buy a white disco suit and matching belt and pronounce himself the Northwest Disco King. Six months later, not being one to let art cloud reason, he'd been right up there shoveling disco records into the fire when they'd staged Disco Inferno Night down in the Kingdome parking lot. Whatever he may have lacked in consistency of vision, he more than made up for in continuity of effort. No craze was too crazed. No fad too fucked.

By the time the mid-eighties rolled around, Gregory Conover found himself on the outside looking in. To the local punk and grunge players, he was just a nasty reminder of the omnipresent sixties, which, as far as they were concerned, relics like Conover and I could feel free to stick where the sun didn't shine. They were looking for walls to break down; they wanted to thrash rather than embrace that which had come before. Who could blame them? Rock and roll was never meant to be polite.

Conover went back to doing his radio program, classic rock now. Led Zeppelin and Traffic. Never missing an opportunity to rail embarrassingly about the myriad failings of modern music. Until that day when a skinny kid dropped a two-dollar tape on the desk in front of him and said his name was Lukkas Terry.

Four albums later, the rest was history. Once more, he was the man. The man who, if the papers were to be believed, stood to end up with no less than half of Lukkas Terry's estate and royalty checks once the current court case got sorted out. He had moved from being the ringmaster to being the Godfather. All things considered, this was a man I needed to meet.

I knew where the house was the minute I saw the

picture in the paper. It was that white stone mansion that lounged out over the side of the hill on lower Broadway. The house had always fascinated me. From the street it seemed completely surrounded by a stone wall, covered since my childhood with ivy. The single entrance was an ivy-covered arch cut into the wall, barred by a black iron gate. The look called for a monk in a hooded robe.

From the waters of Lake Union, however, the place looked more like the Hanging Gardens of Babylon, as it cascaded in a series of vine-covered terraces down toward the lake. Whatever ascetic quality it may have possessed from the street, the view from the west most surely denied.

It was a party. At eleven o'clock on a friggin' Sunday morning, it was a full-blown bacchanalia. The street was filled with cars. The private alley that ran next to the house was stacked. Fleetwood Mac drifted out into the street. Something middle-aged in me was nearly offended. I got over it in a hurry.

I pushed the buzzer again. Up close, it wasn't ivy at all, but instead some wiry little African vine with leathery leaves and needle-sharp thorns the size of my thumb. Body piercing au naturel.

He waddled up the brick walk, whistling, twirling a gold key on a silver chain, his right index finger pointed right at me as it circled. He waddled because his thighs were so monstrously muscled as to have nowhere to go but out. Hell, his calves nearly touched. Spotless white shorts, just a bit too tight. Nice little woven belt. A behemoth with a twenty-four-inch neck, maybe bigger. Easily the biggest mass of muscle I'd ever seen in the flesh. Thinning blond hair combed straight back. Blue eyes, almost white. A living testament to the power of anabolic steroids and the joys of protracted leisure.

"Yo," he said.

"I'd like to see Mr. Conover."

"Your name?'"

"Leo Waterman."

He scanned the clipboard in his left hand. A plastic picture badge was clipped to the collar of his bright yellow shirt. It said Cherokee. I guess, with some guys, one name is enough.

"You're not here," he announced.

"I wasn't expected," I admitted.

"Then you don't come in."

I pulled out a business card and a pen. On the back I wrote "Representing Lukkas Terry's mother." I stuck it through the bars.

Cherokee used the clipboard to knock it to the ground.

"Beat it, bub."

"Bub?" I said. "You would bub a guy this early? On a Sunday?"

"What I'd do is beat your ass, you don't get out of here, bub."

I reached through the bars and snatched the badge from his shirt. I took a step back and looked it over. "You got your own bar code. Dude. How about that? If they run that little wand over you, you'll come up as yourself. Could completely eliminate the need for therapy. You ever think of that?"

Apparently he hadn't. "Gimme that thing," he snarled.

"Wait a second." I stepped over to the right of the gate.

"Don't make me come out there, motherfucker."

"Tell you what—"

Cherokee was a poor listener. He untwirled the key, stuck it in the inside lock, and came barreling out through the gate. The second his shoulders came through, I hooked him hard with my left arm, getting an arm under like a defensive lineman, hurrying him the way he was already moving, using his own bulk for momentum. As he staggered past, I stepped into the breach, pulled the key from the lock, and closed the gate behind me. I stood two paces back, twirling the key.

"Beat it, bub," I said.

"I'll break you," he said. "I'll tear your—"

"See. It doesn't feel good to be bubbed, now does it?"

"—and stuff it up your—"

"Especially not on a nice Sunday morning."

"—and use your tongue for a—"

I pocketed the key and left him to reflect upon the error of his ways. If his red-faced attempt to tear the gate from its moorings, however, was any measure of his contrition, I believed further anger management work was going to be required.

14

THE ENTIRE CENTER OF THE HOUSE WAS OPEN. Six French doors at each end created a tiled breezeway running from street to garden. On the right, down a short flight of stairs, what I imagined used to be the solarium had been transformed into a recording studio. The control panel ran the length of the room. Tilted my way, its maze of gauges, needles, switches, and slides suggested a NASA moon shot. A stooped guy with waist-length hair and granny glasses was fiddling with the controls.

Out in the garden, knots of people wandered in and out of my field of vision, clutching highball glasses and passing joints to the throbbing of the music. *Players only love you when they're playing*.

Except for the guy in the studio, the house seemed empty. I walked down the three steps and stepped through the open door into the glassed-in control room, which served more as a crowded balcony, hovering over another large room six feet below, where pools of coiled cable surrounded numbered islands of green carpet where the musicians stood.

The longhaired guy looked my way as I stepped into the room. Despite the hair, he was no kid, closer to forty than twenty, his kinky locks flecked with gray. He said, "How ya doin'?"

"Doing great," I said. "This is some setup."

"The best that money can buy. Can I help ya?"

"I was looking for Gregory Conover."

"He's probably outside"—he waved that way—"where the party never ends." He went back to moving slides and tapping the glass faces of dials. "Got a bad relay in here somewhere," he mused.

"You ever work with Lukkas Terry?" I asked.

"Nobody worked with Lukkas Terry. You just opened the door and threw cheese sandwiches and Pepsi at him."

"Nobody?"

"Lukkas didn't need any help."

He stopped his fiddling and seemed to take me in for the first time.

"Hey, uh—"

"Leo Waterman," I said, offering a hand. His grip was firm, his hand surprisingly hard and rough, like a carpenter's.

"Marty Stocker. Nice to meet ya," he said. "You know Mr. Conover or something?"

"I'm afraid I haven't had the pleasure."

He found this amusing. "How'd you get past Cherokee?"

"Cherokee stepped out," I said.

He liked this too. "Far out." He looked around. "Keep away from that fucker," he admonished. "He's crazy. Likes to hurt people."

I promised I would. "Did he really do it all on his own, like they say?"

"Swear to God," he said. Again, he checked the general area.

"Let me tell you a little story. When I first met Lukkas, we were still over in Bothell at the old place, but we had pretty much the same shit in the studio. You know, we've upgraded a few things since then, but it was pretty much the way you see it. Anyway, Mr. Conover brings this skinny kid in and introduces us. Happens all the time. Friends of friends. Plain old wanna-bes who hitchhiked in from Minnesota. The whole thing. Hands me this cheap shit tape the kid put together. I stick it in the deck and, you know, I'm ready to run the usual number on the kid, yeah, not bad, got a hell of a future, don't call us, we'll call you, the whole dog-and-pony show. But I notice right away that the boss's got this gleam in his eye." He stopped.

"And?"

"So I actually listen, for once. And it takes about one minute to figure out that this kid's got more music floatin' around loose in his head than most anybody else is ever gonna see."

"Just off a little demo?"

"One minute flat was all it took."

"Amazing."

"No. Here's the amazing part. He leaves the kid with me. Lukkas starts asking me what everything is, what it does. He knows from nothing. Never seen a real tape machine before. We've got a couple of Studer 800 MK3s that just blow his mind. He wants to know everything. We go through the whole she-bang. I start him out with the tracking console, the mixing consoles, the Nevi and SSI compressors, the Moogs and the expanders, the sequencers, the pre's, the eqs. Everything, all the way down to the guitar pedals. He's like this sponge, just takin' it all in." He took a deep breath.

I folded my arms over my chest and waited for him to continue.

"So anyway, later that afternoon Mr. Conover sends me down to the Moore to fix some sequencer problems they're having down there. Things are a mess. I don't get back into the studio for about two days, and guess what?" He didn't make me guess. "I walk back in here two days later and the kid is still here. Never left. Been sitting right here playing with the equipment all that time."

"Really?" I said.

"And here's the wild part—he's got it all figured

out. He's already recorded three songs. The first three on his first album. Absolutely unbelievable. I've been engineering for twenty-two years, and I've never seen anything like it. He's sittin' in here singing all the parts in all these different voices. The stuff comes out of him whole. It's not like he writes one part and then another; he hears the entire song at one time. Damndest thing I ever saw. After that, all you did was just leave him alone."

"What was he like? I mean personally."

He was tapping gauges again, flipping switches. "Hard to say. It's that genius-madness thing, man. You always hear about that fine line between them. But this was the real deal. First time I ever really saw it. Talked to himself in all these voices while he worked. The boss had to remind him to take showers. Couldn't care less about anything except his music. The ultimate perfectionist. Kept going over and over everything, until it drove everyone crazy. Always late on deadline. Heck, on the last one, *Crotch Cannibals*, he was three months late and talking about trashing the whole thing and starting over. One weird dude."

He stepped around me, walked to the far end of the console, and made some adjustments. "World isn't made for people like Lukkas Terry," he said finally. He walked to the door at the far end of the room. "I gotta get to work here," he said.

"Thanks for the help."

"Try outside. The boss is probably out there."

The outdoor festivities consisted of maybe thirty-five people, settled in knots of five or six, milling about the three levels, nursing cocktails and pretending to listen to one another. Fleetwood Mac had been replaced by the Stones. Mick was on his way down to the demonstration to get his fair share of abuse.

As I came through the doors, I stepped to the right, liberated a glass of champagne from the buffet table, and took stock. Two Korean men in spotless white livery attended the table from either end. Ornamental cold cuts. A little ice sculpture of a dolphin. Lots of fruits and salads.

Gathered to the right of the food and drink, five young women stood transfixed, facing my way, forming a loose arc about Gregory Conover, whose arms swung expressively from the loose sleeves of a gold caftan as he held them, mesmerized.

I went down to the Chelsea drugstore, to get my . . .

They were all maybe twenty-five or so. I'm not good with ages anymore. They all look like kids to me. Black was the predominant color. Black boots, black tights, black leather jackets, four miles of chain, and enough black eye shadow to paint the porch. As I approached him from the rear, their expressions caused him to turn my way. He looked me over carefully, from head to toe and back, before he spoke.

"Can I help you?" he said in a neutral tone.

. . . but if you try sometimes, you just might find, you get . . .

If the hair was all his, it was truly a gift from God. A wondrous thick mass of salt-and-pepper plumage, it feathered back about his head like a storm cloud helmet, nearly forming a mane or perhaps the vestige of wings. Despite a general puffiness, his face still retained its youthful sheen of accessibility. His big brown eyes seemed open to the moment, making the lines in his face seem out of place and artificial.

. . . And she said one word to me, and it was . . .

I stuck out my hand. "Leo Waterman," I said.

He was a two-hand shaker. "Gregory Conover," he replied.

"I was wondering if I might have a word with you," I started.

He was focused back out over my shoulder toward the house, as if expecting someone. The whole chorus sang.

. . . You can't always get what you want . . .

"Regarding?" he said, without making eye contact.

"Lukkas Terry."

For the first time, I had his full attention. "And you're from?"

I handed him a card. He read it carefully. "Perhaps we should step into my office," he said with a smile.

Without a word to the young women, he spun on his heel, took me by the elbow, and guided me back the way I'd come, through the French doors, down the long breezeway, and through the last door on the right.

I was expecting a dark gentleman's-club decor. I was wrong. The room looked out over the alley beside the house through a half a dozen large leaded windows, which bathed the room in gentle southern light. The wallpaper was a small floral print. The furniture was bleached oak. The paintings on the walls were Impressionist garden portraits. He closed the door behind us and then read my card again. "If you don't mind my asking, Mr. Waterman, how did you get in here?"

I pulled the gold key and chain from my pocket and handed it to Conover. "I had a difference of opinion with a guy called Cherokee."

He looked shocked. "About what?"

"Manners."

"And you—"

"Locked him out," I finished.

"You didn't—" he started. "I mean, there was no violence?"

"Nope."

He gave me a big smile. "Extraordinary," he said. "So, now he's outside, and—" He pointed at me.

"And I'm in here," I said.

"Far out," he enthused. Again he glanced at my

card, as we stood in the center of the room. "And what interest would a private detective have in poor Lukkas at this late date?"

"I represent an attorney who has taken an interest in the case."

"That's not terribly informative."

"I know."

He seemed to be losing patience with me. I expected him to throw me out. Instead he asked, "Do you have a license or some such thing?"

I showed it to him. He took his time going over it, and then handed it back. "I have to be very careful about the press," he said. "They'd keep poor Lukkas's death on the front page forever, if they could."

"It sells ads."

"Lukkas Terry was like a son to me," he said sadly. Before I could open my mouth, he started in on the canned spiel. The same mythic tale I'd gotten from the papers and from Marty Stocker. I let him ramble. I was used to it. It was the same thing they did when they talked about my old man, that mixing of tinted recall and tainted desire that makes the person simultaneously both more and less than he actually was and blurs forever the boundaries between fact and fiction for all who hear the tale.

"So he lived here with you," I said when he'd finished.

"Right up until the end."

"How come he moved out?"

He looked wistfully out the window. "My fault," he said quietly. "I told myself I was weaning him. That I was getting him ready for the real world. I mean—" He threw his hands up and then let them drop to his sides. "I thought I was doing the right thing."

"Did you know about—you know that—hard drugs," I blurted.

"I should have suspected," he said. "God knows, I've been around the business long enough. It's always there." He turned back my way. "He'd lived with me for two years. I hadn't heard from him in several days. That should have put up a red flag for me. Lukkas was very dependent on me. It wasn't like him to be out of touch for three days." Gregory Conover pinched the bridge of his nose and took a long, deep breath.

"How did you—" I began.

The banging of doors and a series of coarse shouts filtered in from the center of the house. Several voices could be heard through the door. Conover stepped around me toward the office door when it suddenly burst open, banging back twice against the wall.

Cherokee looked as if he had either survived the Death of a Thousand Cuts or recently been threshed and baled. Every square inch of exposed skin was crosshatched with deep scratches. Several leathery leaves were stuck in his hair. His bright yellow shirt was streaked with sweat and dirt. He was missing one sneaker. He seemed to be annoyed.

He pointed at me with a bleeding finger. "You," he bellowed. "I'm gonna take you and tear your—"

Conover put a hand on Cherokee's overdeveloped chest. "Whoa, now, whoa," he said, as if gentling a horse. "We have to get you something for those scratches." Cherokee was trembling all over like an over-amped retriever on the first day of pheasant season. I backed to the far wall, rolling my shoulders, feeling the comfort of the 9mm beneath my jacket. I had no intention of fighting him. I'd take my chances with a jury of my peers. I figured they'd give me a commendation for not shooting him in the head. If he got anywhere near me, I was drilling him in the foot.

The doorway was filled with wide-eyed partygoers, pawing past each other for a better view. Holding Cherokee by the shoulders, Conover spoke out into the hall. "Brittany, you and Melody go upstairs into the main guest bath. Start a bath. See what you can find for these scratches." I heard heels clapping across the tiles and a buzz of conversation from the hall.

Cherokee shrugged the hands from his shoulders and started for me. I moved to the left, keeping the couch between us. Like most farm animals, he was a lot bigger indoors. Conover hustled back between us, steering him toward the far corner over by the windows, where he administered a hushed lecture to the big fellow. Conover looked back over his shoulder toward the doorway.

"Reenee," he called.

The shortest of the five young women stepped hesitantly into the room. Her jet-black hair was cut in a severe pageboy, bangs low over the forehead but cut up high in back, leaving only stubble on a long, thin neck. Conover pulled the key and chain from his pocket and waved it at her. "You'd better show Mr. Waterman out."

She crossed the room, her eyes locked on Cherokee, took the key from Conover's hand, and backed her way out. She met my gaze but didn't speak. I sidled slowly around the end of the couch and followed her out the door. "I'll find you," Cherokee growled from behind me. "I'll find you, and when I do—"

Whatever atrocities he had in mind were lost as I brushed by the gaggle of guests and followed the young woman down the breezeway.

She slipped the key in the lock but didn't pull the gate open. Instead she looked past me, back up the path toward the house.

"Somebody needs to look into it," she said.

"You mean Lukkas Terry?"

"Yeah."

"You knew him?"

She shook her head. "Nobody knew him. He was too weird to know." Before I could speak, she went on. "I mean, like, you know, everybody, all the girls anyway, tried to put the moves on him, but he was just too weird. But—" She pulled open the gate. "You want to know about Lukkas, you find his little girlfriend."

"He had a girlfriend?"

"Ditziest honey in America," she said with a laugh. "After years of every light hook in the music scene trying to get in his pants, he finds this little piece from Utah on his own." She shook her head. "Beth Goza is her name."

"You got any idea how I might find her?"

"She used to come over here once in a while. I took her home one night when Lukkas had locked himself in the studio and wouldn't come out. She lives on one of those streets that run between Pike and Pine up on the hill. I always get them mixed up. Got these big white rocks out front so you won't park there. That's all I remember."

I figured that was all I'd need.

15

I STARTED DOWN AT THE FREEWAY and worked my way up the hill, slaloming back and forth between Pike and Pine streets, among the pubs, tattoo parlors, vintage clothing stores and omnipresent espresso bars that defined the neighborhood as generic Generation X.

Reenee's memory had been good. About six blocks up, I turned onto Boylston, and there they were. A dozen good-size stones, once painted white, haphazardly filling the muddy area between the apartment building and the street, denying this hallowed space to all but monster trucks.

The building was a throwback to a less pretentious age of traveling salesmen, of single nights in shirtsleeve rooming houses with bathrooms just down the hall. The windows on the ground floor were covered with square black wrought-iron bars. Brown composition shingles covered the outside in what, before slippage, had been some sort of weave pattern, its geometric unity now eroded into a series of senseless waves that frittered aimlessly about the building.

I slipped around the corner and parked in front of the Mercedes dealership. For some reason, the sight of me and the Fiat didn't give either of the car salesmen the urge to so much as twitch.

I stood on the blue AstroTurf in the covered vestibule and tried to make sense of the door security system. Somewhere in the distant past the rain had blown in, smearing the ink on the resident list, rusting and running the cheap metal of the frame, creating a mushy mosaic where the names should have been. I began pushing buttons. I didn't answer the garbled voices screeching from the ruined speaker; I just kept pushing buttons until the woman appeared.

She looked like an anorexic member of the Munster family. Five foot four, maybe eighty pounds, in a tight print dress and knee-high black boots. The skin between the boots and the dress had surely never seen the sun. Her black hair suggested a recent dose of high voltage. She banged open the door. The blast of hot air smelled like a giant cat box.

"What the hell is the matter with you?" she demanded.

"I'm looking for Beth Goza."

"Then why don't you just push *her* button, man?"

I tapped the filthy glass next to the buttons. "What,

you can read this crap? Am I missing something here? What are these, ancient runes or something?"

"That's shit, is what it is, buddy. It's broken shit like everything else around here. Once it breaks, it stays broke. You can call 'em till your ass falls off, and they won't come out and fix it."

I spent a few minutes and scored a few points by sympathizing about the plight of helpless tenants caught in the grip of pitiless slumlords. Finally she said, "This time of day, Beth's always down at that books-and-coffee joint on the corner." When I looked blank, she went on. "You know, the one over on Pine. I see her every day when I drive to work. Hell, most times she's still there when I come home."

She didn't stick around for thanks. As she motored back up the narrow stairs, I concluded that she had, as she'd so colorfully suggested, dialed for repairs till her ass had fallen off. I smiled as I turned, the image of her sliding out of chairs onto the floor significantly brightening my little morning. What can I say? I'm a man of simple pleasures.

I stuffed my hands in my pants pockets as I rounded the corner onto Pine Street and headed downhill. She meant the Bauhaus, four blocks in front of me, one of those books-and-coffee bars that have puffed up like hives all over the city in the last five years. Watering holes for the thousands of melancholic intellectuals who need some place to get their backpacks in out of the rain, get wired to the

ears on designer coffee, and discuss how the retro
values of post-industrial America no longer hold
meaning. Staring at a lifetime of diminished expec-
tations and menial employment, they've opted to
Free Tibet.

The place was just like I remembered. It had a
vaguely East European quality. Sedition City. This
week only. Forty percent off purges. On my left a
guy with a long, unkempt beard muttered as he
scribbled on a yellow legal pad. He looked as if he
might at any second jump to his feet and begin an
impassioned denunciation of capitalism and the
running-dog lackeys of the imperialist state.

Maybe a dozen people were scattered about the
tables. My finely honed skills of deduction and
detection told me that if I discounted the anarchist,
the four gay couples, and the two African-
Americans, Beth Goza was probably the willowy one
with the cranberry-colored hair over by the books.

She was reading a trade paperback copy of *Men
Are from Mars, Women Are from Venus*. She didn't look
up as I stood next to the table.

"Are you Beth Goza?" I asked.

She looked up from the book. She had a pair of
nearly yellow eyes that seemed to glow without pre-
tense.

"Yes," she said.

"Could I have a few words with you?"

I pulled out a chair and sat down. Except for the

ten or fifteen eyebrow rings, the pierced nose, and the four pounds of metal she carried in each ear, she looked a lot like an occidental version of a Japanese dancer, bright red lipstick offsetting perfectly white skin, eyebrows drawn perfectly in place. She wore black tights, a short black leather jacket decorated with enough chain to pull a propane truck, and a short plaid skirt. Industrio-leather Catholic school.

"I don't know you," she said. Quick, this one.

I fished a business card out of my pocket. She held the card with two hands, running her eyes slowly over the surface rather than just reading the words. "What are you investigating?" she asked.

"Lukkas Terry," I said without hesitation.

I wouldn't have thought it possible that one who had so perfectly achieved the Seattle never-seen-the-sun, dead-for-a-couple-of-weeks skin pallor could actually blanch, but she did.

Without a word, she pocketed my card and hustled for the door. I followed along, watching the yellow soles of her new Doc Martens.

"Go away," she said over her shoulder. Her legs were a bit shorter than mine, so I had no trouble keeping up.

"This is dumb," I said as we cleared the door frame. "I'm not here to make any trouble for you, but I'm not going away either. I'm yours morning, noon, and night until we have a little talk." She lengthened her stride. "I know it was you who called the cops. You're the one who found him, I know you did," I said.

She turned and poked me in the chest. "You know nothing. Now, get away from me."

Again I found myself staring at her back as we hurried up Pine Street. Beth had not done nearly as much dialing as the other one and was symmetrically the better for not having done so. I tagged along for another half a block, where she again turned to face me. She put her hands on her hips and faced me like an impatient parent. "What is it with you, Mr.—"

"Waterman," I said with a Bondian air. "Leo Waterman."

She favored me with a sneer. "Take a hint, detecto boy. Buzz off. It's almost over. Just leave it alone. Okay?"

I made eye contact and held it. "Listen to me, Beth. You seem like a nice kid." Her eyes flickered. Been there. Heard that. "Let me finish," I said. "If, when you tell me to leave *it* alone, if by *it* you mean this whole deal of Lukkas's estate being divvied up between Sub-Rosa Records and Gregory Conover, well then, honey, you better make other plans."

She started to speak, but I waved her off. "'Cause that little scenario is over." She held my gaze now. "A lawyer friend of mine is going to throw a jumbo monkey wrench into that little arrangement first thing tomorrow morning. It's a done deal. I'm telling you the truth here."

She bared her teeth and leaned forward. I made sure I was on the balls of my feet. I thought she was going to go for my face, but instead she regained her composure.

"You're contemptible. You know that? You're just trying to scare me. I won't let you frighten me," she said.

"Your lawyer friend has no connection to Lukkas Terry. None. N-O-N-E," she spelled it. Correctly, too. "You're sooo full of it."

"Yeah, but my lawyer friend represents someone who *is* connected to Lukkas."

"Like who?"

I shouldn't have. I should have told her it was confidential and let it go at that. Instead, I showed off.

"Like Lukkas's mother," I said.

Her eyes narrowed. "You're a bad man, Mr. Waterman."

She could have said nearly anything else. She could have questioned the viability of my genetic material, the bona fides of my parentage, the nobility of my appointage, or the quality of my tumescence. Anything would have pissed me off less.

"I am not," I shot back.

"Are too."

"Am not."

"I can see it in your aura."

"I don't have an aura."

"Do too."

"Do not."

If necessary, I was prepared to carry on at this for another couple of weeks. I didn't care. Whatever it took.

"You leave me alone," she said.

"No."

She shifted her weight to her right foot. "I can't believe it. You're *sooo* lower vibrational."

"What's that supposed to mean?"

"The fact that you don't know proves it."

She leaned back against a shop front and brushed at her skirt. Something about the way she patted herself clean slipped an odd gear somewhere in the mess of my mind.

"So help me out," I said.

"You need way more help than I can give you."

"'Mighty oaks from tiny acorns grow.'"

"What's that supposed to mean?"

"The fact that you don't know proves it."

"Grow up," she said.

"My immaturity keeps me young."

Traffic on Pine had picked up. The hissing sound of bus brakes approached from the east. Without warning, she pulled the jacket tight about her middle and took off up Pine Street like a greyhound. She caught me flatfooted. Cursing silently, I trotted along half a block back. She was in good shape. Even encumbered by the little skirt, her long legs ate up the uphill ground. I concentrated on finding my rhythm and moving my arms. Two blocks up she cut off slantwise across the street. Afraid I was going to lose her, I picked up my pace and tried to close some of the distance. No need.

The girl was still running smoothly when she unexpectedly went to the ground in the doorway of the Mars Cleaners. She threw her back into the right rear corner and slid to the pavement. The studs on the jacket screeched down the tiles like fingernails across a blackboard. I stopped running. The street was deserted. I approached her slowly as I traversed Pine Street.

Her mouth was open, but she was only slightly winded. She held her sides with both hands and looked me in the eye.

"I didn't think you could keep up."

"You were right," I wheezed.

"Lukkas said he'd seen her," she said.

"His mother?"

"Right at the end. Right before he—" She mustered her reserves. "One night coming out of the Moore. The first night there was ever really a band. He swore he saw his mother in the crowd there in the alley when they were getting him into the limo. He swore. And I didn't believe him," she said with a shake of her head. "I didn't believe him."

"Why not?"

"Because he was already so freaked out. You know, about having to play in public. Lukkas never wanted to play in public. He wanted to make studio music. But Greg kept at him, you know, this was the nineties. That there had to be a band, like, that people could see. That they had to do videos and stuff. Lukkas was blown away. That night, the night he said he saw his mom, the night the band played its only gig, he musta puked about twenty times before they went on. It was—"

She sat there slowly shaking her head. I stood in the doorway and watched as she worked her way through it. Watched until a hand on my shoulder spun me around.

A kid. Maybe twenty. Long blond hair in dreadlocks. Scuffed leather bag over one shoulder. Nice knit cap, red, yellow, and green, pulled rakishly over one eye. "I don't know what's goin' on here, man. But this don't look good to me. Maybe you ought to—"

I cut him off. "Everything's cool here, kid. Thanks for being concerned. We need more concerned citizens."

He dug his fingers into my shoulder. "I think you better—"

I grabbed the thumb with one hand, the forearm with the other, and commenced introductions. He went to one knee. I relaxed a little.

"You need to go away now, kid."

When I let go, he backed down the length of the block, mumbling, "Hey, fuck you, man," bobbing his head, assuming combat stances. A Mighty Morphine Power Ranger. Way too much time spent playing Mortal Kombat, I suspected. We silently watched his exit.

"You hurt that boy," she accused.

"Not much."

Rasta Boy was one block down now, other side of the street, pointing a particularly vicious tai chi exercise my way.

"It's all my fault," she said, looking down at herself.

I took a chance. "You're pregnant, aren't you?"

She threw her eyes toward the sky. "I can't believe it," she said.

"Believe what?"

"That I'm pregnant, you dolt. He told me right away. No kids. Said he had bad blood. Lukkas used to call himself the Bad Seed. Like after this old black-and-white movie about a little girl who—"

"I've seen it," I said.

"It's all my fault."

"No way."

"Way."

"It takes two to tango," I insisted.

"Or three, or four, or five," she mused.

"You didn't put that needle in his arm."

"In a way I did," she said.

"No way?"

"Way," she said. "See"—she pointed at me—"you're just like the rest of them. Just because he's a certain age and a musician, you just assume he must be some kind of drug addict. Just like that." She snapped her fingers in my face.

"He had other needle marks," I said.

"Duuuh. Like migraines, retardo boy. Lukkas was very tense, very tight. When he got stressed, he got these migraines. He was such a wuss he couldn't even give himself the shots. Had to get other people to do him up with the medicine. It was pathetic. Lukkas Terry was the straightest mother on the planet, man. Lukkas fired people for using drugs. I never so much as saw him have a beer."

"So what are you saying?"

"Duuuh. Don't you get it? You must have gone to school on the little bus, man. It was just too much for him."

"What was?"

"All of it. Moving out of Greg's place." Her emotions began to slide toward sadness. "All that money. All that fame. And you know what?" She didn't make me guess. "He'd never even had his own place before. Never. We were gonna move in together—" She bit it off.

"You found him, didn't you." I said it as a statement.

Another nod and the beginnings of tears. "I just told him that night. You know, about being late and doing the test and stuff. He went ballistic. He hung up on me. Took the phone off the hook. It was still off when I—you know."

"What time did you call him?"

"About seven-thirty."

"What time did you find him?"

"Around eleven-thirty."

I cocked an eyebrow at her.

"I kept trying to call him. I didn't know what else to do. Then I got dressed and got to the bus."

"The bus?"

"I don't drive."

"A cab?"

"I didn't have any money, man. Okay?"

"But Lukkas Terry—" I started.

"Lukkas never had a dime, man. You gotta get that crap out of your head. All he had was this credit card Greg gave him, and most of the time he didn't remember to bring that. Greg just paid for whatever Lukkas wanted, which was musical equipment and grilled cheese sandwiches. He didn't want anything except to do his thing with his music."

Just short of maudlin, she snapped herself upright and recited a much-practiced litany. "There was no accident. He killed himself, man. He couldn't take the pressure, so he took himself out."

I changed the subject. "Trying to find his mother how?"

"He hired some dude. Some ancient ex-cop like you."

I ignored the insult. "What's this guy's name?"

"Who cares? Lukkas got his name from somebody. Some old fart looked like the dude in the Monopoly game."

"Big white mustache," I said.

"Yeah," she agreed. "That's all I know."

That was all the info I needed. It had been so long since I'd laid eyes on him, I'd assumed Charlie Boxer was dead. Charlie had operated for thirty years as a PI-cum-bunko-artist. The kind of operator who creates his own clientele. When he wasn't extricating a customer from some mess or other, he was out running some con game, getting somebody into some mess or other so he could get them out of it later. For a nominal fee, of course. All very smooth and dirty.

About five years ago, the last time I'd seen him, he was sitting in a battered gold Buick; the aluminum bar running across the whole center of the car held his legendary collection of sport jackets. Scrunched hard together in bold plaids, abstract patterns, and phosphorescent hues, they could have formed the international symbol for bad taste.

I'd leaned in the passenger window and said howdy. He'd looked bad. Wasted and wounded.

Embarrassed for me to see him like that, he'd made a quick joke about his fall from grace—reckoning how he'd gone from living *on* the Riviera to living *in* a Riviera—and then, without warning, he'd fed the peeling sled some gas and gone bouncing off down Western.

"Go on, take a hike," Beth said.

"No, I won't."

"You're so—so—" She finally settled on "old."

I could feel my blood rise again. "I am not."

She rolled her yellow eyes. "As if—" We stood in sullen silence. "I can't believe you fucked this up for me," she said as much to herself as to me.

"Way," I said.

She cast me a pitying gaze. "That's not where you say 'way,' you retard. It's like when somebody says 'no way,' then you—" She noticed me grinning at her. "Oh, God," She held a hand to her head. "You're *soooo* sixties."

"Who's paying your bills?" I asked.

"None of your busin—" She caught herself. "What makes you think anybody—"

"You've got a roof over your head. You're wearing nice clothes. A brand-new pair of Doc Martens. What are they, a hundred and a quarter, someplace in there, with tax? You sit around on your ass all day drinking five-dollar cups of coffee. The money has to come from somewhere."

"Maybe I have a trust fund."

"You can't even spell trust fund."

"If I tell you, will you go away?"

"Sure," I said.

"Okay, then, if you must know, Lukkas's manager, Gregory Conover." She studied me carefully. "Even an antique like you must have heard of Mr. Gregory Conover."

"I've heard of him."

"Unlike some people." She stared me down. "Mr. Conover is a gentleman. Unlike some people, he knows how to act. How to treat a lady."

She actually tapped her foot while she waited. "Well?" she said.

"Well what?"

"Well, go away like you said you would."

"I lied."

"You're execrable," she hissed.

"I'll help you," I said suddenly.

She was dubious. "How could *you* possibly help me?"

"You might be surprised."

"Oh, here it comes," she said to the sky.

"Come on up to the coffee shop on the corner. Tell me your story. If you're straight with me, I'll be straight with you."

"Oh, let me guess. You want to work out your middle-aged hornies on me. It's the little plaid skirt. Something like that. Maybe have me tell you about what a bad boy you've been?"

"Just talk," I said. "I'm just old, not blind."

"You should get so lucky," she hissed.

"I just want to talk," I said again.

She looked me over. "How do I know—"

"You don't. The only thing you know for sure is that whatever deal you've had working up till now is history. First thing tomorrow morning that all goes down the toilet. I was being straight with you back there. Believe me, honey, it's time for plan B."

At first, I thought I'd crapped out. She brushed past me and started up the hill. I stayed where I was and watched as she banged open the coffee shop door and went inside.

I got her settled in a booth with a double mocha decaf. She pulled her jacket tighter around her. "Where should I start?" she said with a sigh.

"Howzabout back at the beginning."

"My parents live in Orem—"

"Whoa, whoa," I said. "Too far back."

"When I began my career?"

"What career?"

"Rock and roll."

"You mean your career as a music groupie."

"God, I hate that word. It's *sooo* retro. What's next, love-ins? Be-ins? We all sit on the ground and sing 'Michael Row the Boat Ashore'?"

"Well, what do *you* call it?"

"I'm a professional musical companion," she said.

"Okay, start there." I sighed.

I got out my notebook. She took a moment to organize her thoughts.

"Actually, Jesus was my first."

"Oh, Christ," I groaned.

"Not that one, you moron. Greasy Jesus. The band." She looked to me for recognition. "You're *sooooo* lame," she said.

"Greasy Jesus, eh?"

"Actually it was Wound."

"Wound?"

"The lead singer. That was just his stage name. He had this scar on his side. You know, like where Jesus was supposed to have one, only his wasn't from a spear or anything; it was from chicken wire. His real name was Howie Dickman." She checked the restaurant for spies. "That's strictly hush-hush, though. Like, nobody, but nobody, knows his real name."

"Your secret's safe with me," I assured her.

Three pages in, we were through a couple more lead singers, a keyboard player, and a road manager and working on our first drummer. I was wishing I'd taken shorthand in high school.

16

IT WAS ONE OF THOSE what's-wrong-with-this-picture? moments. An instant when the general order of the universe is sufficiently askew to automatically command the eye. I was still dodging traffic when I spotted the Speaker tramping in a solitary vigil up and down the cul-de-sac that fronted Providence Hospital. The sight brought me up short. The bright overhead lights surrounding the driveway showed me that the cellular phone message was gone. He was serious today. Today, both sides of his sandwich board read the same: "Rehab Is for Quitters." He'd attracted other attention as well. A trio of security guards stood just outside the automatic doors, thick arms folded over two-tone blue shirts, eyes following his solitary shuffle, desperately hoping he'd stray onto hospital property so they could clean his clock. The Speaker, however, was way too sly, staying exclusively on the public access strip between the sidewalk and the street.

I stepped up onto the curb and watched as his board-covered back marched to the far end of the building, where he executed a crisp military turn back in my direction. The sight of me waiting for him suddenly spun him again like a shooting gallery bear. He wide-eyed me over his shoulder as he hot-footed it back up the block and disappeared around the corner of the building.

The guard on the right, a balding specimen whose name tag read T. Parker, appeared at my elbow. "You know that schmuck?"

"I may have seen him around," I hedged.

"He seemed to know you."

"A lot of folks know me."

Before he could reply, the black plastic radio pinned to his epaulet emitted a stream of static among which some unintelligible verbiage seemed to float. Numbers maybe. Two forty-three. Something like that. Whatever it was brought all three of them to point. Without a word they rushed in through the automatic doors and disappeared down the hallway to the left.

I stopped at the front desk. Whatever chicanery was going on hadn't filtered down to the blue-haired volunteers at reception. According to them, Ralph was in 509. I headed for the elevators.

I was one step onto the fifth floor when I suddenly knew what was up. Each end of the long central hallway was capped with a white bench. Mary sat at one end, Earlene at the other, pretending to read magazines, just like I'd taught 'em. Lookouts. Like the Speaker, they took one look at my cherubic countenance and went scurrying out of sight, heel-and-toeing it down parallel halls toward the back of the building. I followed the signs to 509.

I stepped into the room and took inventory. The room was empty. The bed was gone. On the night-stand, a blue plastic cup with a bendable straw sat on a rumpled newspaper. An IV stand, its plastic bottle of saline solution still hooked on top, lay sprawled on the floor like a remnant pruned from some aluminum cybershrub.

I turned to leave and bumped into T. Parker, who filled the doorway.

"What are you doing here?" he demanded.

"They told me Ralph Batista was in this room," I said.

"Who told you?"

"The ladies at the front desk."

"You better come with me," he said.

"I don't think so."

He hooked a thumb in his cop belt. "You don't want to be giving me a hard time now, do you, Sparky?" He gave me a big shit-eating grin.

"Oh, I don't know," I said evenly. "I think maybe I do."

He began to fiddle with one of the snaps on his belt.

"You pull out that cute little Mace can and I'll give you a high colonic with it," I said with an even bigger smile.

He took two steps back. I kept pace, crowding him, staying right in his face. We stood there, nose to nose, grinning like a couple of idiots until a voice behind Parker broke the reverie.

"What's all this, Parker?"

"Got us a smart-ass here," T. Parker said without turning.

Either the new guy had a stethoscope fetish or he was a doctor. Clad in blue disposable overalls, little white booties, and a matching shower cap, he looked like an accountant caught in his jammies. His bare arms were covered with thick black hair, giving the impression that he was probably furred all over like a rhesus monkey. I decided to take the initiative. "I'm here to visit a guy named Ralph Batista. They told me downstairs that he was in this room. Where is he?"

I shouldered Parker aside and stepped in close to the doc. I stuck out my hand. "Leo Waterman," I said. He glared at my hand like it was radioactive. I stuck it back in my pocket. "Where's Ralph?" I said.

Parker and the doc passed meaningful glances but stayed mute.

"They move him to another room?" I tried. Nothing. "Where do I find an administrator?" I asked.

This query seemed to have the desired effect. Dr. Jammies immediately softened. "Well, Mr. Batista . . . at the moment—" He started again. "As we speak—"

"You lost him, huh," I interrupted.

He showed me a palm. "Not lost, exactly." He glanced from Parker to me and back. "Why don't you continue with your duties, Parker," he said finally. "I'll—eh—have a few words with Mr.—"

"Waterman," I prompted.

"Of course—yes, with Mr. Waterman."

Parker left slowly, sullenly, like an errant schoolboy consigned to his room for the rest of the day. He gave me his most terrifying stare as he boarded the elevator. I gave him a nice little wave in return.

"Now. Mr. Waterman—I wouldn't have you getting the wrong impression."

"Oh?"

"This is a big hospital. Sometimes the lines of communication are not what they might be."

"You mean like when they cut the wrong leg off that guy a couple of months back?"

"Oh no." He checked the hall. "That was most unfortunate. No, no. Nothing like that at all. I merely mean to suggest that Mr. Batista is most likely just out for tests in some other department, and somehow— you know, the lines of—"

"You don't know where he is, do you?"

"Well, perhaps not specifically, but—"

"Then howzabout generally, or maybe cosmically?"

"Excuse me?"

I tried again. "Where's Ralph?"

He took a deep breath and held it. "I'm not sure," he said finally, exhaling. "We had some trouble the other day with a bunch of hooligans showing up drunk to see Mr. Batista. We were forced to remove them from the hospital. That's what Parker—we're concerned these"—he searched for a word—"people may have—you know." He stopped. "Security is looking for Mr. Batista right now. It's quite unlikely that any of those same people could have gained entry. Our staff was briefed. They all saw the security camera film. So you see, it's almost surely a communications snafu. Mr. Batista will—"

I let him off the hook. "Okay," I said. "I'll come back later when this is all straightened out." He looked at me like I'd just given him that sled he'd always wanted for Christmas. I turned on my heel and started back toward the elevators. I stopped. His back was to me.

"By the way," I said. He stopped and screwed his neck my way. "What's the dirtiest, crappiest job in the hospital?" I asked. He looked as blank as a melon. I tried again. "What's the job with the biggest turnover? Where they constantly need new people?"

"Why, the laundry, I suppose. You know, with sur-

gery and incontinence, all of that, it can be rather—
"

"Thanks," I said. "Where's the laundry?"

"In the basement. Basement two. All the way down."

I ambled back to the elevator. No basements listed. The door began to close. I stuck my arm in, muscled open the doors, and went looking for a nurses' station. Yes, as a matter of fact, there was a freight elevator. In the back of the building. In the northwest corner. Over that way. Yes, that was indeed how one got down to the laundry. Thanks a bunch. Adios.

The floor of the elevator car was rough scarred wood like the bed of a boxcar. The walls were draped with heavy olive-drab padding sheets hooked to brass eyelets. I pushed the button marked B2. If the crew hadn't come in through any of the conventional entrances and hadn't been spotted by anybody in all the time it took to find Ralph and get him out of his room, then they must have had some kind of inside help. If they knew anybody who worked in a hospital, in all likelihood it wasn't a neurosurgeon. More likely it was somebody whose parole officer had found them the job and dogged their ass into showing up. The laundry was a good place to start.

I'd expected a great deal of sloshing and tumbling, but instead the basement was strangely quiet. I followed the black-and-white linoleum down a long hall lined with lockers and then around the corner into a large central room. Huge silver commercial washers and dryers, maybe twenty of each, lined two sides of the room, their empty glass windows staring out like the portholes of some sunken liner. A long white folding table ran the length of the center.

Surrounding the room were meshed-in storage areas bursting with freshly washed linens piled floor to ceiling on gray Erector set shelves. A small woman in a fresh white uniform walked out of the nearest storage area. She stopped in her tracks. Her name tag read Betty.

"Oh, you scared me," she said.

"Sorry," I offered. "Where is everybody?"

"A staff meeting, I think. I'm not sure. I don't work here." She wrinkled her nose and stepped around me. "I'm helping out in obstetrics today. They told me that if the laundry didn't answer the phone that they were probably all in a meeting and I'd have to go down and get it myself." She patted a thick blue blanket under her left arm. "Every Sunday, one to three. That's what they said."

"On a Sunday?"

"For the night and weekend people," she said as she rustled around the corner. I listened until I heard the groan of the elevator and then turned back to the room. Behind me, to the south, a flight of concrete stairs followed a bright blue railing up to the exit sign. Unless I was turned around, the door would lead out onto Eighteenth Avenue, at the very back of the old wing.

I allowed myself a moment of pride. Not bad, I thought. Considering how lubricated they all probably had to get before attempting anything this audacious, the plan really wasn't half bad. The Speaker keeping security occupied out front. The girls keeping lookout and watching everybody's back. A staff meeting keeping the laundry staff out of the way. For the boys, this was tantamount to arranging peace in the Middle East. Not bad.

At the far end of the room, a ten-by-ten steel door with a pull handle like an old-fashioned refrigerator occupied the entire wall. It looked like a big walk-in freezer. For no better reason than because I couldn't imagine why a laundry needed a freezer, I headed that way. Grabbed the handle and pulled. The door began to open but was suddenly jerked shut from the inside. I pulled again, harder this time, and the door started to come open. I could hear shoes sliding on the floor inside the door, fighting for traction. With a final grunt, I gave it all I had and jerked it open. It banged hard against the old steel radiator along the wall, sending a dull ring throughout the bowels of the building.

Ralph was still in bed. Sitting up. Oval eyed. A bottle of Potters vodka clutched in his lap. Earlene and Mary peeked out from over his shoulders. To my left, Billy Bob Fung was plastered against the wall, shaking his hand. Out in the center of the room, two masked figures in surgical gowns were rooting through a pair of huge canvas laundry hampers.

"Holy shit," said Ralph.

I spoke to the nearest brain surgeon. The one with the mismatched Nikes and the wet spot in the center of his mask where he'd been drinking through it. "You want to explain this crock of shit to me, George?"

"You're not gonna rat us out, are ya, Leo?" asked Ralph.

"George," I repeated.

He yanked down his surgical mask. "He's got no goddamned clothes. They burned his clothes. Said they were a health menace."

"A *public* health menace," Ralph corrected, after a quick pull on the bottle.

"Leo won't rat on us," Mary said without believing it.

George pointed to the piles of stained garments littering the floor and covering his feet. "He can't wear any of this shit. We won't get a block. This shit looks like somebody butchered an elk on it."

He had a point. The garments on the floor looked more like they belonged in a slaughterhouse than in a hospital. I suspected they used this room to isolate surgical supplies from the rest of the laundry.

"I don't believe you guys."

"We don't want to hear it," said Earlene.

"Yeah, stuff it," said Mary.

"Don't you realize—" I started.

Harold cut me off. "Oh yeah, Mr. High and Mighty gonna make a speech now," he slurred through his mask.

I opened my mouth to speak, thought better of it, and closed it again. I checked my watch. Two thirty-three. Wouldn't be that long. Meetings usually got out a bit early.

"I'm getting out of here," I said. "I don't give a shit what you guys do. Just give me two minutes to get clear." I turned and walked back through the door.

"He's got no goddamn clothes," George shouted at my back. "We can't get him home with his ass hanging out. Goddamn it, Leo. You gotta help us. Loan us your shirt."

"Oh no," I said. "I've got work to do and then a dinner date. You guys are on your own on this one."

"What are we gonna do?" Mary whined.

"Try the lockers," I suggested as I headed for the stairs.

17

"ARE YOU LISTENING TO ME, GODDAMN IT?"

I rolled over and pulled the phone out from under the covers. "I'm listening," I said. Seven-fifteen A.M. Arrrrgh.

"Where the hell have you been, anyway? I called you all the way past midnight last night."

"Letha's cruising."

"Not the downtown bars, I trust."

"Alaska with her sister."

"How nice for you."

"I sure thought so, until just a few minutes ago."

"You get that goddamn bed back. You hear me? I don't care how you do it. You find those maniacs and you return that bed to Providence Hospital, or I swear to God it's going to appear on your bill. You'll be working for me pro bono well into your dotage. Am I making myself clear? You have any idea what a hospital bed costs?"

"I don't wanna know," I said.

"And speaking of your bill, what's going on with that little matter I'm paying you for? Pleased as I am that your sex life has taken an upturn, I thought maybe—"

"You're a bit cranky this morning," I ventured.

"Cranky? Me? Why would I be cranky? Just because I had my dinner interrupted by an irate hospital administrator, who tells me that someone who's there under my auspices—"

"Nice word, auspices."

"Shut up. Who's there under my auspices has broken out and taken a four-thousand-dollar hospital bed with him."

"Four thou?"

"On your bill."

"Jesus. I'll find them. Trust me. Consider it done."

"Trust you? I trusted you to find the Mendolson girl."

"We're making progress," I objected.

"Such as?"

"Such as she's not visiting anybody in northern Michigan."

"Your man is sure?"

"He's a good man. If he says she's not there, she's not there."

"Shit."

I'd tottered in about two-thirty this morning and decided to check my E-mail before falling into bed. I had two messages. The first was from Tim Miller.

No go. The girl was not hiding out with either her father or her brother. Ron was sure, which was good enough for me. The second message read:

Date: Sun, 18 Feb 96 08:51:24 EST
From: "Kara L. Robinson"
<KROBINSO@KENTVM.KENT.EDU>
Subject: Re: subscription
To: Leo Waterman <LeoxxW@ESKIMO.COM>

Hi,

To join DorothyL, follow the attached instructions
EXACTLY!
1) send an email message to LISTSERV
@KENTVM.KENT.EDU
2) the text of that message should read ONLY:
subscribe DorothyL
Leo Waterman
you will receive a message back from LISTSERV
asking you to confirm your subscription (this is
to check your address). To confirm, Replyto the
message, with the only text being the word ok (this
will be explained more clearly in the message from
LISTSERV)

Once your subscription has been added, you will
receive a copy of the user education/welcome
memo. PLEASE read through this memo carefully

as it contains valuable information about DorothyL.
Also, please be aware that on DorothyL the ONLY
email option is a daily digest version.
If you have any questions or problems, now or in the
future, please let me know.

Danger Mouse AKA
Kara L. Robinson
Co-Listowner: DorothyL

I followed the subscription directions, watched
slack-jawed as the message went through, and then
shuffled in to bed, where I dreamed of lime green
icebergs floating just above the surface of bright blue
waters until Jed roused me.

"Well, that about leaves our asses in the wind, now
doesn't it?"

"Not quite," I said. "I'll hear from Paul today
about whether she's been using her credit cards or
not. Maybe we'll get something there."

"You think so?"

"No," I said. "But I've got another idea."

"What?"

I told him. When I finished, he said, "That's the
most ridiculous thing I ever heard. Investigation
over. I'm calling the cops."

"Just give it till the end of the week," I pleaded.
"If I don't find her by Friday—"

"You're out of your mind. It's from hanging out

with those lunatic friends of yours. You need to keep better company. That's your problem, Leo. Are you nuts? You think I'm going to hold back a police investigation for a week because you think this girl is going to write in to some mystery fan Internet thing?"

"I can feel it in my bones. I just know it's gonna happen."

"If you'd spent more time pursuing the Mendolson investigation instead of sticking your nose into this Lukkas Terry thing, maybe we wouldn't be in this—"

"I'm telling you, Jed, this girl didn't have a hell of a lot going on in her life. She's addicted to this thing. That's why she took her computer with her. Desktop computers are not generally on the list of stuff people take with them when they go into hiding. She's hooked on it. Hell, *I'm* addicted to it. You gotta trust me on this, Jed. All I've got to get her to do is send me a piece of E-mail and I've got her."

"How's that?"

"I've got this piece of software that Carl gave me last summer called SuperFinder. It's like caller ID, except it works for E-mail. It works its way back through the system and finds the phone number that any message originated from."

"Really? You can do that?"

"Guys like Carl can do that. It's not commercially available."

Carl Cradduck was a former AP photographer who, after being consigned to a wheelchair by a couple of drunken kids, had worked his way into being the Pacific Northwest's premier surveillance expert. C&C Technical was the cutting edge in everything from sophisticated industrial espionage to recording those long phone calls your wife kept making to that downtown plumbing shop. Not only had Jed and I used Carl on numerous occasions over the years, but Carl had, over time, become a close friend of mine. I was hoping his name would lend some credibility to what I had to admit sounded like a pretty far-fetched scheme. "Just to the end of the week," I said.

"No can do. Wednesday is the longest I can wait."

"I need the whole week. I don't know how long it's going to take to get connected to the list. It's automatic, so it shouldn't take too damn long, but I can't be sure. Friday. Close of business."

Jed heaved a huge sigh. "What makes you think she's going to write in to this—this—"

"Digest. It's a compiled digest, and I think she's going to keep participating because the thing has a strange, hypnotic quality to it. Once you start reading it, it's like you don't want to stop. She had digests everywhere. At home, at work. I'll bet she took a bunch with her when she left."

"You need more to do."

"No, I'm serious. By the time I'd gone through all

the digests she'd downloaded to disk, I was like really disappointed when I got to the end. It was weird. I was depressed, like I'd lost a bunch of friends in an airplane crash or something."

"I stand corrected. You don't need more to do. You need a nice long rest, is what you need."

"Friday. Close of business."

"God help me, Leo."

"And you're going to file that paperwork on behalf of Serena Dunlap this morning."

He heaved a sigh. "Already done. I had it messengered to both Sub-Rosa and Conover. I've already heard from both of them. They want to meet this afternoon."

"What time?"

"Two."

"I want to be there."

"Why? It's just going to be the kind of legal posturing you hate."

"I want to watch them squirm."

"What is it with you and this Lukkas Terry thing? You, my friend, are definitely not one for crusades. You've always been old Mr. Live and Let Live. This is way out of character for you, buddy. What's the deal here?"

He had a point. I'd been asking myself the same question for the past couple of days. "I don't know, man," I said. "I was thinking about that the other day when I was on my way down to Vital Statistics."

"And?"

"It started out to be just idle curiosity."

"And?"

"And the minute I started to poke around in it, I got all these discrepancies. A bunch of stuff that didn't fit. Just the kind of crap that tends to get my attention."

"Like?"

"Like, I've got a competent police force under heavy public scrutiny saying the kid died by misadventure. Accident, period. No-brainer."

"So?"

"I've got a girlfriend. The one who found him, by the way, who says they were about to move in together, saying he killed himself because she told him she was pregnant. She swears Lukkas Terry didn't use drugs."

"Really?"

"On the other hand, I've got a manager, a guy who takes it upon himself to support half the down-and-out musicians in town, so damn nice he's still paying Terry's girlfriend's bills out of his own pocket, probably the closest guy in the world to Lukkas Terry—and he's strictly noncommittal on the drug issue. He says you never really know what goes on behind closed doors with these rock stars."

"Probably a wise approach," Jed offered.

"I agree," I said. "Buuuut—" I drew it out. "Number one, I'm told that Terry had real bad migraines and was forever hitting Conover up to help him with his shots. Couldn't do it himself. Too squeamish."

"Do tell."

"Which, the way I see it, makes him real vulnerable to somebody slipping him something other than medicine."

"It do indeed."

"Yeah, and number two—we're in a situation here where millions upon millions of dollars are at stake. I don't need to tell you how that gums up the works."

"Be like preaching to the choir."

"That about covers the range of possibilities, now, doesn't it? Accident, suicide, murder. Other than dying of old age, that's about all there is. And then— just about the time I'm asking myself these same questions and thinking about bagging it—"

"Somebody tried to run your big ass over," he finished.

"Correctomundo. Always an attention-getter with me. You want to pique my interest, try to run me down. Works every time."

"You said that's how it *started*."

"Yeah, well, you know, it's gotten to be more than that, too. It's as if I'm pissed off about something. About Elvis getting fat and wearing those stupid jumpsuits in fucking Las Vegas. It's about every dead musician I ever liked. From Buddy Holly and

Elvis, Jimi and Janis, all the way up to Stevie Ray and Lukkas Terry—you know, all of them. What happened to them. What they did to themselves. How record companies end up with all the fucking money and the families get screwed. All of it. Like I feel cheated or something and now suddenly, just this once, I've got this chance to fuck with somebody over it, and I seem to be determined to make the most of it."

Jed took a minute and then said, "Yeah. I know what you mean. Let's kick some ass." Before I could reply, he said, "You find that goddamn bed and get it back where it belongs."

"Scout's honor."

"I mean now. Right now. First thing," he insisted.

"I won't be able to find them until about one, one-thirty, when they start to wander into the Zoo. They move so often. I don't know where any of them flop anymore."

"All right," he said without enthusiasm. "But you round up that goddamn bed, you hear me?"

He was still grumbling as I set the receiver in the cradle and sat up. Without rising, I pulled the cord on the Levolor and took a peek at the day. A thick drizzle hissed against the glass, distorting the newspaper-headed creatures trotting up Fremont Avenue. Back to normal. Arrrrgh.

The coffeepot had progressed from drooling to dripping to a full-throated gargle by the time I configured and clicked my way to my E-mail. *Ta ta de da*. You have mail today. Mr. Happyface. Nobody loved me. One measly message. Oh, goody. A big one. This would require coffee and possibly an onion bagel. Life was good.

Date: Mon, 19 Feb 1996 00:00:00-0500
Reply-To: Mystery Literature E-conference
<DOROTHYL@www-test.kent.edu>
Sender: Mystery Literature E-conference
<DOROTHYL@www-test.kent.edu>
From: Automatic digest processor
<LISTSERV@www-test.kent.edu
Subject: DOROTHYL Digest—17 Feb 1996 to 18
Feb 1996
To: Recipients of DOROTHYL digests
<DOROTHYL@www-test.kent.edu>

There are 26 messages totaling 1046 lines in this issue.

Topics of the day:
  1. A basketball mystery
  2. Phoenix and Tucson mystery tips?
  3. Fair Dinkum
  4. Anti-semitism
  5. Dropshot
  6. Inappropriate Places to Read
  7. Dealbreaker/Series/LOC

I KEPT IT SHORT. "I'VE GOT NOTHING TO SAY about what you assholes pulled off yesterday. That's your business. I'm talking about today. And TODAY, I want that bed back up at Providence Hospital by two. That's it. End of story."

They'd come out of the woodwork for this little gala. The Return of Ralph. People I hadn't seen in years. Waldo and Big Frank. Heavy Duty Judy, still wearing that friggin' tiara. The little guy with the brain damage. What was his name? Soloman. Something like that. Poor guy had this neurological problem that kept him from approaching anything directly. Instead, he was forced to close in on things in a series of oblique tacking movements, like a sailboat. Slalom. That was it, they called him Slalom. Flounder in a brand-new Mariners cap. Red Gomez and some Asian woman. Half a dozen younger guys I didn't recognize. All gathered around the regular crew.

They were a sullen lot. I'd interrupted a perfectly good party, and they didn't like it one bit. The Speaker's board read Free at Last.

"I never thought of you guys as thieves," I said.

George gave me the reaction I was fishing for. "We ain't no goddamn thieves." His scalp glowed red beneath the carefully combed rows of his white hair. "Don't you be callin' us no thieves."

"Then return the bed to the hospital."

Harold spoke up. "Ya know, Ralph lost his shopping cart down there at that hotel. We just figured, you know—"

"That bed's a four-thousand-dollar shopping cart," I said.

"Are you shittin' me?" said George. "Four grand?"

"The crux of the healthcare dilemma," intoned Normal.

"Four grand. Grand theft. Hard time," I chanted.

The mention of hard time sent the crowd scurrying for the dim corners of the bar. A week or two in the King County slammer was one thing. Sometimes, if times were tough, when that belt of arctic air slipped down and decent flops were hard to come by, a roof and three squares wasn't the worst thing in the world. Hard time was a whole 'nother matter.

"You shoulda seen him coming down Cherry Street," Earlene said with a huge grin.

"He passed an old broad in a Buick," added Big Frank.

"Sucker's got good brakes," said Ralph solemnly.

"By two," I repeated. Nothing. I went for the throat.

"Have it back there by noon, and I've got work for all of you."

A murmur ran through the crowd. "Detective work?" asked Ralph.

"Yep. Twenty-five a day, plus twenty-five for expenses."

"Each?" asked Harold.

"Each," I confirmed.

"Wadda we gotta do?" asked Earlene.

"Go to bars," I said.

"Dickie," George bellowed. "Get the truck."

As the kid hustled out the front, George turned to me. "How many guys?" he asked.

"As many as you can find. But I need real quick

results. I'm paying the freight on this one. There's no client."

"What's the job?" he asked.

"I need to find Charlie Boxer."

George's shoulders slumped. "That fucker's dead," he whined.

"I don't think so."

"Nobody seen that bum since—"

"I seen him." Heavy Duty Judy strode over, wearing a truly awesome collection of junk jewelry that rattled as she walked. "Maybe two months ago. He come into Spins'. Bought me a beer."

This last statement precluded further argument. These were not people to forget anybody who bought them a drink.

"He told me he had a woman," Big Frank offered.

Heavy Duty Judy shook a massive, segmented arm in his direction. It sounded like a car wreck. "That's what he told me, too. Told me he had some old dame takin' real good care of him."

"He say where?" I asked.

"Local," said Judy. "At least, that's what I figured."

I reached in my pants pocket, pulled out five hundred in twenties, and dropped them on the bar in front of George.

"I need to find him. That's all I could get out of the cash machine. When you need more, call me."

George pulled me aside. "I'm worried about Ralphie," he whispered.

"What's the problem?"

"They done somethin' to him. Drugged him or somethin'."

"How can you tell?"

He leaned in close. "He's been wearing his teeth."

"In public?"

"Wearin' 'em right now," he affirmed.

The back door opened. Dickie appeared in silhouette. George addressed himself to the younger guys. "If you'll leave Ralph's stuff on the porch and then load that bed into the truck, I'll put you guys on with the crew. Wadda ya say?"

He turned, squinting toward Dickie. "Tell 'em you found it in the street, kid. Who knows, maybe they'll give you a reward. Then hustle back here so we can get to work."

As the door hissed us back into blackness, the crowd formed itself into small whispering knots. Harold made an expansive gesture, indicating that another round was in order for the assembled multitude. Terry began to pour. I turned to George.

"Get the best people you can, okay? People who will actually look." I shot a glance over my shoulder at Slalom, who seemed to be stuck in the corner like some berserk windup toy.

"You'd be surprised, Leo," George assured me. "Slalom finds some interesting shit in his travels."

"Yeah, I'll bet. Here's my pager number. I reactivated it this morning. Give it to everybody. Have them look in twos. Anybody finds him, one goes and calls me, the other keeps an eye on him."

"Got it," he said. "We'll start downtown and work north."

"Why north?"

"He don't drink in the Square, or everybody'd know about it. And old Charlie was never any too fond of fags, so that about lets out the whole Hill. So if Judy's right and he's still in the city someplace, that pretty much leaves downtown and north. Don't worry, Leo. If he's out there, we'll find him."

I had no doubt. What was for sure was that, wherever he was, Charlie Boxer was a regular at some bar or another. It was his life. Charlie Boxer extracted from bars the same range of succor and support other people get out of their families. If it's true that it takes one to know one, then I definitely had the right guys for this job.

18

SURROUNDED BY A GALAXY OF GOLD RECORDS and celebrity photographs, a life-size bronze John Lennon sat barefoot and cross-legged, just a couple of sinews short of the full lotus position, staring serenely down at his National steel guitar through wire-rimmed glasses. At the other end of the room, a massive font of red-and-white tulips erupted from a bright blue handblown vase, fabricating a sense of spring having sprung from somewhere among the framed testimonials. In between, a massive central staircase wound up to the second floor.

She was just short of forty and wore a black wire harness across the top of her head, allowing her to answer the phone and stuff envelopes at the same time. Waste not, want not. The simple black dress seemed to hover about her without landing, while the beginnings of a double chin mocked the hard health-club tone of her body. A small sign, Madelaine.

"Can I help you?" she asked.

"I'm here for a meeting with Arthur Prowell," I said.

She twitched a thin eyebrow my way. "You have an appointment?"

"I'm expected at two."

"Regarding?"

What the hell, I handed her a business card as I said it.

"Regarding highly confidential matters." She gave a couple of those contact-lens blinks. "We detectives can't be too careful, you know."

She came out from behind the desk on a pair of tightly muscled legs. With a three-inch fingernail, she gestured at the two green leather chairs in front of the window.

"If you would care to have a seat," she said.

I said I would, but instead stood my ground and watched as she mounted the staircase; from the knots in her calves to the roll of her shoulders, everything seemed to tingle as she motored up and out of sight. She watched me watch. I watched her watch me watch her.

She was gone quite a while, finally reappearing at the far end of the room, down by the tulips. Her hips seemed to move with an exaggerated swing as she sashayed the length of the hall toward me. "Top of the stairs. The office at the far end of the hall," she said.

This time, she stood her ground and watched as I headed up. As I negotiated the stairs, she watched me watch her watch me follow the thick red carpeting down the hall toward the open door.

The space was decorated in the same gold-record, testimonial, smiling-group-picture motif as downstairs. There were four men in the office. Seated at a black enamel desk was a balding little guy of about fifty, whose nine remaining hairs had been grown to truly prodigious lengths and then wrapped—almost woven—about his head like a hair yarmulke. He rose as I entered, holding out his hand.

"Arthur Prowell," he said.

I took his hand. His grip was firm and dry.

"My associate, Leo Waterman," Jed intoned from the red leather chair on my left. "Fashionably late, as usual."

To my right, a guy in a crisp gray suit stood in the north window, smoking. He had pulled the top sash down and was leaning out into the alley, allowing the smoke to drift up and over the roof. He was a sinewy fellow, with tightly curled blond hair and a shiny, pitted face.

"This is our corporate attorney, P. J. Papa," Prowell said.

Papa threw a nearly imperceptible nod my way and went back to his smoking, completely turning his back on the room now. The humming of the copy machine filled the room with the low sound of moving air.

Behind me, Gregory Conover was studying a pair of framed guitars—John Lennon's, according to the plaque. If he was surprised to see me again, he didn't let on. Instead, he gave me a conspiratorial wink and went back to his scholarship.

Prowell motioned me toward a suede chair directly in front of the desk and sat back down. He laced his fingers together in front of him as if praying. "Well, gentlemen," he started. "I don't mean to be impolite, but something unexpected has come up, and we've only got a few minutes before Mr. Papa and I have to get downtown to a meeting, so if you don't mind, perhaps we could dispense with the niceties and get right down to business." When we didn't seem to object, he went on. He was a man of his word.

"This restraining order," he said. "Prohibiting any and all transfer of funds connected in any way with the estate of Lukkas Terry." He brought it close to his face and read the fine print. "Filed by one Jedediah C. James, acting as counsel for one Selena Dunlap. It would appear this Dunlap woman claims to be the mother of the late Mr. Terry."

He looked at me quizzically and then set the paper back on top of the file and spread his hands. He addressed himself to Jed.

"So, what can we do for you gentlemen?"

"We intend to file for survivor's rights on the Terry estate."

"Go right ahead," Prowell said affably.

Nonplussed, Jed jumped back in. "We intend to see that, in keeping with current legal precedent, Ms. Dunlap receives equitable treatment."

"What can we do to help?" Prowell asked. He gestured over our heads toward Conover, who waved his full-hearted assent. "I think I speak for everyone in this room when I say that, granted your client is able to document her supposed relationship with Lukkas Terry, we shall be quite happy to comply. Eager, even." He gave a conspiratorial wink. "There is, as they say, more than enough to go around." He continued. "Being able to share with his mother the fruits of his genius would, in some small way, perhaps help mitigate the pain of losing one so talented and yet so young."

If his feet hadn't been up under the desk, I'd have surely puked on his shoes. I bit my tongue. Jed went for the throat, pulling a black calfskin notebook from his inside pocket and opening his pen. "What's the current distribution situation of Lukkas Terry's royalties?" he said.

Prowell gave a silent chuckle. "I'm sure you understand, that kind of information is quite confidential."

"Not for long," Jed said quickly.

The implied threat merely amused Prowell. His

eyes crinkled. "Be that as it may, Mr. James. Mr. Papa and I were just going over our contract with Lukkas Terry. We remain confident of our legal position in this matter." He rested both hands on the brown folder.

The conversational ball flew back and forth over the net for another five minutes or so. Jed seemed to be getting nowhere. I jumped in.

"Are you the one who had Selena Dunlap declared dead?" I tried. Papa gave another grunt.

"Oh no," said Prowell. "A clean estate and line of inheritance is part of the package. We don't sign distribution agreements unless that's all been taken care of. That's all strictly SOP."

"I would like to see a copy of that agreement," Jed said.

It was Papa's turn to chuckle. He flicked the butt out into the alley and turned back toward the room. "Then all you're lacking, sir, is a Superior Court subpoena demanding those documents. Should the court in its wisdom grant you gentlemen your request, we will most surely comply with the wishes of the court." He had a drawl. Texas, maybe. The words oozed out in an almost courtly manner. As if they were written down somewhere.

"I'm sure Mr. James is prepared to take whatever steps are necessary to ensure his client's rights," I said evenly.

Papa snapped the window up. "I have absolutely

no doubt," he said, smoothing his suit. "Mr. James, if you'll allow me to say, you are preceded by a considerable reputation for both success and, if I might be so bold, also for your particularly"—he went shopping for a word—"how shall we say . . . *vigorous* style of litigation. I have no doubt your client is in capable hands."

"Oh, stop it; you're spoiling him now," I guffawed.

"Now, now." It was Conover, wandered over from the wall, standing now between Jed and me. "Why can't we all just get along?" he asked with mock sincerity. "We're all brothers and sisters here, you know. We're all on the same page here. No need for animosity."

Another five minutes of legal repartee, and then suddenly, as if on cue, the three of them passed a look that said school was out. Whatever curiosity they'd had about us had been satisfied. Jed slipped his notebook back into his pocket.

Papa rubbed his palms together. "I'm sorry we couldn't be of more help," he said.

"Really?"

"Really what?"

On my left, Prowell spun in his chair, opened the bottom file drawer, M-Z, and slipped the brown file back into its rightful place.

"Really sorry you couldn't be more help."

"Within the context, of course," he said affably.

"What else is there?" I inquired with a big grin.

"Should I discover anything, I'll most certainly call," he said, matching me ivory for ivory.

Jed rose. "Thank you for your time, gentlemen," was all he said.

Suddenly Prowell was out from behind the desk. Somehow he'd reannexed my hand and was stroking it like a pet ferret. "I'm sorry, but we've got to be on our way. We're running a little late. If there's anything else we can do to help, don't for a minute hesitate—" Arrrgh.

Without further ado I extracted my hand from his grip and followed Jed back down the hall, waving good-bye over my shoulder as I ambled toward the stairs.

I pulled the door closed behind us and turned to Jed. "You detect any squirming in there?"

"Not unless you count Prowell rubbing his thighs together with glee," Jed answered.

"Fill me in. What just happened in there?"

"We were slimed," Jed said as we crossed the sidewalk. "They just wanted to see who the hell we were."

"Was it just me, or were those assholes sneering at us?"

"The sneer meter has seldom reached such lofty realms. If somebody weren't trying to run you over, I'd have to swear to God nobody in that room gives a shit whether Lukkas Terry ever had a mother or not." He waved a hand at me. "I'm going to have to think about this a bit. We may need to explore other avenues. Less conventional avenues," he said with another wave. "Gotta go." As he legged it around the corner, I wandered over to the side of the Key Bank and stood in the shadow of an unconventional blue spruce.

Cheokee was at the wheel of the new blue Range Rover as it crossed the near lane and turned left. Conover sat in the passenger seat, twisted toward the driver, his face contorted with invective. He punctuated his points with insistent jabs of his finger. Cherokee appeared unmoved.

Prowell and Papa couldn't have been any too late for their meeting. It was another ten minutes before they rolled out of the alley into the gathering gloom and bounced into the street. Prowell sat low behind the wheel of a green Cadillac DeVille, his hair-beanie curled just above the top of the wheel like a lacquered cat. Papa rode shotgun with the window open, his hand, cigarette stuck between his fingers, rested on top of the car. Prowell turned left on Third Avenue and headed downtown.

I watched until they'd cleared three lights and then pulled myself from the Fiat and trotted back across the street. Less conventional, he'd said. Madelaine was whispering into her headset and stuffing envelopes as I strode in. I held up a hand and kept moving fast.

"Left my day planner up there," I said loud enough for her to hear above the phone call. I started for the stairs.

Her eyes widened. She put a careful hand over the mouthpiece. "They're not—" she started. "You can't—" Her eyes showed that someone was speaking on the line. "Oh, no, sir. I was—no, not you, sir. Yes, sir, I'm writing this down. Yes, please go ahead."

"Be right back," I said, taking the stairs two at a time.

I took the hall as fast as I could without making too much noise. The door was open. The copy machine was still on. Ready to copy. The file cabinet was unlocked. Lukkas Terry's file still stood just a bit higher than the others. I straightened the thin metal tines at the top of the folder and slipped the contents off. Felt like six or eight pages. I peeked around the doorjamb, out into the hall. Empty. I could hear the muted sounds of Madelaine's voice repeating what she was hearing on the phone.

I hurried over to the copy machine and slid the papers into the top feeder. Two sides to two sides. No collate. No staple. With a rush of mechanical air and a snap of paper the first document disappeared down into the machine. One by one the machine swallowed the documents, and then whirled out copies into the stacked trays at the far end of the machine. I had already returned the originals to the file cabinet and stuffed the copies beneath my shirt when Madelaine came bursting in. The cord from her headset dangled by her right hip. I pulled my notebook from my pocket.

"Got it," I announced.

She strode across the room, brushed me aside, and went right to the files. She fingered her way through the bottom drawer, found the Terry file, and checked the contents. The deep hum of the copy machine found my ears as she rifled through the documents. I'd forgotten to turn it off.

She kicked the drawer shut and started for me.

"You get out of here right now, or I'll call the police," she said.

"I was just—"

"Mr. Prowell would lose his mind if he knew you were up here alone. Not to mention my job," she added accusingly.

I opened my mouth, but sorry wasn't going to cut it. She put both hands on my left shoulder and pushed me out the door into the hall.

"Get out," she repeated.

"Take it easy," I said. "I was just getting my notebook."

She stood, flexed in the doorway, until I started down and then watched me leave from the top of the stairs.

19

I STOOD WITH MY NOSE PRESSED TO THE SILVER GLASS, watched the kid cross the black-and-white diamonds of the lobby to the receptionist and jack himself up on tiptoe to make conversation across the wide counter.

Darkness was driving the express lane tonight. Behind me, low over the Olympics, a thick band of braided clouds squeezed the remaining light into a thin low-wattage line, recessed behind the tops of the mountains, leaving even the early commuters to chug home in the dim fluorescent gloom. The kid came bouncing out the revolving door.

"I done it," he announced.

He was about ten, maybe sixty pounds, in an oversize Oakland Raiders pullover, a pair of black canvas pants that would have fit Orson Welles, and Reeboks with no laces. "She say she send it right up."

"Good job," I said. I pulled a five-dollar bill from my pocket and held it out. The kid snatched the bill and began to skip backward, as if I were going to change my mind and try to take the money back. When I didn't move, he stopped. "You a spy or somethin', man?" he asked.

"Bond," I said. "James Bond."

"My ass," he said with a grin and turned and left.

I retrieved the Fiat and fought the traffic north, up Third Avenue with the buses, sliding down to Mercer, facing the bobbing web of lights now, as the late-afternoon flow of the interstate began to swell in the deep cuts along the side of the hill, where a bazillion highways, state routes, arterials, just plain roads, and maybe even cul-de-sacs parceled out their meager portions of the swell and began to move it toward home and the dubious promise of another morning commute.

I followed a new black Jaguar up Eastlake, where the uneasy tension between tradition and the profit motive hung in the air like diesel smoke. The new Seattle has for twenty years been chipping away at the rough-handed, old-time commercialism that surrounds the city's downtown lake. Wedging fancy eateries in along the shore, cheek to jowl with the commercial fishermen, the shipyards, the smalltime maritime fabricators who stubbornly cling to their soiled lots like fifth-generation barnacles. Unable to either muscle or buy them out, the city now sought to displace this tawdry blue-collar enclave by making the whole damn thing a park. Someplace nice for the kiddies and the cocker spaniels, you know. Fuck the jobs. We'll put it on the ballot. Progress is, after all, our most important product.

For the second time this week, I could hear my phone ringing through the door. This time, though, I didn't hurry. I hung my jacket on the oak stand in the hall and my keys on the hook by the breakfast bar. Thus organized, I ambled toward the phone. No matter. It kept ringing.

"Leo Waterman," I said.

"I seem to have forgotten the part of the meeting where they opened their files to us."

"The ravages of advancing age," I suggested.

"Can they be traced to you?"

"Only through rumor and innuendo. Nothing that will stand up in court," I assured him.

"You're sure?"

"Positive."

A lengthy silence ensued. "Why am I overcome with the feeling that a similar level of commitment to finding Karen Mendolson just might produce similarly startling results?" Jed said finally.

"A jaded and churlish nature?" I suggested.

"I'm serious, man," he snapped.

"That makes two of us," I said. "I'm doing everything that can be done. This girl kept to herself. She's not using her credit cards."

"You heard from Paul?"

"I stopped by his office after I saw the boys. We did lunch."

"Shit."

I tried to cheer him up. "The boys took the bed back."

"I know. I called."

"Ye of little faith."

"Shit," he repeated. "I was hoping—goddamn it, Leo, you said—"

"It was always a long shot. I was just covering our bases," I interrupted. "She's a bright woman. She reads a lot. She knows the score. She's got a nearly unlimited supply of cash. As long as she keeps her head down and doesn't leave a paper trail, not me, not the cops, the friggin' FBI, nobody is going to find her ass." Now it was my turn to get nasty. "If you've got somebody you think can do a better job, maybe you better trot them out now, because other than this Internet thing, I'm fresh out of ideas."

I spent the next minute or so listening to the static on the line.

"Close of business Friday," he said sullenly.

I changed the subject. "You get a chance to look at that paperwork?"

"It'll be tonight before I have time. For obvious reasons, I'm not going to be able to farm it out to one of the kids."

"Thanks for filing the order."

"No problem."

"Heard from any of them again—Prowell, Conover—?"

He wagged his big head. "Nary the peep."

"We may be losing our touch."

"Sorry about before," he said suddenly. "I know you're doing the best you can. I'm getting a lot of pressure from the mayor's office, that's all."

"Don't worry about it," I said.

"Actually, fucking around with these music types is fun."

"Ain't it, though."

"Later."

Five-twenty. A little over an hour and a half until I was scheduled to pick up Rebecca for dinner. Freezing in here. I turned the thermostat up to eighty, punched the red button on the surge protector, and headed for the shower, where, due to the special acoustic qualities of my glass-walled stall, I was able to simultaneously warble all four parts of the Dell Vikings' doo-wop masterpiece "Come Go with Me," melting the seemingly disparate parts into a sonic stew of such harmonic richness and tonal quality as to surely warrant professional archiving.

Five-thirty-five. The place was a sauna. I lowered the heat to sixty and opened the office window. After configuring my PPP, I checked my E-mail.

I pulled the little West Bend timer from the top drawer of my desk and set it for an hour. Rebecca had bought me the timer for my last birthday. It was

all she'd bought me for my birthday. I was fresh out
of mistakes. No more innocent faces about how I'd
gotten involved on-line and lost all track of time.
Absolutely none of that shit was going to float anymore. I was ready.

Twenty minutes later, right at the beginning of
the second part of the digest, nestled between a rave
review of an L.A. detective novel called *Violent Spring*
and a call for mystery titles involving sleuths who
were also gay exercise therapists—I made a mental
note to check back on this one—Karen Mendolson
got her two cents' worth in.

Date: Mon, 19 Feb 96 18:21:42-0600
From: J.P.Beau@magic.net.com.
Subject: Sayers' Values

In a recent posting by Jeff Meyers he quoted Tracy
Sheen as saying "The writer has an obligation to
rise above the petty prejudices of his or her time".
I would be much obliged if he or Mrs. Sheen would
give me a list of precisely which current social
attitudes will be deemed incorrect sixty or seventy
years from now and a complete list of the reasons
why this has transpired. How could anyone doubt
that the reason anti-semitism is now unacceptable
is because of the Holocaust and the lessons people
have (hopefully) learned about the ends of prejudice.

J. P. Beaumont (J. A. Jance's Seattle Detective.)
J.P.Beau @magic.net.com

I copied her address into my address book and then read the rest of the digest. Good thing. Right near the end, the handwriting showed up on the wall. It was now or never. Karen's pet issue was about to become a thing of the past.

Date: Mon, 19 Feb 96 15:13:41 EDT
From: "Kara L. Robinson"
<KROBONSO@KENTVM.KENT.EDU>
Subject: Re: SAYERS AND ANTI-SEMITISM
To: ALL

Okay My loyal DorothyLers,

The time has come to put an end (as in halt, desist, stop already) to this Sayers thread. It is time to agree that we will never all agree on the issue of Dorothy L. Sayers and her purported anti-semitism, so it is time to put down our keyboards and move to other issues.

Thanks a ton for your cooperation in murdering this thread:)

Danger Mouse AKA
Kara L. Robinson
Co-Listowner: DorothyL

I clicked and scrolled my way back to Karen's
message and put together a pithy reply. This was
going to be the only chance I got.

Date: Mon, 19 Feb 1996 18:21:42-0600
From: LeoxxW@eskimo.com
SUBJECT: Sayers Thread
TO: J.P.Beau@magic.net.com.

JP,

I couldn't agree with you more; hindsight is always
twenty-twenty. I can't believe some of these people.
Alas, perhaps Danger Mouse is right. This particular
issue does seem to be particularly contentious. It
doesn't seem to be bringing out the best in any of
us. As she suggests, this might be best discussed
off line.

Leo Waterman

I wasn't at all sure about the *alas*, but the rest of it
sounded pretty good. Send. I followed Carl's directions. Leave the computer on-line. Unpack the
SuperFinder. Click the installer. Wait. Make sure the
program completely loads. Okay. Clicking find pro-
duces a dialogue box. The directions say to type my
own E-mail address. LeoxxW@eskimo.com. Click
OK. Another dialogue box. Type "all," lowercase.

Click OK. Big black letters moved across the screen like marching soldiers: . . . R . . . E . . . A . . . D . . . Y . . . R . . . E . . . A . . .

The timer went off. I took the machine at its word and went in search of some clothes.

20

I DIPPED THE TWISTED END OF MY NAPKIN back into my ice water and went to work on my shirt. Just to the left of the fourth button, a jeering glob of barbecue sauce the size of a fingernail had welded itself to the fabric and was worming its way into the heart of each tiny fiber, where it would surely dwell and stain forever. Arrrgh.

"I wish you'd told me you wanted to eat here," I whined. "I'd have worn old clothes."

"You're such a slob," she sympathized.

"It's not that I'm a slob," I protested. "It's merely the luck of the draw. Some people are just born to stay clean. Some aren't. That's it. End of story. You"—I pointed with the wet napkin end—"could snort a bowl of chili and not get anything on you." I rubbed harder. "I, on the other hand, am destined to always wear my lunch. That's just the way it is." The deep blue of the shirt had begun to come off on the napkin. Not surprisingly, however, the glob of sauce remained unscathed.

Willie's Taste of Soul was, if food was the sole criterion, perhaps the best restaurant in Seattle. If the location at the top of the hill off the Swift-Albro exit in South Seattle was a bit out of the mainline, the mouthwatering beef brisket more than compensated. Whatever the small dining area may have lacked in ambience, Willie's homemade Louisiana Hot Links would make you forget about in a hurry. By the time you'd choked down a piece of his legendary sweet potato pie for dessert, you were way past thinking about restaurants; you were thinking about cardiologists and dry cleaners.

I gave up on the shirt, leaned back in my chair, and watched the thin line of traffic making its way down Beacon. From the corner of my eye, I could see Rebecca was studying me like a lab specimen. Instinctively, I knew it was one of *those* moments. The ones where you don't get the test results until years down the road, when, smack-dab in the middle of some seemingly innocuous and totally unrelated conversation, she throws back a shawl, tosses her hair, and says, "And then there was that time my mother was thinking about moving in with her sister, and you—" God help you then.

I decided to take the initiative. "So," I started.

"What do you figure are the chances of the old girls actually moving in with each other?"

"I think time doth make cowards of us all," she said, eyeing me.

I figured she probably didn't want me to tell her how the Vince Lombardi quote really went, so I said, "All? Us too?"

She held my gaze. "Us especially."

"You really think they'll do it, huh?"

"I've got a feeling they will."

I took a deep breath, cleared my throat. "Okay, I'll jump right in here. If that happens—are you in favor of making some, like, major adjustments in our . . . our . . . current relationship?"

"Are you?"

"You're not going to let me palm this one off on you, are you?"

"Not a chance."

I was ready. "I think we ought to talk about it."

Worst-case scenario. "All right. Let's talk about it," she said.

We were still talking about it thirty minutes later as we cruised under the green lights of the Washington State Convention Center, tacking back and forth through the hazy heart of Seattle.

"I was just saying that first we ought to analyze whether we want anything to change before we go plunging in and screwing up a good thing," I wheedled. "I never once said I was or was not in favor of making any changes of any kind."

"What is it you're not satisfied with?"

I was barely holding my own. A babe in the woods. Each statement, no matter how closely couched, seemed to tip some cosmic scale further against me, leaving me naked and defenseless against unimaginably Florentine translations of my own seemingly simple phrases. Mercifully, my beeper went off. I checked my hip. The pay phone in the Zoo.

In spite of being no more than two miles away, I nearly killed us both as I cut across two lanes of traffic, leaving a white Mercedes weaving in my wake. An angry blast of a horn followed us up the Olive exit, left, and up to what used to be a Red Robin burger joint but had recently transformed itself into a more egalitarian Boston Market. Good Hearty Fare. *Fair* being the key word.

The restaurant and its parking lot sat on a little disconnected triangle of land where Olive, the aptly named John, and Summit all came together to form one of the busiest intersections in the city. I cut left on Summit, rolled the forty yards to the rear point of the triangle, and double-parked below the phone booth. I flipped the emergency flashers on and pulled the door handle. "Be right back," I said. No response. "I'll leave it running. In case, you know . . . a cop." I swear she growled. I kept moving.

The line was busy. I waited and dialed again. Still busy. Third time was the charm. I punched the buttons and spoke into the grimy mouthpiece. "It's Leo."

"Leo," George's voice rasped, "ya gotta get down here."

Through the smudged plastic of the booth, Rebecca appeared to be passing kidney stones. I gave her my best smile.

"It's not a good time, George."

"It's Selena," he whispered. "She come here to the Zoo. She needs to see ya bad."

"Okay." I sighed. "I'll—" I slouched back into the corner of the booth, rummaging around for what I was going to tell Rebecca. No need. She must have read my mind. She was all the way out of the Fiat, running in that high-knees style of hers, pointing at me, a round mouth shouting my name. Prison-break lights swept across the apartment building behind her. I turned toward the source of the lights.

The gray-primered van, its left front grillwork smashed and swinging below the bumper, bolted down the sidewalk at me like a headlong drunk. Its dual antennas wildly whipped side to side as it careened directly at the booth, right wheel on the sidewalk, left wheel in the parking lot, straddling what was soon to be two levels, the single headlight beginning to move above the body as the left wheel rose dramatically. Too late to get the right wheels up, the driver jerked it right, pulling the left wheels down from the shelf, bouncing hard. Fishtailing wildly, the rear panel of the van sideswiped the booth on its way down. I had the door handle in one hand and the receiver in the other when the booth snapped loose and began U.S. West's first pathetic attempt at manned flight. I could tell right away that the booth was short on lift.

I'd like to say that the world suddenly went into slow motion, that the impact of the van tore the breath from my body, leaving me gasping at the horrid hissing sound the booth made as it slid along Summit Avenue and bounced to a rough stop against the far curb. I'd like to tell you all that, but it wouldn't be true.

Truth be told, the whole thing was over before my tiny brain showed even the slightest glimmer of recognition of the extreme seriousness of my circumstances. Next thing I knew, I was lying face-down in the street with a half inch of scuffed plastic between my drooling lips and the pitted pavement, the inside door handle causing me a type of profound discomfort that can generally only be reproduced by urologists and certain Argentinean sadists. The phone seemed to be ringing.

Someone was yelling at my shoes. "Leo! Leo, can you hear me?"

"Arrrgh," I said.

"Don't move," the shoe screamer shrieked. "You're lying on the door; I'll pull you out from the bottom." Strong hands encircled my ankles. I can't be sure. I may have whimpered. Wedging my hands along the sides, I levered myself off the handle and rolled a quarter turn to the left, thus making my weight easier to pull and retaining my future propagation possibilities.

The aluminum bottom molding clipped my chin, gnashing my teeth together as I slid into the street. My toes hit the pavement. I rolled over on my own. Rebecca stood, brushing off her hands, looking down at me.

"Holy shit," I said.

She knelt by my side, looking hard into my eyes. "Lie still," she whispered, putting a hand on each side of my head. "Lift your head."

I lifted my head.

"Can you put your hands together?" I nearly missed, grabbing my left thumb with my right hand.

"Wiggle your toes." I did.

She stood back up. "Holy shit is right," she said with a sigh.

I sat up and extended my arms. Rebecca reached down and pulled me up to one knee. I looked around, expecting to see the sidewalks filled with gawking onlookers. Nothing. Not a soul.

"Let's get the hell out of here," I said, rising, unsteady.

"You mean flee the scene?"

"A lot like that, yeah," I said.

"What about the cops?"

"Did you get a license number?"

"No. It all happened so—"

"You were there for the whole schmeer with Tommy's car. What do you think? You got a couple of hours you want to donate to that kind of crap tonight?"

She checked the street in all directions. Checked the apartment windows. The street again. A careful woman.

"I can't believe nobody's come out to see what happened," she groused. "In my neighborhood—"

"It's Capitol Hill," I said. "You could cut the seat out of your pants and not attract attention up here."

She pointed at the booth. "It's right here in the street—somebody might—an accident."

"More likely, in this neighborhood, somebody will move into it."

The phone began to ring again. I looked down stupidly at the booth.

"It's your pager, Leo," she said impatiently.

I smiled a thanks and tried to push the button. My hand didn't work.

"Maybe you ought to leave that here," she droned.

Six inches of cord dangled from the receiver locked in my right hand. I willed my fingers open.

The receiver clattered on the pavement as I pushed the little red button. The Zoo. George again.

"I'm driving," she said. "Where to?"

"The Zoo."

21

GEORGE AND SELENA SAT AT THE FAR END OF THE BAR, an empty stool between them, half-finished beers and empty shot glasses arranged in front of them like the pieces of some alcoholic board game. The usual collection of eight or ten neighborhood stiffs lined the walls. Three couples were trading off playing pool at the extreme rear table, while a pair of aging bikers, in black leather vests and pants, their long hair and beards streaked with gray, tried to work their fading outlaw magic on a couple of secretaries barely old enough to be their daughters. Like the secretaries, I had my doubts.

Rebecca and I were nearly at her left shoulder before she noticed we were there. By that time, George had already slid off his stool and stepped back from the bar.

"Oh. Rebecca . . . ah . . . Miss Duvall," he stammered. "Nice surprise. I didn't know . . . What can I get for you?"

"Hello, George," she said, holding out her hand. George polished his hand on his pants, checked it twice, and then offered it up.

Duvall said, "I'm fine, but you better get a double something or other for Leo. He's had a real hard day."

George blinked and focused in on me. "She's right, Leo," he said after a minute. "You look like sh—" He caught himself. "Sorry." He nodded to Rebecca. "You don't look so good, is what I mean."

As George raised his hand to order me a drink, Selena started for me, her bleary eyes ablaze. "You dumb son of a bitch," she slurred, loud enough to stop the bar. "You got any idea what the fuck you been doing? What the hell is the matter with you, anyway?"

She came around George in a staggering lope, her right fist cocked and doubled. Before my battered nervous system could react, Rebecca stepped between us. "Smacking Leo doesn't work," she said pleasantly. "Believe me. I've been hitting him for years. He's way too hardheaded."

Selena stopped in her tracks and waited for her vision to catch up with the movement of her neck. "Who in hell are you?" she demanded.

"Rebecca Duvall."

Selena looked from Rebecca to me and back. "You with old bird dog here?" she asked.

Rebecca turned her gaze toward me. "Funny, we were just discussing that. But, yes, I am."

"Selena's my name," she said. "Selena Dunlap." She made a small, crude bow. "I sure hope you don't mind if I knock this stupid son of a bitch silly. After that, you can have what's left of the carcass."

"That's already been done this evening." Duvall shrugged.

"What?"

Rebecca related the fascinating fable of the flying phone booth.

"This ain't the first time, you say?" George asked.

"He tried to get me a couple of days ago," I said.

"I'd like to buy the son of a bitch some goddamn driving lessons, is what I'd like to do," Selena offered.

"Perhaps I'll pitch in," said Duvall without a smile.

"You *are* lookin' a bit ragged, Leo," George said, handing me a double of something brown.

"What seems to be the problem?" I said to Selena.

"Problem?" she bellowed. "The goddamn problem is that 'cause of your big, dumb, stupid ass, there's people out there lookin' for me. Bustin' heads and looking for me. They busted old Rodney's nose. Spread that sucker all over his face. That sucker heals, they ain't gonna be no space 'tween nose and ears. One just gonna flow into the other." She spread her arms in an expansive gesture. "Stomped on his only glasses, too. Hit Hot Shot Scott so hard he talks funny. Sounds like some goddamn fag from up the hill."

She started for me again. Rebecca put an arm on her shoulder. The two women sized each other up. Whatever advantages in experience and general hardness Selena might have had were more than outweighed by Rebecca's three inches and thirty pounds. Besides that, I could tell that Selena was unaccustomed to dealing with women who were even larger than she was. Her usual unbridled courage was waning.

"He deserves it," Selena said.

"I don't doubt it," Duvall said sincerely.

"You don't understand," she said, stomping in a small circle. "I lost my roof. They went down there and busted the place up. You know how long I was on that damn list. I waited nine months. Nine egg-suckin' months till somebody give the mission a bunch of new mattresses so there'd be room for more folks to sleep. Now—" She waved her long arms. "They gonna gimme the bum's rush the minute I show up down there. My ass is back on the street." She waved a finger at me. "I told you to cut it the hell out." She was stomping again. "But noooo, you just couldn't let that goddamn thing go, could ya, Lucky dog? Just couldn't keep from pokin' your nose up just one more porkypine's ass."

"It's in my blood," I said. "Once I start on something, I've just gotta see it to the end. I've always been that way."

Duvall confirmed. "Thick as a brick. He'll stay at it until he bleeds."

Selena leaned back against the bar. "That's it. That's exactly what you do-gooders never understand."

"What's that?" I said.

"Blood gets spilled, all right. No doubt about that. Surely blood gets spilled." She paused. "And ain't none of it *ever* theirs. Not *ever*. Not *once*. It's always us that does all the bleeding."

I didn't realize that the bar had gone silent until someone behind me with a gruff voice said, "Goddamn right."

"I watched friends go into the ground this winter, Mr. Busybody. You know that? Froze to death, and nobody give a shit. Watched the backhoe push mud into the holes after 'em. Where in hell was any of you do-gooders then? You tell me, huh, where?"

"Fuckin' A," somebody rumbled.

She collected her thoughts. "Met a guy on a train once who put it this way. I ain't never forgotten it. He said that the difference is in the difference between livin' *in* the moment and livin' *for* the moment. He said Mr. and Mrs. John Q Public, they live *in* the moment. Like they just visit the here and now, 'cause they're always really looking toward the future. It's like they live their whole lives for the future. They keep their noses down and get it done, so they can get them a motor home and then tool all over the country with those cutesy little signs plastered all over the damn thing. You know, like 'Grandma and Grandpa's Playhouse,' that sort of shit."

I tried to lighten the moment. "I have days lately when that sounds pretty good to me," I said.

No go. From somewhere in the bar came, "Let her talk, dammit."

Selena accepted the appointment. "People like me, now, we live *for* the moment. I don't have no needs or concerns that get much past right now. This is the whole damn shootin' match. I'll worry about breakfast when it goddamn well gets to be breakfast time." She looked at me hard. "That's what I tried to tell you the other day. Right now is all I got. You wanna help somebody like me, you give me your money. That's all. Just slip me your cash. Or maybe give the mission some dough for more mattresses, so's I can sleep inside. I need religion or a jobs program, I'll let your ass know."

A gentle ripple of applause spread to the walls. Sensing that the mob was with her, she raised her voice an entire octave. "So what the hell am I gonna do now, Mr. Detective? You wanna tell me that, huh? Now that you fucked up my whole gig, what am I gonna do? They gonna find me froze up like some TV dinner or what?"

I longed for the feel of a holster.

"Well?" a shrill voice rose from my left.

I took a long pull on my drink. Bourbon. The good stuff. Heady and tasting of wood. My mind was a complete blank.

Rebecca said, "For this evening at least, Selena, I think the least I can do is offer you a place to stay until you can find something more perma—to your liking," she amended. "I've got this huge house. Lots of room. What do you say? You can hang around until Leo gets this thing sorted out."

"You got your own place?"

"Yep."

Selena threw a glance my way. "You don't bunk with Fido here?"

"Certainly not," Rebecca said seriously. "He snores and picks at his feet. I live with my mother, who happens to be out of town for a couple of weeks."

Selena turned back my way. "Now that you got the cat out of the bag, how you gonna get it stuffed back in? Ya wanna tell me that, Mr. Busybody? I gotta life to lead, ya know."

"It's not going back in," I said. "This can of worms is open, and it's gonna stay that way until we get some answers. I probably best find out who's try-ing to run me over. That's probably a real good place to start. Chances are it's the same people who are out looking for you."

"He is a clever one, isn't he? Not much gets by old Leo," Duvall assured Dunlap. They shared a short laugh. "Leo will get it sorted out. Whatever his other failings, he's good at what he does. It's that thing in his blood."

Selena pinned me with a red-eyed stare.

"What do you say?" prodded Rebecca.

Selena looked around the bar. George piped in.

"Was me, I'd take her up on it in a New York minute," he said.

"Oh really?" said Rebecca.

He looked over at me. "You know what I mean," he started. "You know—" He shot a glance at Duvall. "Not like that," he assured her. "If I was to be— then—" He looked to me for help. "Leo?" he said.

I waved him off. "You're on your own, kid. Keep digging."

Rebecca leaned over the bar and said something to Terry the bartender. George looked stricken. Selena clapped him on the back.

"It's okay, Georgio," she said. "Hell, iffen I didn't come up with somethin' better, I was thinkin' about throwing a move on you myself."

"What?" George stammered.

"Probably ain't aired that thing out in years," she said to nobody in particular. A general titter ran about the bar. In the back, someone snorted. A moment of silence, and then, as if prearranged, the

crack of pool balls signaled the end of the show. The
bar settled in.

"I don't know," Selena said quietly. "I don't like to
feel beholden to people. I just can't do it."

"It's Leo who's beholden to you," Duvall said.
"He's the one who started this whole ball rolling,
and now he's the one who's got to get to the bottom
of it. The way I see it, he owes it to you."

The front door opened. An Asian guy in a Sonics
cap held the door open. "Somebody call a cab?"

Rebecca waved at him over the crowd and then
turned to Selena.

"It's up to you," she said.

Selena looked at the floor and then stuck her
hands in her pockets.

"I'll get my stuff," she said, heading for the back
of the bar.

"You didn't need a cab. I would have—" I started.

"Are you daft?" Duvall said. "People are trying to
kill you. I'm not riding anywhere with you until you
get this all cleared up." When I started to protest,
she said, "We'll meet on street corners like in the
movies. It'll be romantic."

"You sure you want to do this?" I asked.

"We'll get along famously," she assured me.

The driver poked his head back in. Selena
arrived. She had a blue sleeping bag, tied with thick
brown twine, hanging from a sawed-off broom
handle, which she slipped over her shoulder.

"Thank Ralph for the loan of the bag," she said to George, who was still contemplating the general unfairness of his lost opportunity.

Duvall pointed at the bag. "You probably won't be needing—"

Selena took her by the arm and started for the door. "Miss Duvall, I'll tell you what. You plan for your future, and I'll plan for mine."

Rebecca's response was lost in the whooshing of the door.

George and I stood alone at the corner of the bar. "Where's Ralph?" I asked.

"Back home," he said. "Said he'd been spendin' too much time down here lately. Can you believe that shit?"

It were fearsome strange indeed, but I was too dim to think about it. I polished off the bourbon and slid the glass across the bar.

"Once more with feeling," I said to Terry. He looked dubious. "It's a special occasion," I said. "George almost got laid."

22

MIDNIGHT WAS WAY PAST MY BEDTIME. All things being equal, I would never have checked my E-mail. I would have shuffled in and gone to bed in my clothes. That was my fondest dream as I opened the door.

But the damn thing was sitting right there twinkling at me as I passed the office. A bold-type banner running across the screen: 206-567-8980 . . . 206-567-8980 . . . 206-567-8980 . . . 206-567-8980. I shook my head and walked on past, rolling toward my beckoning bed like a stakes horse beaten by twelve lengths, headed for the paddock and the promise of oats. Inexplicably, I stuck out my arms and martyred myself in the doorway. Arrrrgh.

I called Carl. "Yeah," he said on the first ring.

"It's Leo."

"Be still my heart."

"How you been?" I started.

"Sittin' down," was his answer.

I hadn't known him before the accident claimed his legs. Some had assured me that he was every bit as caustic and argumentative before as after. I prefer to think not. Carl had this cute little conversational habit, whenever he wanted to make your life difficult, of mentioning his handicap, almost daring your acknowledgment of his predicament. I was ready.

"Makes you a bunch easier to find," I said.

"Cute, Leo. Real cute. Wadda you want?"

"That finder program you gave me worked good."

"Yeah, don't let it get around, though. Most of those yodels out there on the Web think they got privacy rights. They think they're out there in these chat groups and that they're the only one's listening." He gave a short, dry laugh. "Most of 'em would shit if they had any idea how public it all really was."

"I've got the number where she is now. Looks like a Bellevue exchange to me," I commented.

A long pause. No way Carl was going to make this easy on me.

"Lemme guess. Now you need the address."

"It's too new, man. It's not in my reverse phone book. Besides that, it's inside that big condo development up there by the crossroads. I'm gonna need building and apartment. Be a sport."

"A sport, huh? A sport? Tell me, Leo, you generally call folks after midnight and ask 'em for favors?

Is this a regular occurrence with you? You think maybe that explains your vast and continuing popularity?"

"I only call vampires like you this late."

Within our mutual circle of friends, Carl was renowned for, among other oddities, apparently never sleeping. No matter what time of day you called or arrived, he was up, dressed, and sitting in his wheelchair.

"I'll have to call you back," he said with a snort. "I've got all my lines except this one dedicated to something useful at the moment. And Leo—"

"What?"

"You okay? You sound a little—"

"Wasted," I helped him out. "I've had a few."

"Careful," he said.

"Always."

Carl hung up. I shuffled into the kitchen and put together a pot of coffee. Just as I snapped the little basket into the machine, the phone rang. Carl with the address. I stood around until I could pour myself a cup, spent a few minutes with a map of the Eastside, then called Jed.

"Hello," he answered immediately.

"You're up late," I commented.

"Trying to figure out what in holy hell I'm going to tell the library board tomorrow night."

"You'll be pleased to know that may not be necessary."

"You got something?"

"Just Karen Mendolson."

"You have her? Dammit, Leo, you're—"

"I know where she is," I amended.

I could hear him gritting his teeth. "Where's that?"

"Bellevue," I said.

"You sure?" he said.

Before I could answer, he said, "Have you—?"

"I've had a few," I said.

I gave him a detailed rundown of the night's activities. "You better find out who's trying so damn hard to off you," he said when I'd finished. "Seems like they're not going away."

"Amen, brother," I said. "I hear you. What do you want to do about the girl?"

"I'm thinking."

"I don't suppose you want to just call the cops."

"Are you crazy? The vote is less than a week away. No. No. The cops are out of the question. We've got to keep this thing under wraps. We gotta do this ourselves."

"Do what?"

"Confront her, dammit. We've got to scare the hell out of that woman. Get back as much of the money as we can. I mean, if all she's been doing is hiding out over on the Eastside, she can't have spent a whole hell of a lot of it, can she? It's not like she's been shopping in Paris or something."

"Then we better do it now," I said. "You want to put the fear of God in somebody, you roust 'em in the middle of the night."

He heaved an audible sigh. "Hang on," he said, setting the phone down with a sharp click.

I sipped coffee, hearing the sound of a distant conversation leaking over the line, a man and a woman, something about a wedding brunch, and under that, the electronic echo of a busy signal reverberated from some other wire somewhere on the planet. I was immersed in the electronic wonder of it all when Jed picked up. "You there?" he asked.

"Rooted to the spot."

"All right, come—"

I stopped him. "You'll have to come get me. I took a cab home from the Zoo. Also, if you remember, the last time you rode in my car you ended up feeling a bit queasy."

"Queasy?" he growled. "Hell, man, I blew chunks all over the azaleas. Sarah made me hose 'em off in the morning. She still busts my balls about it. Jesus, Leo, I can't believe you *still* haven't gotten that damn thing fixed."

"It is fixed," I insisted.

"I'll be there in twenty minutes," he huffed. "Have some coffee. Get yourself—"

"Wear jeans and sneakers," I interrupted. "We may have to do a little climbing."

"What climbing?"

"I'll tell you about it when you get here," I said.

I took my own advice, changing into a pair of gray jeans, a black sweatshirt, and an old pair of black basketball shoes from the seventies. I strapped the little Beretta .32 to my left ankle, standing, walking around the bed, finding it moved a bit, and then tightening the straps until I was confident it would stay put even at a dead run. I slipped the big 9mm into the shoulder harness and donned my old green canvas jacket over it. I shimmied my shoulders, allowing the big automatic to fall comfortably into place. Until further notice, I was only taking it off to shower.

By the time I slid into the seat next to Jed, I'd had another full cup of coffee and was beginning to come around. Jed's deep blue Lexus seemed to move without effort or sound.

"Take the 520 bridge," I said as I got in.

"Climbing?" he said.

"According to my map, she's inside that big apartment-condo thing over there in Bellevue. Up by the crossroads."

"The one with the big white wall that the neighbors sued over?"

"Yeah. I think it's called Overlake Village."

"You really think they're going to have somebody on duty at this time of night? In Bellevue?" He chuckled.

"You're way out of date, man," I said. "That part

of Swellvue has gone straight to hell. The state made the city live up to the low-income-housing guidelines. You know, so many low income for so many upscale. They built this huge complex. Put 'em all in one place, then walled the sucker in. It's a Little Saigon, with ten thousand recently arrived Russians thrown into the candy like peanuts. For the 'burbs, it's downright nasty, my man. These days, if I have to go in there on business, I generally hire a couple of leg breakers for backup."

Jed mulled it over. We rolled past the Arboretum and onto the floating bridge in silence. Finally, Jed broke the spell. "Those papers that magically appeared," he said.

"Yeah?"

"Very interesting."

"How so?"

"If I'm reading them right—which I am—Sub-Rosa has nothing to either gain or lose from the question of Lukkas Terry's estate. As near as I can tell, their end of the profits is ironclad. They get their end right off the top. Sure—the kid's death amounted to killing the goose. They'd be better off if he was still making records, but they get their percentage of whatever there is, no matter what. Their asses are covered. The contract's good. In keeping with recent equity rulings, too."

Even at this time of night, the bridge was full, an

undulating backbone of red taillights moving east, and insistent yellow beams squinting west.

"Equity rulings?"

"Courts have been upholding intellectual property rights lately." He could sense my confusion. "You know, like how in the old days guys would make a record, have a huge hit, but not really make anything out of it, because they'd signed these shitty contracts with some record company that ended up with all the cash."

"Yeah."

"The courts have put a stop to that lately. Started right around here, when the State of Washington Supreme Court gave royalty rights back to Jimi Hendrix's family, even though he'd repeatedly signed them away."

"I vaguely remember that."

"The court called bullshit on 'em. Said that when it comes to intellectual rights, contracts that did not meet fairness standards would now and forever be subject to review. Started a trend all over the country. There's enough precedence to choke a goat out there now. You sign a contract with any kind of artist or musician, you better make damn sure he and his heirs are getting what they deserve or you might stand to lose your end of the action."

"Really?"

"Really. And Sub-Rosa's financial position isn't half bad. I had one of the associates run it for me.

They're on a roll. The Terry kid was their biggest star, but they're doing pretty damn good otherwise too. Whenever the new record hits the stores, they're fat city. I just don't see them giving a shit whether the kid had a mother or not."

"They sure didn't seem to."

"That's because whatever she gets is coming out of somebody else's end, not theirs."

"Curiouser and curiouser."

"What's really interesting is the other end."

"What other end?"

"Terry and Conover."

"What about it?"

"They're not just artist and manager. They're full partners, with full survivorship rights."

"Do tell."

"'Deed I do."

"You, of course, know what that suggests."

"Except for the very prominent fact that the kid was the golden goose. Nobody ever profits from killing the meal ticket."

Jed had a point. "Get off at one-forty-eighth," I said.

"And, by the by, Leo—good work. The papers, finding this woman. All of it. Good work."

"We're not home free yet," I said.

23

THE BOOTH WAS SMALL AND WHITE; the guard was big and black. We rolled by close enough for me to see him moisten his fingers at his small mouth and delicately turn a page in a crisp *National Geographic*.

"What now?" Jed asked as we cruised past.

"Go up to the light and take a right."

He followed directions. "Keep following the wall," I said as we headed north down 144th. Piece by piece, a steel-and-Plexiglas Metro bus stop extruded itself into the headlights' path.

"Pull over up here. Up past the bus stop," I said. Jed slipped the car to the curb, shut down, and turned off the lights. We were at the north side of the complex. Ryder Avenue Northwest. Even in the ghostly purple light, decline peeked out from the untrimmed shrubs, littered low with cans and bottles, decorated above with shiny bits of wind-blown refuse stuck crookedly up among the knobby roots.

Middlebrow 'burbs working their way toward low. A scant three blocks from the strip malls, which even here lit the night to the point where no stars were visible in a clear sky. Probably changed hands and lost a lot of equity when they put this pig of a project in across the street. They'd fought in court for years, but eventually lost out to the powers that be. From across the narrow road, the view from the front windows must have been like being in the warden's house of a maximum-security prison. All wall.

We opted for geezer easy, dragging the green metal trash container from the bus stop to the base of the wall, climbing up and over in two long steps. Easy. Getting down the other side was, however, another matter. When I was a younger man, I could jump from considerable heights and land lightly, feathering down quietly, bouncing once on the balls of my feet as if the dictates of gravity had been waived. Nowadays, something has changed. Something scientific, I'm convinced. My specific gravity, maybe. It must be something like that, because lately, if it's much more than, say, six feet, I hit the ground with all the wild-eyed finesse of a dairy cow flailing down an elevator shaft.

My single source of solace was that Jed was even worse, landing piteously, splatting like a rotten melon, barely missing a thick little rhododendron whose pruned, upraised fingers would surely have probed him unspeakably. Instead, at the last moment he landed on his side in a great whoosh of air like some subterranean digging creature found beached in beauty bark.

We both checked for broken bones and chipped teeth as we limped along the sidewalk next to the buildings. Building thirty-seven. We were looking for seventeen. Thirty-eight. Wrong way. To the rear march.

Half a block up, I stepped out into the street to look at the handy map. Even beneath the swirls of spray paint, I could see that the place was drawn out like a wheel. The hub was the office, along with the fitness center, a couple of pools, and some sort of communal party area. The buildings fanned out from there in groups of eight, eventually reaching the round border road that we now were on. The spaces in the corners, where the circle met the square of the outside wall, were little mini-parks and play areas. How nice. Seventeen was closest to the hub five streets up. I stepped back up on the sidewalk and started in that direction.

"Doesn't look so bad," Jed commented as we walked along.

At first glance Overlake Village was much like any other ant-colony apartment complex. I'm sure they wanted it that way. When you forcibly inject thousands of recent immigrants into as chichi and trendy a community as Bellevue, you better do everything possible to be unobtrusive. Of course, it hadn't worked. After a protracted court battle, the result was that Bellevue now had both a right and a wrong side of the tracks.

West of the interstate was the Bellevue of old—Bellevue Square—German car, pinkie-in-the-air rich, spread out along Meydenbaur Bay and Lake Washington, hiding behind gates and shrubs all the way up to Medina, where Bill Gates was building the missus a quaint little bungalow about the size of Grand Central Station.

East of the highway, always the more commercial poor relation anyway, had been thrown to the dogs of development and diversity and summarily swallowed whole. As its opponents had so loudly insisted, Overlake Village had merely been the beginning. Hindsight.

The cars were an odd mixture of older American gas hogs and thrashed imports. Almost nothing new. In the first recreation area we passed, the basketball stanchions held netless rims that had been bent all the way down like dejected lower lips. Jed put a hand on my arm.

Up ahead, several bodies moved about in the shadows. I kept walking. Jed tagged along. "Are you armed?" he whispered to my back.

"Thought you said it wasn't so bad," I said.

Asian kids. Out crawling cars. Looking for trouble while their parents were out killing themselves, working double and triple shifts, earning a living.

Four, maybe five of them, wearing the uniform of the day. Prison chic. Huge saggy pants over expensive unlaced Nikes. Enormous hooded sweatshirts, hood up, covering knitted watchcaps pulled down nearly to their eyes. They milled around, pretending they didn't see us, bouncing to the beat of their internal hip-hop. I kept walking. They had their choreography down. The collective body language screamed that they'd done this before.

The tallest of the group, pushing six feet, leaned back against the peeling hood of a red Camaro, extending his crossed feet over the sidewalk, forcing me to either walk in the flower bed or step over him. I stopped and looked down at his shoes and then back up at the kid. He was maybe seventeen, with the broad, flat face common to Southeast Asia and the lifeless eyes common to wanna-be gangstas. The other four, all younger and smaller than Mr. Feet, began to flare out in a loose circle as we passed. I kept my eyes on Mr. Feet. If there was going to be trouble, and there sure as hell was, it would come from him. I probably should have tried harder to talk us through it, but it had been a hell of a day, and I'd long since used up my ration of patience.

"This here is a toll road," he said without moving.

"You don't say."

"Yeah, but I do." He showed me an acre of teeth, then looked past Jed toward his buddies.

"Nice shoes," I said. "You blow somebody for them?"

His wide nostrils flared and the black eyes twitched, but I'll say this for the kid, at least he wasn't into idle chatter. No threats. No snappy rejoinders. He bumped himself off the car. We stood no more than a foot apart. He covered my eyes with his for a long moment and then looked down at the space between us and turned away. With a resigned shrug, he stepped around to the left into the gap between cars and took a single long stride out toward the street. Just one.

For a kid, he was good. In a single oiled motion, he pulled his left hand from his coat pocket as if to steady himself on the hood and then, using the car for leverage, pivoted himself quickly back my way. His right hand came straight over the top, airmailing a wicked pair of brass knuckles straight at my forehead. I could smell the cheap metal as it whisked just over my head. If I hadn't been ready, he would have checked me into either the hospital or the graveyard.

I moved all of me two feet to the right and stepped quickly into the breach, kneeing him in the balls while the force of his own blow still carried him toward me. With the snap of a sail, my knee drove the sagging crotch of his pants the two feet back up where it belonged. The force of my knee nearly lifted him from the ground. A round mouth sucked in a huge chunk of air. Both hands flew to his groin.

I grabbed him by the back of the hood, spun him, and drove his face down onto the hood of the Camaro with a long, hollow *bong*. His nose made a noise like the snapping of a stale Saltine, mostly crisp but a little doughy in the middle.

The cap came off in my hand as he slid to the pavement. He fought so hard for breath, he hadn't even noticed his nose. I turned toward Jed and the others. Just Jed. The others were slapping soles and fading blurs in the distant streetlights.

"Nice friends," I said.

"Jesus, Leo. You didn't have to—"

"Yeah." I smiled. "I do kinda feel like Bernie Goetz."

When I got through with the laughing fit, I wiped my face with my hands and stood upright.

"I think I'm getting giddy," I said. "Let's go. I don't want to have to worry about those little pricks being behind us."

I took him by the arm and marched him around the writhing figure on the sidewalk. "What about—"

"He'll be okay," I assured him. "Once they clean out their drawers, the others will come back for him."

He kept looking back over his shoulder as I hustled him up the sidewalk, moving around the loop until the much-distressed Mr. Feet was out of sight.

I changed the subject. "How do you want to handle this?"

"Firmly."

"We gonna talk our way in or are we just plain going in?"

"We're going to try the former and be prepared for the latter. I think when she hears what I have to say, she'll come around."

We continued up the sidewalk until the little blue sign on the corner said 7-14. Seven-oh-three was on the top floor of the building, hardly more than a good piss from the back door of the indoor pool. The smell of institutional chlorine levels and fresh paint swirled about our heads as we stood on the ribbed concrete on either side of the door.

Jed tugged the knitted part of his brown leather jacket back down around his waist and then found my eyes. He nodded. I pounded the door hard five times and waited.

From behind the door, "Who is it?"

I pulled my license from my pocket, held it up in front of the peephole for a second, and then snapped it shut.

"Seattle Police, Miss Mendolson. Open the door."

Jed's eyebrows formed a pair of question marks. Hearing a scratching noise on the inside of the door, I stepped back to the far rail. The door opened on two inches of gold chain. One frightened brown eye peeked out. I took two quick steps forward and hit the door with my hip, tearing the cheap hasp from the door frame, sending the woman reeling back into the room. I grabbed Jed by the arm, propelled him into the room, and locked the door behind us.

She wore a burgundy sweatshirt with "Harvard" emblazoned across the front, a pair of gray sweatpants, and fluffy black slippers. No longer reeling, however, she held an aluminum baseball bat in what appeared to be a pair of skilled hands. Down at the end. No choking up. Her feet were spread and moving. She held the bat high and waved the end at us, kind of like Edgar Martinez sitting on the fastball. Her stance suggested competence born of repetition. I kept my distance.

"You're not the police," she said. "You get out of here, you hear me? You get out of here."

We stayed put. "No. We're not the police," I said. "My name is Leo Waterman." I reached into my pocket. She became more agitated, moving around in the batter's box now, more like the manic twitchings of Gary Sheffield than the calm resolve of Edgar Martinez. I held up my license. "I'm a private investigator. This is Jed James." He waved a business card. "Mr. James is vice chairman of the King County library board." Take that.

I'd expected her to wilt. No such luck. She dug in. Moving back in the box. Wiping out the rear line. Spreading her stance and leaning pugnaciously out over the plate like Albert Belle doing his famous impression of Mike Tyson brandishing a big twig.

"You get out," she repeated.

Jed picked up the ball. "You can have us or you can have the police. Take your pick." He suddenly moved across the room to the wooden apple box working overtime as an end table and lifted the receiver from the white princess phone. "Make up your mind, honey. Tell me how you want it. Either put down that bat and talk to us, or let's let the cops sort this out." He started to dial.

The bluff worked. "Stop," she said after Jed pushed the second button. Jed paused, finger poised. A series of thin wrinkles I hadn't noticed before crept out from her eyes, and her mouth turned down. She flipped the bat out onto the blue carpet where the dinette set would have been. She put her hands on her hips and turned her back on us, wandering behind the breakfast bar back into the kitchen.

"It's over," I said soothingly. "Relax. We're going to try to help you as much as we can."

She was every bit as sharp as everyone had said. It took her only about ten seconds to regain her composure and think her way through it.

"Bullshit," she said under her breath. She turned quickly and moved toward the bat. I was standing on it. She began yelling. "You're not going to call the cops. If you two were willing to call the cops, you'd have done that already. You would have showed up with them."

She took another step toward me.

I shook my head. "I generally try not to hit women," I said. "But there have been exceptions."

She stepped right up into my face. "You think you're pretty tough, don't you now, Mr. Detective?"

"It's in the thug handbook." I gave her the scout's honor sign.

"Thou shalt not get beat up by librarians."

"I want to see an attorney," she said.

I poked my thumb over my shoulder. "You're in luck. Jed's an attorney. As a matter of fact, he's my attorney, and a damn fine one, I might add. I couldn't recommend him more highly."

She stepped around me and faced Jed. "If you actually are an attorney—*which I doubt*—then you're an officer of the court, and I am telling you, as an officer of the court, that I, as a person with rights, want to consult an attorney." Same routine I'd run on Gogolac.

"You'll do time," Jed said quietly. "Eighteen months minimum. I don't care who your attorney is or how spotless your record may be—grand theft, public funds, a position of trust—a considerable sum. If you get real good representation, and I mean stellar advice, maybe you get to do it in King County instead of at a state school, but either way, you do some time. The public will demand it."

That one always worked. The mention of specific sentences and institutions, talking of hard time, rife with the veiled threat of unnatural acts always reduced the amateurs to jelly.

"F. Lee Bailey couldn't keep you out of jail," I added for effect.

"F. Lee Bailey couldn't keep himself out of jail," she sneered.

"My point exactly," said Jed.

"Maybe the public would like to know how its cherished library system really works," she spat. "The *Times* has always hated the library system. They've been waiting twenty years to get a story like this."

"Like what?" Jed demanded wearily.

"Like about how this institution has no regard for the people it's supposed to serve. Like how they put people out into the ice and snow because it's too hard on their precious landscaping. Like how public rest rooms aren't really public. About how people are forced to do not only their own work but also the work of people who quit, because the library always tries to circumvent the legal hiring guidelines for as long as possible. Like how half the administration are away half the time on these half-assed conferences which always just happen to be somewhere where the sun happens to be shining. Like how—"

Jed wasn't listening anymore. I could practically

see the wheels turning in his head. Worst-case scenario. A zealot. An articulate zealot, no less. God help us. Bring on the hemlock.

"—and how departments, at the end of the year, spend the last of their money on any old thing. Just anything. Whether they need it or not. Whether they know what the hell it is or not. We've got closets full of equipment nobody knows how to use. Not only doesn't anybody know how to use the stuff, but nobody even knows what some of the stuff was supposed to do in the first place. They spend it just to spend it, because if they don't spend it, they'll lose it in next year's budget. They do this while people are starving and freezing to death right outside the building. And how—"

"Stop!" Jed bellowed in the voice that regularly stopped courtrooms cold. "And when all of that is done—when you have disgraced and discredited everyone you can think of, you, my good woman, are still going to jail for grand theft." He cut a line in the air. "Unless—"

Karen Mendolson gazed down at the bat beneath my feet and then over at Jed. "Unless what?"

"Unless this matter can be handled both legally and privately. Like adults, shall we say."

"Save it," she said. "There's no way they're going to—"

"But there is," he interrupted. "Hear me out."

She wandered back into the kitchen and leaned

on the counter. "Go ahead," she said as if bored. "Spin-doctor away."

"As you so astutely have reasoned, Miss Mendolson, we—I speak here, I think, for the entire board—would prefer that this matter be settled privately. Out of the glare, so to speak."

"Politics," she sneered.

Jed admitted it at length and then went into soothing mode.

"You have been at large now for the better part of three weeks with a substantial amount of the county's money. Is that correct?"

"A hundred ninety-three thousand, six hundred and twelve dollars even," she said with some pride.

"With a clean record, and complete restitution—"

It was Karen's turn to interrupt. "I spent some of it," she said.

"How much?" I asked.

"About thirty-three thousand dollars. Give or take."

Jed's mouth gaped. "In a month? Thirty-three thousand? In a month? What? Did you buy a yacht or something?"

She heaved a sigh. "I gave it away."

"To who?" I demanded.

"Whom," she said. "And I gave it where it was needed. I gave it to that downtown food bank that had the fire. That was five thousand. I gave some to a senior meals program in the International District.

Twenty-seven hundred and fifty dollars, as I remember. Oh, and the literacy program over here. I gave them five thousand too."

"And the rest?" Jed prompted.

"I gave that to the Eternal Mission for mattresses. So people wouldn't have to sleep outside when the weather was—" She hesitated.

"Like Earl," I said.

Her eyes went elsewhere. "Yes," she said distractedly. "Like Earl."

"Who in hell appointed you the champion of justice?" Jed demanded. For the first time, he was annoyed.

"I did," she shot back.

"For God's sake, why?"

"Why not?" she said. Then, "If not me, who? If not now, when?" She spit it out quickly, as if she had been chewing it for a long time.

"Nobody, and never," said Jed.

She bobbed her head up and down as if to say, "I know, I know," and was pulled in a full circle by her thoughts.

"It got out of hand," she said sadly. "I was really pissed at the library for removing the homeless from the windows. Earl, and you know—that was very painful." She paused. "I was pissed about having to do two jobs." She took a deep breath. "I was depressed about my life." She turned up her palms. "Once I started, it just snowballed. Next thing I knew, I'd already cashed the check and given away money that didn't belong to me. By then it was just—" She searched for a word.

"Too late," Jed suggested.

She didn't hear him. "And you know what?" she continued. "I never really had a plan. I just moved in here because I didn't know what else to do." She looked around the dingy interior as if seeing it for the first time. "But that's not the strange part," she continued. "The strange part is that I've never felt better. Never felt like I was getting more done or being more useful. Since I started," she mused, "this has been the best time of my life. I've never—"

"Earth to Karen. Earth to Karen!" Jed shouted. "What you better be thinking about is how you're going to beg, borrow, or steal enough money to give the county complete restitution."

She gave a short, derisive laugh. "I don't have that kind of money. I gave away all of my own to the Capitol Hill Senior Center. That's why I started to— you know—"

"Let's get this over with, then," he said quickly. "Perhaps Mr. Waterman and I can get back to our beds. The question, young lady, is this. Are you or aren't you prepared to do prison time?" Jed asked flatly. "I'm not going to bore you with those film noir stories of women in prison. You're an intelligent young woman. You make up your own mind. But do it damn quickly, because I'm about at the end of the line with you. I'm working my way up to the politics-be-damned stage of things."

She thought her response over. Turning it several times.

"No," she said quietly. "I don't want to go to jail."

"Well, then, what you're going to do is this. You are going to move back into your regular apartment so that it does not appear that you are attempting to flee prosecution. I am personally going to see to that. Right here, tonight. All right?" He waited for an answer. It took quite a while, but she agreed.

"Next, you are going to call everyone you know. Your father and brother up in Michigan, everybody, and you are going to beg for money."

She started to protest, but Jed cut her off.

"Cousins you haven't seen in years. Maiden aunts. All of them. You are going to raise every dime you can raise. Then you're going to go to your bank and borrow every dime they'll give you. Ransom your body on Pacific Highway South if necessary. Do you understand what I'm telling you? If you are going to avoid incarceration, you must make complete restitution. Period."

For the first time, she seemed to deflate slightly. "I understand."

Jed wasn't through. "As I understand it, you siphoned this money off electronically. Is that true?"

"Yes."

"If you removed the money electronically, does that mean you are equally capable of putting the money back in by the same means?"

"Well, if they haven't changed the codes. But by now—"

"By noon tomorrow, the codes will be the same. Can you do it?"

She was reluctant. "Yes," she allowed.

"As you get more money, you must put that back into the acquisitions account."

She nodded silently. "What if I can't get all the money?"

"We'll cross that bridge when we come to it."

"I'll still need an attorney, won't I?"

"Indeed you will," he answered. "Indeed you will."

He leaned on the opposite side of the counter from Karen and examined his nails. "My options are extremely limited," he announced. "I'm already on shaky ethical ground." Raising his head, he looked at Karen. "Give me a dollar."

"What?"

"You heard me. Give me a dollar."

Karen Mendolson leaned back, opened the drawer in front of her, and rummaged about. "Will four quarters do?"

As she counted them out, my beeper went off. I crossed the room and dialed the number.

"Leo. It's George." He was slurring, full-scale twisted.

"We found that old Charlie Boxer," he mumbled proudly. "Holed up just as snug as a rug in a jug." I knew what he meant.

24

CHARLIE BOXER HAD BEEN TALKING for a full half hour.

"I can still see the pair of them. Tweedledee and Tweedledum. Just like it was yesterday. They were firemen for Dave Beck and the union. The teamsters, you know." Charlie gave me a meaningful glance, as if I needed reminding. "That's what they used to call themselves. Firemen. You started blowing any smoke"—he took a quick drag from a Kent and a long pull from his drink—"and those two would put your fire out in a hurry."

His eyes clouded. "Your old man, big as a barn, with these hands the size of hay rakes." Charlie shook his head. "In those days, he never could find a suit that fit him quite right. Always a couple of inches too much arm sticking out. Not like later when he had his own tailor and all. That little Eyetalian guy—what was his name?"

"Hugo DeGrazia."

Another swallow. He waved with his cigarette, as if scratching something into the air. "Always wanted to handle everything peaceable if he could. Always wanted to talk first. Shoulda known he was gonna turn out to be a politician."

As he laughed at his own joke, the laugh suddenly became a phlegmy hack that slid in stages into a tubercular coughing fit of truly epic proportions. He pounded his chest, which sounded as if it were full of Vaseline. I pulled my drink out of range and held on.

His arm flapping, whooping and wheezing he eventually became sufficiently animated to distract the crusty quartet from a spirited game of dollar-bill bullshit at the far end of the bar. George, Harold, Norman, and Ralph were medicating themselves from a second bottle of peach schnapps that I'd tried to buy from Charlie. As with the first one, Charlie wouldn't hear of it. It was on the house.

"Go, go, Charlie, go," George sang to the tune of "Johnny Be Good." This, of course, led to an inevitable round of hip-thrusting Elvis-the-Pelvis impressions. Charlie, meanwhile, was still sucking air and flailing about like a stroke victim.

"Sounds like he's got a hairball," suggested Harold when they'd finally calmed down. This one reduced them to jelly. Fist-pounding, backslapping, knee-buckling jelly.

"Here comes a lunger," intoned Nearly Normal above the din.

Beet-red, teary-eyed, but no longer gasping, Charlie Boxer whipped a soiled blue handkerchief from his rear pocket, lifted it to his lips, and deposited within its folds whatever deeply rooted matter he had just so exhaustively excavated from his lungs.

After returning the hankie to his pocket and mashing it with his right cheek—possibly to forestall an escape—he picked up the still-smoldering Kent and scrutinized it closely.

"Gotta quit these things one of these days," he announced. He took a long pull on the butt and continued.

"Him and that friggin' Tim Flood. They were partners back then. Little bastard could keep right on smilin' at a fellow while he slipped the blade between his ribs. Damnedest thing. Never got anything on him, neither. I hear from reliable sources that back in the early fifties he slit a guy's throat ear-to-ear in a warehouse over on Fourth and just walked off clean as could be. Didn't even have to wipe his hands."

I made a mental note to remember this for Rebecca. This was firsthand proof of the validity of my born-to-squalor theory.

I lifted a glass to the old man. "Like that old toast says: May you be in heaven before the devil even knows you're gone," I said.

He tipped a glass my way. "Thank you, Leo. Have no fear about it. I'll say a few kind words to your old man about you when I get to the promised land."

"You figure that's where he is, huh?"

"Couldn't say for sure, but I'll tell you this, wherever he is, is most definitely where I'll be going, my lad. I'm damn well sure of that. Wouldn't have it any other way," he added with a smile. "If I went any other place, I wouldn't know anybody."

He looked a little better but a lot older than the last time I'd seen him. His hair was pure white and going thin. His trademark mustache, once lustrous to behold, was stained a sickly yellow and singed in places. His puckered hands looked as if they'd been boiled.

It was three-thirty A.M. After hours. The Red and Black Lounge had been closed to the public for the better part of an hour. I'd watched and sipped while Charlie shot the bolts, turned off the neon beer signs, counted the till into the little zippered bag, and poured himself four fingers of Maker's Mark.

Charlie and I sat at the center of the bar, looking over the sink at a bronze hula-dancer lamp whose undulating hips and key-chain skirt caused the fringe on the fancy shade to tremble. Anticipation, I figured.

It was a cute little neighborhood joint up on Phinney Ridge, directly across the street from Woodland Park. It didn't take a detective to see that the place had recently been refurbished. Four black Naugahyde booths, their decorative silver tacks still shiny, ran down the right side of the room, across from the twelve-seater bar. Little kitchen with a delivery window behind the bar. Unless he'd stashed the bag in the freezer, there was probably an office somewhere behind that. At the back, several small tables and a gaggle of chairs competed for space with a new pool table. Behind that, the bathrooms. One on each side. Buoys and Gulls, no less. Blue handicapped stickers on the doors.

"How long has this place been here?" I asked.

Charlie lit another Kent. "Oh hell, fifty years or so," he said. "Helen's old man Ben—" He waved the Kent at me. "Helen—she's my—we—"

"Your main squeeze," I offered.

Charlie liked that. "Yeah, my main squeeze," he wheezed, staring off into space. "Helen, she can't hardly work the place no more. Got arthritis real bad. All her joints. Specially the hips." He caught himself. "Anyway, her old man Ben Cleveland built this place back in the middle forties, right after the war. He was a bricklayer by trade. Helen was just a kid. A war bride. Her parents had the property for years. Couldn't find work right after the war, so he built this place. Turned out real good for him."

"Nice little place" seemed to be what he wanted to hear.

Charlie Boxer sat with both arms resting on the

bar circling the bar towel. He was wearing a Philippine dictator shirt, cut square at the bottom, worn outside the pants. Two solid lines of green leaves embroidered lengthwise down the front. Without moving, he looked at me out of the corner of his eye and said, "I take it, Leo, that you and the Pioneer Square Protection Association here"—he inclined his head an inch toward the boys, at the far end of the bar—"aren't just up here in this neck of the woods by chance. I mean, much as I'd like to think this was a social call—" He let it hang and grinned.

"I've had them out looking for you."

"For me? For old Charlie the Boxer?"

"I need to know about what you were doing for Lukkas Terry."

He lit another Kent. Probably wanted to keep the one burning in the ashtray company. A cigarette's lot is, after all, a lonely one.

"Poor kid," he said. He looked like he was going to get mushy in that maudlin way endemic to drunks, so I pressed.

"What were you doing for him?"

Charlie took a minute to calibrate his position. "Lookin' for his momma," he said through the drifting cloud of smoke that encircled his head. "He wanted to find his momma."

"How in hell did the kid hear about you?" I

asked. He looked hurt. "Not that you aren't a legend in the business—" I added quickly.

"Damn right." He chuckled.

"But you haven't been in the business for years," I finished.

He gave me a look that said I'd pay for that.

"Tubby Moran. You remember Tubby, don't ya?"

Tubby Moran had spent forty years as a low-level grifter and confidence man all over the Northwest, sandwiching brief, publicly mandated vacations around the usual collection of cons and scams that kept people like him alive. Murphy games. Pigeon drops. Kited checks. Aluminum siding. Driveway repairs. Gutter and downspout replacement. All of it.

"Tubby Moran?" I said incredulously. "Tubby the Touch?"

"Works for his son-in-law's janitorial company. Doin' real good. They got the contract over at the Moore. The kid was running all over the theater, telling anybody who'd listen that he needed somebody to look for his momma. Claimed he seen her out back in the alley. Said she looked like a bum. Wanted her found."

"I can't believe you still see Tubby."

"Hell, Leo, he don't live but four blocks north of here. Can you believe it? Comes in all the time. He figured, you know—" He gave me a sly look that said old habits die hard. "Rock-and-roll star. Big bucks, and all that jazz. I figured, you know, what the hell. Maybe a little nest egg; it was worth a try." He gave a dry laugh. "Kid didn't even own a checkbook, for pity's sake. No cash to speak of neither. Had to drag me over to his manager's house so's he could get me some expense money." He snorted. "A real high roller, that one."

"Have any luck finding her?"

"Nah. I dragged my ass all over the city for a week. Hadn't worked that hard in years. Nobody knew dick. Never got the rest of the cash, neither," he groused. "Wasn't so bad, though. Got to see a lot of people I hadn't seen in years. And, hell, it was good to be back on the streets." He gave me a little slug in the arm. "Hell, I don't have to tell you, do I?"

When I allowed that he didn't, he went on.

"Helen was having a hell of a time running the place by herself. You know, you hire help in a cash business like this, they steal you blind. She needed me. I needed to get back. About the time I give it up, that goofy bastard booted himself into never-never land, and that was the end of it."

"That's it?"

"That's it," he said with a shrug. "The whole ball of wax."

I swirled the dregs of my drink in the glass. "Glad to see things are working out as good as they are for you, Charlie," I said.

He sat up and looked around. "Best gig I had in

years. Helen's a good woman. Steady." He slipped off the stool. "I'm damn lucky to have her," he pronounced.

I offered a hand. He took it. His grip was soft and dry. "It was good to see you again, Charlie," I said.

The boys had gathered about us. It was handshakes and pats on the back all around. Free booze made you a viable presidential candidate, as far as these guys were concerned. Sainthood—perhaps. We all moved toward the door together.

"Sorry I couldn't be of more help," Charlie said as he used his bundle of keys to let us out the front door.

"Don't worry about it," I said.

The five of us milled about the sidewalk as the locks clicked behind us. The moon was on its way down. Ralph, Normal, and Harold linked arms and went weaving out into the street. George stayed at my shoulder. "You see what I mean?" he hissed.

I was dumbfounded. "What?"

"You see how quiet Ralph was? Ain't said anything real dumb in almost two days." He shook my shoulder. "Wouldn't even do his Elvis impression, and ya know how proud he is of that."

"He'll come around," I assured him.

I stretched toward the heavens and yawned as I walked diagonally across the street toward Jed's Lexus. Heavy Duty Judy and Big Frank sat on the low cement wall that marked the park's boundary, passing a bag-shrouded bottle between them. The air was heavy, the heady scent of equatorial dung rolling over the neighborhood from the adjacent Woodland Park Zoo. As if to play counterpoint, the muted trumpet of an elephant blatted twice, followed by the strange dry call of a large bird.

"Judy found him," George whispered as we crossed the street.

I pulled out a fifty and handed it to her. "Good work," I said. "Good work all around." High fives all around. I refused a pull at the bottle. "Anybody wants a ride to where they're going better get in the car," I announced. "'Cause this train is headed for home."

It was a state cop's wet dream. George, Ralph, and Harold squeezed into the rear seating area, with Big Frank spread out over their laps like an acrid afghan. Rear vision—zero.

Norman, who generally filled any passenger seating area beyond capacity, had somehow scrunched up and back to accommodate Judy's loose-jointed bulk, most of which had melted over the console and onto the floor. The tiara rested in my lap. Her booted feet bobbed in the breeze. Mercifully, she'd passed out, staring straight up at the headliner with only the suggestion of a smile decorating her otherwise cherubic countenance. The primal stench I had attributed to the Zoo was now in the car with us. I stifled a laugh and turned the ignition.

Whether we violated state visibility constraints was open to question. That we exceeded highway load limits was beyond debate. I eased the car from the curb. The steering wheel passed a scant quarter inch above the tip of Judy's nose. I started to giggle.

25

"**YOU HEARD ME.** That's exactly what Sarah asked me this morning. Her exact words. We're going down to Larry's for a coffee cake and she looks over at me and goes, 'Jed'—very serious-like, you know, and she says—'Have you been transporting wet sheep?'"

"If she has doubts about you, old buddy, tell her to hire me. I used to do divorce work. Either that, or you could just move to Montana."

"I'm serious, man. I left the windows open all morning, I've got those little pine tree things hanging everywhere, and the damn car still smells like old meat."

I searched for an excuse. "It was late. There were a lot of us. Some of them were . . . big and . . . somewhat indisposed." I wondered if they'd found Big Frank's shoe yet. Remembering the ride home, I suppressed a grin.

"It smells as if some of them were wildebeest."

"Take it down to Smith's and get it detailed on me," I offered.

He huffed and puffed a bit more and then changed the subject.

"I have, of course, resigned from the library board."

"Of course."

"I spoke—off the record—to several other members, and we all agreed that, all things considered, this is unquestionably the best way to handle the situation. I've assigned Marty Kroll to the Mendolson woman's case. Kroll's a real go-getter. It wouldn't be right for me to be directly involved as her attorney."

"Aren't you on rather shaky ground here? I mean, like, legally and ethically and other minor details?"

"No charges have been filed," he snapped. "Nothing is officially amiss until the final results of the audit are in. My legal position is, if not altogether pristine, at least manageable. Ethically, it's a bit more of a horse race. What I knew and when I knew it could get quite sticky, but I see no other path that assures both the library's public position and the young woman's legal position so thoroughly."

"Wouldn't it be better if she had an outside attorney?"

"Not possible," he said. "The minute we bring in an outside attorney, we lose all control of the information situation. The guy could go right to the press. I know that's what I'd do. I'd play that whole thing with the frozen bum for all it was worth. I can see it now. Burgess Meredith as Earl. The steaming cup of latte every morning. A little string music. This caring young woman pushed to the brink by an uncaring society. She'd have her own news logo and musical fanfare by the end of the second day."

"Information situation? Now you really sound like my old man."

"A man could do worse," he said seriously.

"And as long as it lasts past the vote on Tuesday—"

"Merely a beneficial side effect," he assured me.

"You got her home okay?"

"Oh yes. She called a bit earlier. On short notice, her father and brother can come up with about fifteen thousand between them. She's still about eighteen short. She's going to sell her car. This afternoon she's going down to her bank."

My phone line gave a click.

"Is that you or me?" I asked.

"You," he said.

It was Duvall, about as excited as she gets.

"You better get over here, Leo. Right now."

"Is there a problem?"

"She's leaving." She added, "For California."

"I thought you were going to get along famously."

"We did until I ran out of things for her to drink."

"Well, give her some more."

"There isn't any more. She got the sherry. Mom's bottle of Scotch. The commemorative champagne.

That half case of chardonnay we brought back from California."

"The Cakebread Cellars?"

"Gone. All of it. And all that beer you left out in the garage. Likewise, gone. Leo, this morning, she was eyeing my Chanel."

"You've got to keep her around till I get there."

"You better hurry. Soon as her clothes are dry, she's out of here."

I checked the clock by the bed. Eleven-fifteen. It had been five-fifteen by the time I'd gotten everybody to where they were going, returned Jed's car, caught a taxi back to the Fiat, and driven home. I sat up. Still dressed. I threw my feet over the side. Nikes too. Just like I planned it.

"Think of something. If she gets out on the loose now, she's going to be hard as hell to find."

"We've already had one shoving match this morning. I'm telling you, Leo, she's leaving. You get over here." I could hear shouting in the background.

"I'm on my way." I checked the mirror. My do had survived the night except for a solitary clump that stuck straight out to the right like a horn. The dreaded hatchet head. Better find a hat. "I need half an hour," I said into the phone. "I've got an idea."

"I'll do what I can," she said without enthusiasm.

I grabbed a Boston Bruins cap from the coat tree and sprinted for the elevator. The day hadn't yet made up its mind about itself. One of those gray

Northwest mornings. Overhead rode a rippled layer of cloud, bumpy and disorganized like atmospheric cellulite, while, to the west, fifty miles out over the snowcapped Olympics, a bright white sun backlit some of the peaks, hinting of better things to come.

I made good time. Seventeen minutes later, I slid the Fiat to a stop in front of the Bauhaus. She sat at the same table, reading a different book. *Snow Falling on Cedars* this time. She saw me as I came through the door and snapped the book shut.

"I need you," I said.

She curled her lip. "I knew it would come to this."

I pulled the book from her fingers. "I need you to meet somebody. Right now. We have to hurry. Come on."

She stood up. "Meet who?"

"Lukkas Terry's mother."

"Me—I—why—"

"You want something out of this other than your rent paid?" I said quickly. "You want something for that baby you're carrying around?"

One hand crept to her midriff. "Sure I do."

"Then get in the car."

She wrinkled her nose at the sight of the Fiat.

"This is your ride?" she said. "This POS?" I didn't bother to answer. She lasted three blocks. "What's wrong with this car?" she asked as we flew onto the freeway entrance ramp. "I think I'm going to be sick."

"It's a bit out of alignment," I said. "Don't look out the front window and you'll be okay."

"Oh God," she groaned. "I'm sick in the morning anyway. Oh God."

Miss Goza continued her devotional services as I ran flat out up to Fiftieth and then cut east toward Duvall's place in Ravenna, avoiding the University Village traffic knot, running behind fraternity row, dropping down the hill onto Twenty-second Avenue, remembering what Rebecca had said about construction in her neighborhood and staying on the arterials.

I took Fifty-fifth all the way to the top of the hill and turned left and then left again toward Thirty-fourth Avenue. I slid to a stop. Goza had stopped groaning and sat white-faced, breathing deeply.

Selena Dunlap, sleeping bag hanging from her shoulder, was striding north down Thirty-fourth Street beneath the arch of bare trees, away from the city. Her loose-jointed stagger suggested that Duvall would be well advised to check the perfume supply. Rebecca was half a block behind, wearing her black spandex biking outfit, her cellular phone dangling from her wrist as she walked along. I got out and stepped up onto the sidewalk in Selena's path.

"Get the hell out of my way!" she shouted. "I've had all a you I can stand. You just stay the hell away from me."

The area adjacent to her left eye was puffy and

beginning to turn purple. She was going to have a hell of a shiner. I opened my mouth.

As if to answer, she spun on her heel, dropped the sleeping bag, and shook a fist at Rebecca. "I told you to stop followin' me," she said.

Duvall had a scrape on her chin and the beginnings of a minor mouse on her cheek. She gave me a sheepish look.

"You ought to see the other guy," she said.

I said I figured I had, stepped around Selena, and inserted myself between the women.

Selena poked me in the chest. "You just don't get it, do you? I'm outta here. You got that? Got some friends hitching down to the Bay Area. I'm goin' with 'em. You wanna play your little games, you do it without me." She turned to leave.

"You want a bunch of strangers to end up with his money?"

She closed the distance between us. "I don't want nothin' from that boy, you hear me? It's me shoulda had things to give him, not the other way 'round. Only thing he ever got from me was the thing that killed 'im. All I ever gave him was the get-high monster. It's hereditary, you know. He'da never been an addict—"

"Lukkas *did not* get high." Beth was emphatic, standing at the curb holding the little jacket around her. "Get a life. An addict. Duuh."

Selena squinted down at her. "And what in hell is this?" she demanded of me.

"Her name is Beth Goza."

"Well, Miss Beth Goza, let me tell you somethin'. What you oughta be doin' instead of standin' out here in the street, pokin' your nose into where it don't belong, is to be lookin' high and low for your hairdresser so's you can kick her ass. Whoever it was give you that rinse surely deserves a whippin', I can tell ya that. Ain't nothin' on God's green earth got hair that color 'ceptin' one of them dumb-ass troll dolls."

Goza looked my way. "What did she say?"

"And what's all that metal shit you got hangin' offa you, girl? Kerrrist, you look like a walkin' junkyard."

The girl opened her mouth, but Selena stayed at it. "And one more thing, while I'm at it, just so's we understand each other. You make that *duuuuh* noise at me again, and you're gonna have trouble breakin' up the lumps in the stew, if you catch my drift."

With that, she pushed me aside and began weaving up the street. I followed, yapping at her heels like a terrier.

"Anybody ever tell you, you're pretty damn judgmental for a woman who once left town on the back of a Harley behind a guy with MOM tattooed across his forehead," I said.

She slowed and then stopped altogether. "Rufus,"

she said. "For crimeny sakes, how do you know about Rufus?"

I told her about old Clark Bastyens's story.

"Busybody," was her only comment before she once again swayed up the street. I stayed with her.

"There's more involved here than just you."

"Not for me, there ain't," she countered.

"I think that girl's pregnant with Lukkas's baby."

Again she stopped. This time she turned back my way. "Well, we ain't never gonna know now, are we? The boy's dead. He ain't here to speak for himself, now is he?" She dismissed me with a wave. "Hell, that's something a live man can't hardly be sure of. The dead, hell man, they got no chance, they're just dead." She started to leave.

"It's easy enough to find out," I said.

"Yeah, and how's that? All we got's"—she pointed back at Beth—"that thing's word."

"Oh, no. We've got a whole lot more than that."

"Like what?"

"We've got the woman who claims to be the mother. And we got—" I searched for a word. I settled for "samples from Lukkas."

For the first time, she seemed to pay attention. "What did you say? You say they got parts of the boy, like, stored away someplace?"

I went for the throat. "A bunch," I said. "They've even got the plate they took from his arm."

She started to speak but instead seemed to fall

inward. I kept at it. "A sample from the girl and a sample from Lukkas, and we can tell for sure. No doubt about it."

"They can do that?"

"Easy," I said. "DNA testing."

"They got that thing from his arm, eh?"

"In a little glass jar," I added.

I thought I detected a slight sag in her shoulders as she walked over and put the nearest oak between us, leaning back into the thick gray bark. I moved forward. She cast me a sidelong glance. "Jesus, bird dog," she said after a minute, "you could fuck up just about anything, now, couldn't ya?"

"Just can't stay away from those porcupines."

"Think you'da learned to run like hell by now."

"You would be the world's foremost expert on running from it, now, wouldn't you?" I said.

She bounced off the tree. "You listen here, you—"

I straight-armed her back against the tree. "She's right, you know. Lukkas didn't take drugs. Didn't drink either. Not even the people who assumed that his behavior must have been caused by drugs can say they ever personally saw him take anything. They just assumed."

Duvall from behind me. "Leo," she said urgently.

She stared out over my shoulder. I turned around. Selena craned her neck in that direction.

The back third of a gray van slid slowly from view behind the corner house.

"That the one been tryin' to clean your clock?" Selena asked.

I made it a point not to look that way. "Yup."

I kept my eyes on Selena's. "We need to get you and Rebecca and the girl out of here," I said.

"I can take care of myself." A wry smile touched her lips. "And your lady friend there ain't no shrinkin' violet neither," she said, gingerly fingering her swollen eye.

"The girl couldn't find her butt in the dark," I said.

Selena bobbed her heavy eyebrows. "Why ain't I surprised?"

"Must be 'cause you're such a fine judge of character."

"It's back," Selena said without moving her lips. "I can just see some of the front end stickin' out. He's turned it around."

"What say we head back the way we came?" I suggested.

She didn't argue. Selena retrieved the sleeping bag as we turned our backs on the van and started back down the uneven sidewalk.

I talked as I walked. "Rebecca. You take these two back to the house. When you get there, call the cops. Stay on the sidewalks and hustle your bustles."

Beth Goza began to object, but with Rebecca

latched onto one arm and Selena lifting her by the other, traction was at an all-time low. Her booted feet barely touched the ground as she flew openmouthed down the street as if swept along by the breeze.

Resisting the temptation to glance over my shoulder, I stepped off the curb and into the Fiat. Before snapping the seat belt around me, I pulled the 9mm out from under my coat, checked and rechecked the safety, and then set it on the passenger seat. I pulled the door in and checked the mirror. The van was now fully out from behind the house.

I pulled the door until it clicked and then backed the Fiat into the street and began a slow K-turn maneuver, taking four tries to do what I could have done in two. By the time I got it finished, the van was no longer in sight. I started back up Thirty-fourth Street.

At the corner, I whipped the wheel hard to the right and gave the little car everything she had. It wasn't nearly enough. The roar of a big V-8 assaulted my ears. The van filled my mirror. As I pulled the shift lever down into second, the van rammed me from behind, sending the car into a series of small swerves. The van hit me again before I could recover from the first. This time I could feel the snapping of the plastic taillights as I nicked one of the cars parked nose-to-tail along both sides of the streets. The wheel tried to escape from my grip, but I muscled the Fiat back under control. Redlined in second gear, I lifted my foot from the accelerator and allowed the force of the screaming engine to slow the car enough for me to slide left around the next intersection.

Unable to react in time, the rocketing van slid past the intersection, screeching to a halt on locked wheels, then burned out backward and followed in my wake. I stayed off the arterials, running in the neighborhood where the blocks were short and the Fiat's cornering advantage could keep me away from my more powerful adversary. By now Duvall had called the cops. In this neighborhood, somebody on every street we went down was probably calling them too. It was just a matter of time.

The van was twenty yards behind and closing fast when I slid around Thirty-first Street and headed north again. Three orange-and-white barricades stood like urban hurdles halfway down the block. Two six-foot piles of light brown dirt bracketed the barricades like bookends. Dig we must. Instinctively, I lifted my foot. Immediately, the van filled my rear vision. I put my foot back down and sprinted down the street. The van was so close that I could hear the squealing fan belt over the roar of the engines.

As the front wheels of the Fiat rolled onto the dirt left behind by the backhoe, I crimped the wheel all the way to the left and stood on the brakes. The residual soil allowed the little car to slide effortlessly around to the left until I was facing directly toward the hurtling van. When I lifted my foot from the

brakes, the car continued left, off the roadway, slam-
ming into the pile of dirt collected by the curb. The
Fiat embedded itself in the fine loam like a horse-
shoe buried in a much-used pit. Dirt and fine pieces
of stone showered over the hood as the van slid by,
locked wheels tractionless on the slippery dirt.

From the side of the rear window that wasn't
covered with dirt, I watched as the skidding vehicle
scattered the puny barricades like tenpins, crushing
the center one beneath the frame, sending the other
two flying toward the gutters.

The front of the van slammed into the far side of
the ditch, centering just below the Chevy emblem,
smashing hard enough to shake the ground beneath
the car like a minor earthquake. The driver's foot
still held the pedal to the metal. The engine, locked
in some lower gear, screamed in protest. The rear
wheels, in the air now, whined around at preposter-
ous rpms. I sat and waited either for the van's door
to open or for the engine to succumb to the abuse.
No such luck.

I grabbed the 9mm from the floor where it had
fallen and stepped out into the street. The noise was
horrendous. I flicked the safety off.

A loud, electronically amplified voice boomed
from behind me.

"Put the gun down. Put the gun down and put
your hands behind your head. Now!" it screamed.
Two SPD blue-and-whites blocked the street behind

me, their doors thrown open, their uniformed passengers spread out, using cars for cover.

I held both hands above my head, making damn
sure to move slowly.

"Squat down. Put the gun in the street."

I did it.

"Back up. Stand back up."

I complied.

"Turn around."

Smoke was beginning to come from the engine
area. The rear wheels were slowing down.

"Put your hands behind your head and back up
toward me."

At about my fourth backward step, a young Asian
officer worked his way around the front and picked
up my automatic.

"On your knees," the voice boomed.

"I have an ankle gun," I said to Officer Park.

"On your knees," the voice repeated. Like hell. I
stood still.

Two pair of hands grabbed my forearms, bent me
forward at the waist, and forced my hands behind
my back. As they applied the cuffs none too gently,
Patrolman Park removed my ankle gun.

"I'm a private investigator," I said. "Both guns are
licensed. Copies of my licenses are in the glove compartment."

From the far side of the trench, two burly officers,
vests worn over their uniforms, approached the van

in combat stances. Park leaned into the Fiat and began rummaging around in the glove box.

One of my keepers, a thin African-American woman, released my left elbow and began to approach from the rear. Gun drawn. One slide step at a time. She put her back against the van and slid slowly up to the driver's door. Her gold plastic tag read B. Ferguson. The two cops on the opposite side of the ditch were aiming over the tops of the piles of dirt, directly into both doors. The one on the driver's side nodded.

Ferguson moved her revolver to her left hand and used her right hand to push the button on the door handle. Without warning, the door sprang open, bouncing on its hinges. A massive ball of pink plopped down onto the pavement, slid feet-first over the edge, and disappeared down into the trench.

Ferguson turned back this way. "Call for an ambulance."

I jerked my elbow loose and hustled over to the side of the hole.

Marlene Jolley lay faceup. Her chest rose and fell. A massive purple bruise had already begun to puff across her forehead. She seemed to be smiling.

From the rear, somebody threw a choke hold on me.

"You know this woman?" Ferguson asked.

"Sure," I rasped. "That's Adrian Jolley's mother."

"That big drug dealer got busted last year?"

"Yeah," I said.

Ferguson looked down into the ditch and then back to me. A smile spread across her face. "You the peeper she bit in the ass?"

"In the leg," I countered.

The grip on my throat disappeared. From behind me the voice said, "Guess she wanted another piece of you."

Ferguson hid behind her hand. I didn't bother with a response.

26

THE LAST TWO COPS FINALLY DRAGGED THEIR ASSES out of Rebecca's house at three-fifteen. Three hours before, they'd let me make a phone call. I'd called George. "Round up the fellas and get up here," I said.

"Us? Miss Duvall's place? You sure?"

"You got any money left?"

"'Bout forty bucks."

"Spend thirty on booze. Save ten for the cab. Tell the cabbie to wait. I'll have another job for you."

They arrived an hour later. I'd immediately slipped George another fifty and sent him out for more liquor. We now had enough alcohol to float a Danish cruise liner. The boys and Selena were partying it up in the kitchen. Duvall burst through the swinging doors, back into the parlor.

"Norman just ate the top of my cousin Francine's wedding cake. He found it in the freezer."

"You had other plans for it?"

"Her youngest is a junior at Stanford, Leo. It must be—"

"Normal's got the tract for it," I assured her.

Beth Goza had been asleep for an hour. Her impossibly red head rested on the arm of Rebecca's black velvet sofa. Her limp hands tugged the jacket tight about her. When she was asleep, it was easier to ignore the eyebrow rings, the pierced nose, and all the other crap and see somebody's little girl somewhere in there. Duvall sat down on the arm of the chair next to me and began to massage my neck with one hand.

"You okay?" she inquired.

"Fine," I said.

"You're awfully quiet."

"I'm thinking."

"About that woman?"

A gust of laughter blew through from the kitchen. I could hear George delivering the punch line: "So the father says to the kid, Son, you ever seen a bulldog eat mayonnaise?" This one left them rolling in the aisles.

"All she needed was some playmates," Rebecca observed.

"Yeah, Mrs. Jolley," I said. "What a weird deal. After all this time, she's still out for my—" I shook my head. "What devotion."

"More like fixation."

"Changes everything, though," I said, closing my

eyes, allowing her massaging fingers to begin to loosen my knotted neck.

"How so?" She was using two hands now.

"I've been thinking all along that we—me and Jed— have really been making some serious waves with this thing we've been doing for Selena. I figured we'd really been making some well-connected folk nervous. I was working up a pretty good set of conspiracy theories."

"And?"

"Hell, we've barely created a ripple. The only damn thing that's happened since we started all this crap is that somebody went around strong-arming drunks looking for Selena. That's it. We haven't amounted to a piss hole in the snow."

"Why is that significant?"

"Because it tells me that nobody is particularly nervous about what we've been doing, which is bad for two reasons. First, it means that they think their asses are covered. And because of that, I probably can't count on them helping me out by doing anything stupid. And that means whoever it was was looking for Selena is my only lead."

"Done a good job of it, though." It was Ralph, trying to be nice. He'd wandered in from the kitchen, still holding a half-full beer bottle. He was wearing his uppers.

Through the door, Harold hollered, "Careful,

Ralphie, that ain't the crapper." Peals of laughter rolled into the room.

"Good job of what?" I groaned as Duvall began to work the golf ball that was lodged at the top of my spine.

"Findin' Selena," he said. "Done a whole lot better than that old Charlie Boxer." He turned and pushed his way back toward the laughter. "I'll tell 'em to keep it down," he said over his shoulder.

I grabbed the arms of the chair and stood up.

"What?" Rebecca asked.

"George is right," I said. "Ralph *is* seriously off his feed."

I pushed through the double doors into the kitchen. Selena, for all her practice, was no match for the crusty quartet. She was curled up on the counter immediately to the right of the sink, snoring quietly.

"Just checkin' her eyelids for holes," Harold assured me, hoisting a water glass full of clear liquid. Normal and Ralph were sacking the refrigerator, peering expectantly down into ancient Tupperware containers, sticking their fingers into the glop, and then tasting.

George proffered a bottle of peach schnapps. I said no.

"George. I want you and Ralph to go find Judy and Big Frank."

"What for?" he demanded.

I told him, but he still didn't like it.

"And what if he did?"

"Then that's the end of it."

"And if he didn't?"

"Then I want you and Ralph to do a quick job on the square. You guys know everybody. See if you can find somebody who remembers."

He looked at the alcoholic wonderland with which he was surrounded and began to bleat. "Send Norman. Nobody bullshits Norman."

"I want Norman and Harold to stay here and keep"—I nodded at the figure on the counter—"Sleeping Beauty company. I need you because I'm going to send you to see my aunt Karen."

"The one with the—" He made a gesture with his hands.

"Yeah. That one. You remember where she works?"

"Eighth floor of the City Building."

I checked the clock over the sink. Four-thirty. "I'll call her. I'll have her wait for you."

"She's probably gone, man," he whined.

I crossed the room, picked the phone from its cradle, and dialed. I gave the switchboard operator my name and waited. George took a long pull and then appeared to be praying. Karen came on.

"What a nice surprise," she said. "Believe it or not, I was going to call you later this week."

"Well—" I started.

"And you would have ignored me as usual, now, wouldn't you?"

"Probably," I admitted. "I was hoping—" I tried again.

"No, no, no, Leo," she chastised. "Just this once, before we get to what you want, we're going to get to what I want."

"Okay," I said. George was smirking at me.

Before it was over I had solemnly promised to attend the wedding of Karen's youngest daughter Mary Alice. In Bremerton. In a suit. With a gift. A week from Sunday. Arrrrgh.

"Now it's your turn," she said amicably.

I told her what I wanted.

"The whole history of the license?" she asked.

"Why not?"

"I'll have it ready. It will be nice to see George again."

I assured her that George felt the same way, broke the connection, and dialed for a cab.

27

SHE ROLLED HERSELF OUT FROM BEHIND THE BAR; the veins in the backs of her hands crawled beneath the skin like thin blue worms. As she forced the wheels forward, her small features became tightly gathered in the center of her face, wired in place by strain and thin silver glasses. She wore a small print dress. The tartan plaid blanket thrown across her lap clashed horribly with the dress's print and seemed to be trying to escape.

Her eyes said worried. "We were just about to close, gentlemen," she said with a wan smile.

I didn't blame her. The sight of George, Ralph, Judy, Big Frank, and me walking into your place at five to two in the morning was surely cause for concern. All things considered, she was remarkably calm. Her stock immediately rose with me.

I quickly took the lead. "We're friends of Charlie's." I walked over and offered my hand. "My name's Leo Waterman."

Her grip was firm and dry. "Charlie said you'd been by." She beamed up at me. "Well, aren't you the fine, strapping young fellow? I knew your father, you know. Even bigger than you, he was. A fine figure of a man, if you don't mind me saying."

I let her ramble on about the old man and how, back in the sixties, he'd intervened on her behalf in a local sewer dispute. When she ran out of gas, she called out over her shoulder, "Charlie—Charlie, you have friends out here." Her tone indicated that this was quite possibly a first.

It was a minute before Charlie came out from the back room. Same shirt. He stopped drying his hands on the white towel when he caught sight of me. His eyes flicked around the room, taking in the others, and then he slowly resumed his wiping, now one finger at a time.

He looked down at the woman. "Helen, this is—"

"Oh, we've already introduced ourselves, silly," she chided. "You should have told me they were coming." She patted at her dress, straightening the fabric across her legs. "I would have—"

"Musta slipped my mind," Charlie muttered.

She retold the story of the old man's stellar sewer stewardage as I leaned uncomfortably against the bar. Down at the far end, George threw a fifty on the bar, stepped around Charlie, liberated a bottle of schnapps and four glasses, and began to pour.

Charlie came around and stood holding the black

handles of her wheelchair. His eyes were flat, telling me nothing.

"I was just gonna take Helen home," he announced. "She—we—just live a few houses down. I was gonna come back and, you know—"

"Take her home," I said quickly. "We'll take care of things till you get back."

Helen started to object, so I stepped in, taking her hand.

"Real nice meeting you, Helen. It was a pleasure."

"I remember now," she said out of the blue. "You're a private eye like my Charlie used to be, aren't you?"

"Yes, ma'am, I am."

She looked up at Charlie. "Charlie doesn't do that work anymore. Just that one last time—" She looked up into his eyes.

"Charlie's a legend in the business," I said. "Whenever I have a real tough case, I always like to get Charlie's opinion."

Charlie sneered over her head at me. As she looked up at him again, he made quick facial adjustments in a vain attempt to transform the sneer into a smile. He managed something transitional. A smile, maybe.

"A legend," she repeated.

Charlie began to move the chair forward. I reached down and straightened the blanket on her legs. "Good night," I said.

She boxed me on the arm. "Oh, I'll leave you to your detective talk. All very confidential, I suppose."

"Very," I confirmed.

She looked my way as she turned left toward the door. "You will come and see us again, won't you? When it's not on business, I mean."

I told her I would and instantly wanted a drink. Dull the pain. Dull . . .

He bunked her out through the door, and the place went silent except for the gentle hum of the coolers and the metallic swivel of the hula dancer's hips. George waggled the bottle at me. I shook him off.

Either they lived in the alley next door, or Charlie took her home in a full wheelie, because the old boy came barreling back through the door in less time than it took Norman to put down his first boiler-maker of the day. Mere nanoswallows, as it were. All righteous indignation.

"You just can't stand it, can you? Just can't put it to rest that you ain't never gonna be nothing but a shitty little shadow of your old man. That you're never gonna personally amount to shit. That all you're gonna end up with is what he gave you, and you'll probably fuck that up too."

"You see right through me, Charlie."

"So you come up here trying to fuck up my gig. You just can't stand it that—"

"Charlie!" I shouted.

He clapped his mouth shut.

"Do us both a favor and just shut the fuck up."

He hustled past me, snatched the bottle from the boys, and replaced it behind the bar. "We're closed," he said. "I'll have to ask you to leave."

"We need to talk."

"I got nothin' to talk to you about. Told you everything I know." Before I could respond, he wagged a finger at me. "You know, it must skip every other generation. Your old man was never mean-spirited like you are, Leo. He was a gentleman. Gracious. I don't know what in hell's wrong with you. I could see it even when you was a kid. You had this little—"

He searched for a word. I filled the gap. "You get straight with me, Charlie, and there's no reason you can't just go on with your life. I'm not the law. I've got no axes to grind."

"I don't know what the hell you're talking about," he said flatly.

"Well, let me help you out, then, okay?"

"Have at it. Knock yourself out." He pointed at the clock.

"You've got four minutes."

"You told me the other night that the kid hired you to look for his mother, right?"

"Maybe you should have taken some notes."

I ignored him. "And that you legged the square and came up dry. Is that right?" He didn't answer. "I know you were actually down there, because you ran into Frank and Judy."

He held his face together well. "So?"

"So, how come you didn't ask either of them about Selena? Frank, I can maybe understand. Maybe Frank's not the most talkative guy in the world. But Judy . . . I mean, there's a woman who knows more about the—"

"Residentially challenged," suggested Ralph.

"—who knows more about the residentially challenged community than just about anybody, and you don't ask her?" I turned to Judy. "He ask you about Selena?" She shook her head. "Frank?" Likewise negative. "So how come a legend in the business like you can't turn up a square regular in a whole week?"

"Maybe I'm losing my touch."

"What you must be losing is your voice."

"What?"

"Nobody down in the square remembers one damn thing about you trying to turn up any woman named Selena Dunlap. Not one. Not a bartender. Not a regular. Nobody. I sent George and Ralph down there today, and you know—they came up just drier than hell." He looked to his left at George, who met his gaze and then reached around him for the schnapps.

"So what?"

"So, just this week, some guy nobody ever saw before, some gorilla, managed to damn near find old

Selena in one day's time. Kicked up her flop. Smacked a couple of her friends around. What do you make of that?"

He turned back my way. "What are you, the better business bureau? So what if I took the kid's money? Maybe I didn't hoof it all over. What business is that of yours?"

"I'm making it my business, Charlie. I'm making it my business to find out what you spent your time doing when you were supposed to be out looking for the kid's mother, and I'm not going away until I'm satisfied. If that fucks up your present gig, so be it. The way I see it, that kind of depends on you."

I could almost see the gears turning in his head. "Why you all over my ass?" he demanded. "What have I ever done to you?"

"Because, sometime about when you were supposed to be looking for the kid's mother, somebody got nervous enough about something to slip Lukkas Terry enough heroin to kill a cow. And I think whatever in hell it was you were doing is what set it off."

He showed me a palm. "I don't know nothing about no death. You got that? Nothin'." He took a deep breath.

"I never said you did."

He wiped his hands down over his face and walked out into the seating area. "Okay," he said. "So I didn't look for the woman. Maybe I'm not Sam Spade. So what?"

"What happened?"

"Well, you know, like I told you, the kid didn't have a goddamn dime. Took me over to his agent's place. Had this big old party going on." He stopped. Considering his options. "So we just get there, all these fucked-up people milling around, and the kid gets lost. Leaves me standing around with my thumb up my ass. Turns out later he's downstairs fucking around in this recording studio they got right there in the house. I mean, you oughta see this place. Christ. I'm wandering around checking out the sights when this Conover guy takes me into his office. I figure he's either gonna write me a check or throw me out, right? But instead he up and asks me what I know about the kid, and I tell him I know nothing. Like I'm just being hired to do a job."

He stopped. Another deep breath. Charlie sat down backward on one of the black chairs, leaning his forearms on its rounded back.

"So?" I pushed.

"So the guy goes into this big song and dance. Tells me this sob story about the kid. About this really weird life he's had. All alone in the world. How he's more like a father to the kid than a manager. How the kid is wired real tight, and how concerned about it he is and how he, first off, don't think the kid really saw his mother and how, second off, he don't think the kid's any way capable of handling anything as traumatic as finding out his mother is a bag lady."

"How much?" I asked quickly.

He almost smiled. "You got a nasty mind."

"How much?" I persisted.

He flashed a certain pride. "Twenty-five hundred."

"Not to look."

He nodded. "Just keep the kid happy and get lost."

"Then what?"

"There's no then what," he said. "That was it. I took the money and ran." He pushed a finger in my direction. "And I don't care what you say. You would have taken it too." I didn't argue with him.

A silence, punctuated by the clink of glass on glass, settled in.

"You remember my aunt Karen?" I said finally.

He knit his brow. "Which one?"

"The one just a little older than me. Used to be married to Bert."

"The one with the—?" He used his hands.

"Yeah, that one."

"What about her?"

"You remember what she does for a living?"

"Sure as hell must be something for the city," he quipped. "Everybody in your family's out there on the city dole somewhere. Your old man saw to that."

"Licenses, building permits. Business licenses, shit like that. That's what she does." I reached into my inside pocket and pulled out a wad of paper, which I smoothed on the bar in front of me. I looked over at Charlie Boxer. He looked old. "Before we go through this," I said, "I want to say again that I'm not the law. Whatever I might personally think of what you did, it's not my place to be cleaning up after the cops."

"I told you what I did."

"And you know, Charlie, if it wasn't for this stuff"—I tapped the pile of paper—"I probably would have just let it go at that."

He didn't say anything, so I asked the question for him.

"It's the liquor license for this place."

His face turned the color of old custard. He gripped the chair back with both hands. I went on. "It's weird too, Charlie. Because if some woman hadn't gotten me thinking about building permits and my aunt Karen, I would probably never have thought to look it up. Strange how life works, isn't it?"

I thumbed through the pile. "Tell me how I should interpret this, Charlie, and if it's good, I'll just go away. How's that?" Stony silence.

"Beginning about three years ago, the city licensing bureau and the county health department started trying to get the Red and Black Lounge and its registered owner—one Helen Cleveland—to clean up a number of serious health and safety violations." I wet a finger and worked down through the pile. "They've cited the place here no less than thirteen times. Bad ventilation. No handicapped access. Sanitation concerns about the bathrooms." I flipped through the citations.

I pulled a piece of violet notepaper from amid the pile. It was covered with a fine and quite precise handwriting. "All this time Helen has been claiming that the bar barely supports itself, that she is crippled and has to hire help, and there is no way she could possibly get the place up to code. Asked the city to work with her."

I pulled out a piece of city stationery. I waved it at the inert Charlie Boxer. "And, believe it or not, the city actually tried to help. They came up with a bare-bones renovation plan. They estimated it would come to about fifteen thou to get the place up to snuff and made some suggestions as to contractors. Pretty nice of them, I thought."

I looked over at Charlie. He didn't seem to agree. He was doing uninterested. I fanned the pile of paper. "To make a long story short, about three months ago, the city, as cities will do, finally lost its patience and gave your Miss Cleveland ninety days to get up to code or get out of business. Guess what?"

Apparently, Charlie wasn't in the mood to guess, so I helped him out. "On March fourth, a mere twenty-five days before the place is going to be padlocked, out of the blue, like a gift from the heavens,

Helen Cleveland suddenly finds the cash to get the place fixed up. She beats the deadline. Spends twenty-five grand on repairs. The place looks great. The city's happy. She's happy, and"—I let it hang—"your name suddenly appears on the license as half owner. Wadda you think of that?"

"A major step up," said George.

"A dream come true," agreed Ralph.

"Must be his animal magnetism," suggested Judy.

"Isn't it weird how all this stuff—Lukkas Terry's death, the remodeling of the bar, all this shit coming down at the same time?"

"Get the fuck out of here," Charlie said, rising to his feet. "I don't have to talk to you. Get out of here."

I stayed where I was. "Call the cops," I suggested. "So, what did you think when the kid turned up dead?"

"Go on, get out of here."

"You gonna try and tell me it didn't cross your mind?"

"I'm not telling you anything."

"I know, Charlie, and the bad news for you and your little love nest here is that I'm not leaving until you do."

For a brief second I thought the little guy was going to rush me, but the moment of anger washed completely through him, leaving only resignation behind.

He wandered about. There were tears in his eyes.

He held out his arms. "I can't lose this, man. This is all I got. My whole future."

"You didn't believe a word Conover told you, did you?"

His anger came flooding back. "He was full of shit. Twenty-five hundred not to work. Just 'cause he was such a nice guy. Who the fuck was he kidding, anyway? Thought he could con a conner."

"What did you do?"

"I started to look anyway. That's when Frank and Judy saw me. At first I thought I'd see if maybe I couldn't turn the woman. You know, see what it was was making him go jumpy about turning her up."

"And then?"

"Then I had a better idea. I figured, what the hell, I'd been paid, I might as well put in a little time, so I camped out up the street from that mansion of his and followed him around."

"The whole week?"

"Yeah. The whole week."

"Don't make me pull this out of you, Charlie. Let's get this thing over with as quickly as possible."

He seemed to be ready for it to end. The last of it came out of him in a rush. "Auburn. The Muckelshoot Casino. Every day around three. Stays till around eight and then back home."

"Gambling?"

"With some folks, it's a gamble, but not with him; with him it's a sure thing. All that son of a bitch does is lose. He couldn't pick a winner in a one-horse race."

"You saw this yourself?"

He moved to the back of the room now, leaning against the wall between the rest rooms. "I followed him in. Watched from the bar. He plays that James Bond game. The one where you try to make eight."

"Baccarat?"

"Yeah, that's it. I got friendly with a couple of waitresses who work the tables. Fucker's famous down there. He's the biggest loser any of them have ever seen. Said it was nothing for him to lose thirty grand in a weekend. Ten, twelve, easy, four or five days a week. None of them could even begin to guess the total. Hundreds of thousands, anyway. That's what they said."

"So you put two and two together, didn't you?"

"Didn't take no genius. We got this high roller, with expenses through the roof, with a gambling jones that's pissing away money hand over fist down in Auburn, and he's managing this golden goose who don't give one flying shit for his money." He shrugged. "So why does Conover give a shit whether the kid finds his mother or not? Unless of course he's so deep into the kid's pockets that he can't afford any change at all in the status quo."

"So you shook him down."

"He didn't take much shaking," Charlie Boxer said quickly. "He's a smart boy, that one. I knew what I needed. I didn't get greedy. I kept my end reasonable. He could see right away that if he paid me off, I was going to be in no position to come back at him. I'd probably have done more time for the extortion end than he ever did for skimming the kid. Just good business, really," he said finally.

"And when Lukkas Terry turned up dead? What, it never crossed your mind? You gonna try to run that shit by me?"

"What crossed my mind's none of your damn business."

"Sure turned out to be Lukkas Terry's business."

"The kid was crazy as a shithouse rat, Leo. Had whole talks with himself. Just sittin' there. No telling what mighta actually happened. What is it you want from me anyway, huh?"

It was my Catholic upbringing. I wanted contrition. Instead, I bit my tongue. I want to tell the old man that he may as well have just shot the kid himself. That just walking up and blowing Lukkas Terry's brains all over the wall might have been kinder and gentler. But I didn't. Instead I said, "Hope this works out for you, Charlie."

28

IT LOOKED LIKE A TIME WARP. As if some ancient wandering band of Goths had suddenly stumbled into a modern dining room, found the fare to their liking, and begun setting up their hide tents.

We'd had to put both extra leaves in the table, which now spread out before us like the banquet plank of some medieval keep. The five chairs on the left side were occupied by George, Harold, Big Frank, Judy, and at the far end, Normal, towering up into the morning light as if he were sitting in a booster chair. At the foot of the table, Ralph shoveled scrambled eggs into his yawning mouth. The better part of an egg and a half adorned his faded shirt-front. As a fellow spiller, I knew in my heart he'd get to it later.

Selena sat next to Ralph and across from Judy. Way up at this end, Beth Goza sat directly across from George. She and Selena had been allotted the extra bedrooms. Everybody else had bunked in the basement, whose palatial appointments had been the major topic of breakfast conversation prior to the arrival of food.

Duvall had elbowed me awake a bit after seven. "This is your party, Sherlock. I suggest you beat feet to the store."

I'd begun to protest. "There's some eggs and stuff, isn't there?"

"There's no nothing." She kneed me in the back. "I've never seen anything like it. They're like locusts. They got the last of the rice and canned peaches at two." Another knee. "Norman used my pottery project for dip. It was hideous." She elbowed me again. This time harder. "Go to the store."

I went. But not before I called Jed. My turn to wake his ass.

"Jed James," he said crisply.

Damn. He was up. "Top of the mornin' to ya," I said.

"And to you, my good man."

"Can you come over to Rebecca's?"

"Now?"

"Yeah."

Before he could ask, I filled him in. Mrs. Jolley. The Goza girl. Selena. Charlie Boxer. The whole thing. I heard him sigh.

"Are you thinking what I'm thinking?" he said when I'd finished.

"You know me, Jed. I'm universally renowned for

my keen perception of the obvious. You show me
you had motive, means, and opportunity, throw in
millions of bucks, and I'm just dumb enough to
figure it was you."

"Give me half an hour," he said.

I went to the store.

Now Jed came bustling back into the dining
room, holding several more pounds of crisp bacon
on a blue platter. "Right now, as we speak, in a little
cemetery on Long Island, my mother is turning over
in her grave," he announced. "To my knowledge, no
member of my family has ever been so exposed to
bacon."

He divvied the slices between the greasy plates at
each end of the table. The crew dove in and made it
disappear in a heartbeat.

I was ahead on the eggs and toast, leaning against
the wall watching Beth Goza, who looked as if she
had awakened to find herself locked inside the
gorilla cage at the zoo. She took minuscule bites
from an onion bagel with no-fat cream cheese and
watched, wide-eyed, the carnage going on about her.
Duvall stood back to the window, taking pictures of
the assembled multitude with her Pentax. For insurance purposes, she'd said.

Norman strode over to the Igloo cooler in the
corner and, with one massive hand, fished out three
fresh beers. His other hand was clasped across his
middle. "You okay, Normal?" I asked.

"Musta ate somethin' a little heavy last night," he growled. "Just gotta wash it down."

Duvall lowered the camera and bent an eyebrow my way. I peered out over the length of the table, pretending not to notice her.

From the far end of the table, Selena picked up the thread of the conversation. "Much as it pains me," she said between bites, "I agree with old bird dog on this one. Catchin' him for stealin' somehow just ain't enough. If he done what Leo says he done, then he's gotta pay."

Jed repeated himself. "I'm telling you, Selena, unless somebody turns up who was in that room when Lukkas got that shot, no DA is going to be willing to try it, because no jury is going to convict. It's not even circumstantial; it's inferential."

"Ain't right," she insisted before wedging another piece of toast into her mouth.

"I refuse to believe it," Goza said for the umpteenth time. "Greg loved Lukkas. It's not possible—"

Jed interrupted her. "I know it's difficult for you, Miss Goza—"

"Ms.," she corrected. I could hear his teeth grinding.

"Try going slower," I suggested.

"Ms. Goza. I understand that he's been quite good to you. For that matter, he's been quite good to a number of people." He took a deep breath. "And don't for a minute think I enjoy making accusations against a cultural icon like Mr. Conover. Among other things, he's something of a hero of mine." Goza started to speak, but Jed carried on. "But—but—Leo's scenario as to what happened is not only the obvious answer, it's the only explanation that makes any sense at all." He used his fingers to count. "This all starts when Lukkas sees Selena in the alley behind the Moore and hires this Charlie Boxer to look for her."

"Strike one for the kid," said George. "Conover really don't need no extra cards in the deck. He's into the kid's poke in a big way."

"Then he really screwed up," I said, "when he tried to run a number on old Charlie. He'd have been much better off if he'd just sent Charlie off to look for Selena. If he finds her, he finds her. So what? Anything would have been better than trying to con Charlie. All he managed to do was get Charlie's attention. That's when the shit really hit the fan."

"So Charlie made Conover for his gambling jones," Big Frank rumbled. "And shook him down for the twenty-five to fix up the bar."

"For at least twenty-five," I said. "Knowing Charlie as I do—" I let it hang. At last we had consensus.

"Strike two for the kid," said George. "By now, Conover's gotta be crappin' bricks. The kid is looking for his mama, which has got serious fly-in-the-ointment possibilities. He's moved out on his own. He's fixin' to move his girlfriend in. The boy's gettin' more independent by the day. On top of that, Conover's been shook down by Charlie for God knows how much. He's gotta be sure he's lookin' at the end of the world."

I jumped in. "And, I think maybe worst of all, the kid is in no hurry to release the album. As a matter of fact, he's telling anybody who'll listen that he's gonna scrap everything and start over. The minute anybody asks for an accounting, Conover is screwed. He's so far into Lukkas Terry's pockets, only his feet are sticking out. What he needs more than anything is for that new CD to hit the stores."

"And then he gets the call," George finished.

My turn again. "Lukkas has been ranting and raving around his new apartment ever since Beth called and told him she was pregnant. Doing that weird role-playing thing of his. I'm bettin' that's the voices the neighbor swears she heard. He works up this screaming migraine. He needs a shot. Who does he call?"

"Not Ghostbusters," offered Ralph.

"He calls Conover. Come over and help me with a shot." I shrugged. "Look at the position that puts Conover in. He's just flat losing control of the kid. And then what happens?"

"Manna," said Normal.

"Help me with my shot, Greggy," Ralph gargled through a mouthful of scrambled eggs.

"And Conover carpes the diem," I finished. "Whatever else you can say about the guy, he's always known an opportunity when he saw one. It's the whole story of his career."

"Strike three," from George.

"Dirty bastard," Selena said under her breath.

"I still don't believe it," Goza said.

"Let me ask you this. When Conover came to you at the funeral and offered to help you, did he know you were pregnant?"

She stared at me blankly. "Sure," she said. "He, you know, said how sad it all was. What a great loss, you know, all that stuff, and then he said something about how he understood how a woman in my condition could use some help at a time like this and how he hoped I'd let him be the one. He was such a gentleman."

"'In your condition' were his exact words?"

"Exactly." She put her chin down. "He knew; I know he did."

"So—how did he find out?"

She knit her creamy brow. "That I was—am—pregnant?"

"Yeah. Who told him? Did you?"

"Not me." She shrugged. "Must have been Lukkas."

"And when did that happen?"

She thought it over. Stopped. And then thought it over again. "Must have been the night I . . . he . . . that night. He was . . . It could only have been . . . before I got there—" It dawned on her slowly. As she thought it through, she began to relive the sorrow. Tears began to pour down her cheeks. "He looked so sad lying there on the floor," she sputtered. Whatever she said next was washed away. Everyone went silent as she cried.

When she regained some measure of control, I said, "Conover claims he hadn't spoken to Lukkas in a couple of days. That's what he told the cops. That's what he told me."

"Me too," she sniffled and then again began to cry.

The crew went back to eating. The sounds of working jaws and gulping throats filled the slack air. More beer.

"Damn near worked, too," Jed said. "If Leo hadn't been so dead set on messing around with this, Conover would have just waited for justice to run its course, released the new record, and buried whatever shortages there were in the ocean of money that was about to come rolling in. He was almost home free."

"Then you guys served them papers on 'im," Selena said. "And that's when they come around lookin' for me." I nodded.

"Probably a leg-breaker named Cherokee. He

works for Conover. He'd be the one. Probably figured they could scare you off."

"Or worse," observed Ralph.

"Wadda you figure Conover's doin' about now?" asked Harold.

"Shittin' his pants," said Judy.

Jed shook his head. "Uh-uh. He's hiring counsel and preparing to hunker down and ride out the storm," he said. "As long as he's in line for the proceeds of the new record, he's high on the hog. Misuse of funds is one thing. So maybe he loses the radio show. Maybe he doesn't speak at any more charity dinners. That he can live with. Murder is another matter. He's clean on the murder. That's what's important. At this point, he's probably better off in court than anywhere else. No, his pants are clean."

That's what I was afraid of. Once it got reduced to the level of lawyer fodder, all things were possible.

"Before it gets down to lawyers, guns, and money, maybe we ought to make one last effort at actual justice," I said. "Give him one last chance to save his own ass altogether. Just one last chance to stay the King of Seattle Rock and Roll. What say?"

"Wadda you mean?" asked George.

I turned to Jed. He met my gaze. "I think this might be where you exit stage left, buddy. No self-respecting officer of the court should hear what I've got in mind. They'll disbar your miserable ass."

I knew he'd be torn. That part of him would want to see this thing through. To jump in and work with the crew. So I made a joke about how he was the attorney of record for all of us and reckoned how we would probably be needing good legal advice. After a moment's consideration, Jed reluctantly agreed and then worked his way around the table to hand-shakes and hugs.

I walked him to his car and bent his ear. "When you get home, call Conover. Tell him we're with-drawing our restraining order. Tell him that our client has proved to be unreliable and that we're no longer convinced she's who she says she is. Apologize. Do that semi-humble thing you do. Hell, he was trying to get rid of her. Let him think it worked. Put him into party mode. And then—" Now I squinted at him. "Just when it seems like he might skate again, we'll lay it on him."

As I spoke, his eyes screwed down to mere slits.

"Be careful." He wagged a finger at me. "If you're thinking what I think you're thinking, and it goes wrong, you could all end up wearing those nifty orange coveralls."

"I know. That's why we need you on the outside. In case we all end up on the inside."

"You think he'll go for it?"

"I think he's real cagey. He's one of those guys who instinctively know when to step in and when to step out. He's like my old man that way." I held up a finger. "Where he differs from the old man, though, is that he's got no distance at all from it. No perspective. He's been on top for so long he thinks he belongs there. I think if he sees a chance to hang on to it, he'll do it. Besides that, if I'm right, he's already gotten away with it once. I hear it gets easier."

"You think the girl is up to the task?"

I sighed. "That, my friend, is the sixty-four-thousand-dollar question."

"How's the Mendolson woman doing?" I inquired.

We stood in the driveway. The sun was sucking up the last of the morning fog, drawing it heavenward, leaving the street seemingly draped in translucent lace. He put a hand on my shoulder. "She's still about six thousand short."

"She couldn't get anything from her bank?"

Jed heaved a sigh. "That asshole Fortner refused to verify her employment at the library. The bank gave her bubkis. I'm giving her the weekend. After that—"

I was thinking that after that it would be Tuesday and the election would be over, but I kept my lip buttoned.

I went back inside and let the congregation in on what I had in mind. About halfway through, the eating and drinking stopped. Forks were poised in midair. Everybody was suddenly paying attention.

"You figure he'll do it again, don't ya?" Selena asked.

"Last time he found himself in a similar situation, that's what he did," I said. "Old dogs, new tricks, and all that shit."

"'Specially if we bait him right," slurred Selena. "Somethin' easy. Somethin' he can take care of quick and simple and then all his trouble will be over and he'll be back in the catbird seat."

"A no-brainer," said George. "Somethin' too simple to resist."

"Something pathetic and vulnerable." Norman grinned.

"The old free lunch," leered Ralph.

She'd stopped nibbling.

"Why's everybody staring at me?" Beth Goza demanded.

29

"SCARED?"

She nodded. We sat at the top of a long flight of concrete stairs, the high-fenced city reservoir covering our backs. Twenty-five steps down to the level of the natural amphitheater and the band shell. Volunteer Park, the venue for Conover's famous Summer of Love concerts. A little irony never hurts.

I'd coached her to insist on meeting in a public place, just before dark. I'd wrapped the mouthpiece of Duvall's cellular phone in a dish towel. Even so, I'd held my breath as she'd dialed the number. No need; she was magnificent. A woman answered. Who should she say was calling?

"Beth," he oozed onto the line. "How you doing, Lady?"

"I know what you did."

"Excuse me?"

I thought I detected an involuntary intake of breath.

"I know what you did to Lukkas."

A long pause. "Whatever are you talking about, girl?" he joshed.

"I know you killed him," she whispered.

"Don't be absurd."

"I want a hundred thousand dollars for the baby," she blurted. "And that's just for now."

"Beth, honey—"

"Now!" she screamed. "You bring it to me."

"I'm afraid—"

She was ranting now. "You better be afraid, you— you—pigman," was the best she could come up with. Tell him he's old, I thought. "You bring it to me tonight."

"Beth, honey, you need help. Let me call my—"

"Ten o'clock tonight."

"I'm going to hang up now," he said calmly.

She looked up at me. I nodded. Time to play the trump card.

"You haven't gambled it *all* away, have you?"

"Excuse me? What did you say?"

"I know about you," she said musically. "You just bring me that money, mister." Before he could speak again, she told him where to bring the money and broke the connection. The Goths gave her a standing O.

She shivered once as the sound of shoes came down the black path at our feet. George climbed the dark stairs and squatted below us. He was winded and bleary-eyed.

"Everybody's in place," he huffed. "The big monkey—what's his dumbass name."

"Cherokee," I helped out.

"Yeah, he took a couple of laps looking for citizens. Told Waldo to get lost or he'd kick his ass. He jimmied open the women's crapper. He's in there now."

"Which way does the door open?"

He thought it over. "Out."

I told him what to do. He liked the idea. "We ought to leave him in there for a few days. Those crappers have been closed for twenty years. There ought to be some serious livestock living in there by now."

"Just make sure he doesn't get out until we're ready."

George gave me a two-fingered salute.

"Where is everybody?" I asked.

"Normal and Ralph are down there in the trees." He pointed east, behind the band shell. "Judy and Frank are on the far side of the grass under one of them picnic tables." He gave a dry chuckle. "They started making like they was doing the hokeypokey every time the big monkey came by. Even Godzilla wanted no part of that shit."

Nobody was better than the crew when it came to surveillance in public places. The old, the poor, the addled, have become so unpleasantly endemic that our species has systematically learned to shut down those portions of our brains that recognize their existence. In Seattle, the destitute and the depraved have become so prevalent that the crew could loiter places for days on end without attracting unwanted attention. They seemed to operate from beneath a cloak of cultural invisibility. They were there, but they didn't count.

"Harold?"

"He's holdin' Selena's hand back at Ms. Duvall's house."

"You've got Rebecca's cellular?"

He yanked it out of his pocket. "Just like you said."

"The second anything starts, you call the cops. If you even think anything is going to start, you call the cops. You understand what I'm saying here?"

Without a word, he picked his way back down the stairs and disappeared into the gloom. It was five to ten. I turned toward the girl. "You ready?" I took the shaking to be affirmative and helped her to her feet.

"What if he doesn't come?" Her eyes were the size of saucers.

"Then he's who you think he is, and we're probably going to end up explaining to the heat why we were trying to shake him down."

"And if he does?"

"Then he's who I think he is, and unless we fuck up, he's going to be the one doing the big-time explaining."

"Well, I guess we'll see, then, won't we?" she said and turned away.

As she started down the steps, I moved up onto the path that surrounds the reservoir, walked about thirty yards west, and slipped down into the thick bushes. I stayed low and duckwalked out to the front of the shrubbery. I was forty yards from the lip of the bandstand. The hundred-year-old bricks had been tagged so many times that the spray paint had come to form something abstract and vaguely impression-istic. Beth appeared from the left and walked slowly to center stage, where she wandered about in small circles, hugging herself.

I could hear the water falling behind me as the aerator fountain in the reservoir frothed and recy-cled its brackish charge. A black Mazda pickup buzzed up the park road toward the top of the hill and the main entrance, the buzzing of the engine eventually losing itself in the overhead rush of the breeze.

Beth's pacing was becoming more frenzied, tak-ing her nearly to the edges of the stage, back and forth. Five miles later, she stopped, put her hands on her hips, and looked impatiently in my direction. I stayed put. She returned to walking back and forth.

Conover was late and lazy. It was ten-fifteen when

he pulled the Range Rover to the curb at the right of the bandstand and turned off the lights. Beth Goza stopped walking and focused on the car like a pointer. The engine hummed quietly. He stayed inside. She looked my way.

I'd coached her to stay out in the open, not to go anywhere near the car, but her anxiety seemed to be getting the better of her. She began to walk toward the road. I reached for the 9mm and began to rise. Suddenly, as if reading my thoughts, she turned back my way and stopped. She took an audible breath, stuffed her hands into her jacket pockets, and strode back to the center. I settled back down on my haunches and waited.

In the brief flash of the dome light, I could see that Conover was clad in a pair of gray stonewashed jeans and a black leather jacket. Leaving the car running, he clicked the door shut and walked around the rear. I stepped out of the bushes and began moving down the tree line, staying in the shadows, holding the automatic down by my right knee as I shuffled forward. As I'd hoped, Conover was so focused on Beth Goza that I was nearly in his pocket before he noticed me. When he turned my way, I held the gun up above my shoulder, eliminating any doubt as to what I was carrying.

He stopped three paces short of the girl and swung his leonine head back and forth between us. "And what is this?" he wondered out loud.

"That's what we're here to find out," I said.

"This is a very troubled girl—" he started.

I waved the gun in his face. "Show me what's in your jacket pockets," I said.

"My pockets?"

"Is there an echo out here? Show me," I said. "Slowly."

As he pulled the pager from his left jacket pocket, he pushed the button. A dull thump came from behind the bandstand. Then another, louder this time. Muffled shouts, and then a series of rhythmic crashes began. Conover kept looking over his shoulder. I helped him out.

"Cherokee will be spending just a bit more time in the ladies' room than he anticipated."

He looked around, confused. "What?"

"The other pocket. The right pocket now."

His hand stayed put. His car suddenly stopped running. His head jerked around just in time to see Earlene and Mary scurrying off into the darkness with his car keys. Frank and Judy were on their feet now, closing the circle from the south end. My feet could feel the force of the blows being delivered to the rest-room door. I could hear the sounds of shoes and strain. He suddenly pulled his hand from his right pocket. I aimed the gun at his head. The hand was empty.

"What's in the pocket?" I repeated.

"You're going to be sorry for this. Do you have any idea—"

I stepped right up to him, grinding the barrel into his forehead, cutting him off. "If I'm wrong, I'll apologize later. Empty the fucking pocket." He stood stock-still.

"Put your hands on your head." He did it.

"Beth," I said. "Reach in his jacket pocket. Be careful."

Hypnotized by the gun, she obeyed, slipping her hand into the jacket and coming away with a small brown paper sack.

"Open it," I said.

She placed the bag on the edge of the stage. Instinctively, Conover started to move. I pressed harder with the barrel. "Don't," I suggested.

When Beth Goza turned around she was using only two fingers to hold a large syringe with red markings. A blue plastic safety cap protected the business end. Her disappointment was palpable.

"In case she had a migraine?" I asked Conover.

His jaw muscles worked overtime, but no sound was forthcoming.

From behind the bandstand, the shouting grew louder. The timbre of the blows became sharper and the sounds of struggle more intense.

I grabbed Conover by the collar and forced him to his knees.

"Lie down. All the way," I growled.

He unlaced his fingers and complied.

I handed the 9mm to Big Frank. "Protect the girl," I said. "If he tries to get up, shoot him in the leg."

I sprinted around to the right, just in time to see the first rusted hinge pop, allowing the door to swing free at the top, making it impossible for Norman and Ralph to keep the door in its frame. As I stepped up to lend my weight to the project, the door burst from the frame, sending Ralph reeling backward and burying me beneath Norman's bulk, which was in turn buried beneath the door. Cherokee's great weight drove the wind from my body as he ran across the shattered door and then turned back to face us. He paused just long enough to sneer down at me.

I'm sure, in his own mind, Ralph thought he had Cherokee just where he wanted him. Somewhere, he'd found a stout four-foot piece of tree limb, which he held straight over his head like an ax as he moved forward. With a mighty grunt, he brought it down, swinging for all he was worth. Cherokee never even flinched. He merely hunched his shoulders and allowed the blow to be absorbed by his overdeveloped pile of trapezius muscles.

The limb shattered. Ralph stared dumbly at his hands. Cherokee reached out, wrenched the remaining piece of stick from Ralph's shaking fingers and backhanded him across the face with it.

Once in each direction. Ralph staggered back, turned a clean half circle, and went down in a pile.

Just as I jerked my leg free from the door, Cherokee pulled me close and butted me in the face. My nose exploded. My vision went haywire. I seemed to be looking in four directions at once. Everything was red. He was going to beat me to death with the stick. I cowered and waited for the rain of blows. Nothing followed but a series of low grunts.

I autofocused in time to see Norman riding Cherokee's shoulders in an insane game of piggy-back. Cherokee reached over his back, took hold of Norman's coat, and threw him to the ground as easily as if he'd been removing a sweater. With a great whoosh of air, Norman hit the ground and rolled away. Blood rolled down over my chin and onto the front of my shirt. My upper lip felt stuffed and heavy. Norman's shirt was ripped to the waist. A swollen purple bruise was forming along his right cheekbone. The right eye was nearly closed. The left eye was on fire.

We moved in a tight little circle. Cherokee divided his attention between Norman and me. Keeping casual track of me. Then Norman. Then me again. He appeared unmoved and unhurried. Norman now stood between Cherokee and the car. Norman made a dive for his ankles. He never made it.

I never saw the sneakered feet move. One second,

Norman was in the air. The next second, Cherokee had anticipated the move and delivered a roundhouse kick to the middle of the back. Norman's own considerable bulk, augmented by the force of the blow, nearly drove him through the sod. He bounced twice, hunched himself into a ball, and began to gasp for air.

Cherokee hurdled the gasping Norman and started toward the car. Working purely on instinct, I started after him, in spite of having absolutely no idea what I was going to do if and when I caught him.

Turned out not to be a problem. As I left the ground in my best hurdle form, Norman levered himself up onto his knees. We went down together in a heap. We sat with our legs tangled and watched as Cherokee tore open the door and got in.

We scrambled up and started after him. At least I started after him; Norman ran like he was dragging a safe. From within the car came a frustrated scream. "Fuck!" he bellowed. No keys. He slammed the door hard enough to set the car rocking on its springs and began jogging uphill toward the conservatory.

"The hill's going to kill him," I shouted back at Norman. "He's not built for hills." I hoped it sounded more hopeful than I felt.

Cherokee jogged up the park's paved road until the parking lot came into view and then, curling off to the right, ran along the sidewalk, past the big piece of modern art, to the far side of the reservoir. I was twenty yards back when he turned again downhill, moving out among the bushes and shrubs, following the hard-packed runner's path that wound serpentine throughout the park.

I lengthened my stride and allowed gravity to force me into a full sprint down the matted track. In the semidarkness, the running took on a hypnotic quality, becoming merely a series of cadences rather than a specific action. I was gaining ground. My strides were becoming uncontrollably long. I gave it all I had. My hip joints felt like they were about to rotate right out of the sockets.

As he rounded the corner in front of me and reached out to use a massive Douglas fir for support, I noticed that he was limping slightly. My running got easier, but more out of control.

I almost piled right into him. He'd come to bay in the darkness on the far side of the tree. I skidded and staggered to a stop about ten feet from him. Closer than I wanted to be. He sensed it and began to slowly make his way up the slight slope at me. He was smiling. He beckoned. Come on. No fucking way. I backed up.

"I was hoping it was you," he wheezed. "Don't be going nowhere. Papa's got something real special for you." He began circling me. I thought I could hear Norman's heavy footsteps somewhere on the path.

I kept my hands low and circled with him. We

switched positions. His back was now facing up the path. He was still smiling. I was ready to duck or parry any type of blow. Instead, he tackled me like a linebacker, dragging me to the ground while his thumbs searched for my eyes. I twisted my head violently from side to side and rolled over onto my back. Big mistake.

He rolled with me, locked to my back like a shell. His iron forearm snapped across my throat. I pushed my chin down toward my chest. I had no doubt. If he got a clean grip on my throat, this was going to be over before it began. I took a chance and threw my head back as hard as I could. I made contact with his face, and for a split second the grip loosened enough for me to slip my whole chin under his massive arm.

The pressure was ungodly. My head was roaring. I was beginning to see spots. I clawed at his hands, searching for a finger to mutilate. The pressure only increased. Great silver flashes of salmon filled my brain. The fish had faces. I kept prying at the interlocked fingers. I was fading. Other fingers pried at my fingers. Lots of fingers.

The grip on my throat eased slightly and then slipped altogether in the collected sweat and blood. I rolled away. Kept rolling until I hit a tree. I rose and stood, swaying. Norman was there. The extra fingers. Above the roaring of my head, a siren approached. Cherokee knew what it meant.

He rushed Norman. Norman hit the dirt. Cherokee sailed over him. Before he could right himself, I waded in, throwing haymakers. The first one landed behind his right ear, drawing a grunt. I landed a wild right flush on his nose, feeling the warm spray of blood and spittle in the air around me. Norman waded in, throwing vicious punches of his own. Even against the two of us, Cherokee gave as good as he got. The years of self-defense classes faded away. This was primal. I was back in the schoolyard, bringing them up from my knees with my eyes closed.

With a sick tearing sound, Norman went down to a straight-legged kick to the knee. Cherokee now turned his attention to me. He shot a karate punch to my face. I parried. My forearm went numb. There was no pain, just the big smile as he loaded up for another attack.

Norman grabbed him around both ankles and pulled. Cherokee went down hard on his chest. At the moment when he looked up at me, I attempted to break Tom Dempsey's NFL field goal record with Cherokee's head. I missed. My toe landed squarely on his throat. He croaked and gasped at the impact. He stared bug-eyed at me, tearing at his own throat with puzzled hands.

Norman and I no longer mattered. Something had broken in there. He clawed at his throat. He began to convulse, shaking so violently he tore himself free from Norman, who still had him by the shins.

Suddenly he lay still, only his mountainous chest moving up and down as he fought to force air in and out of whatever small opening still remained in his throat. His fists were clenched in the effort.

The *whoop, whoop* of the sirens was close now. Everything was quiet except for Cherokee's labored breathing. Norman stayed down. I swayed in the breeze. My right arm hung useless at my side. Norman's leg jutted from beneath him at an impossible angle. He stared at it. We still hadn't spoken when the first wave of cops arrived.

30

I leaned back against the bar and watched. If you didn't know any better, you'd swear they were partying *again*. That they'd all gotten up early and taken up precisely where they'd left off the previous evening. The fact that they were partying *still* could only be properly appreciated by trained medical professionals and similarly disposed degenerates.

I'd taken Selena and Beth to see my cousin Paul the banker. At first he'd been dubious about arranging a line of credit for either of them. As he began to check out my story, his veneer of bored cynicism was replaced with an escalating sheen of corporate greed. After fielding a series of return phone calls, he'd leaned over to me, eyes hooded, whispering in my ear. "Conservatively, after Uncle gets his bite, after the state, after every damn thing, allowing for a twenty-percent deviation and possible massive embezzlement, these two stand to split about fifty-five million."

He held up a finger. "And that's without the new CD. The service fees alone on this account—" he started. Overcome with emotion, he waved himself off. "Boggle the mind," he finished.

If my lip had been smaller than a pizza, I would have grinned. As it was, I contented myself with a meaningful nod. Credit was forthcoming.

Selena had been standing for drinks for the better part of three days. The party was in full swing. Norman tromped to the far side of the snooker table. His right leg encased in a blue plastic walking cast, he bent awkwardly at the waist, took dead aim, and miscued the ball up over the rail and onto the floor, where, much to his displeasure, it was kicked, soccer style, from patron to patron as he limped vainly about attempting to reacquire the vagrant sphere.

The rest of the crew was sitting at the bar lending support to the Seattle Supersonics, who, by virtue of having won sixty-four games, were now engaged in a spirited second-round playoff encounter with the Houston Rockets. Having won the first two games here in Seattle, they had gone into Houston for game three carrying the highest of hopes. With six minutes to go in the third quarter, they were down eighteen.

The door opened. Jed James and Karen Mendolson stepped inside and waited for their eyes to adjust. Jed caught my profile and wandered over.

"Hey, big fella."

"Hey," I said.

Karen was still standing just inside the door, her hands thrust into the front pocket of her sweatshirt, looking as if she'd rather be modeling thumbscrews.

"You think this is gonna work?" Jed asked.

"God only knows," I said.

"The girl *really* didn't want to come."

"You got any better ideas?"

Selena looked up from her drink and caught my eye. I used a big wave of the arm to beckon her over. She showed a lopsided grin, said a few words to Big Frank, and rolled my way, walking as if the soles of her boots were rounded, dragging the butt of her pool cue along behind her like a stubborn puppy.

"Hey, bird dog," she slurred. "Where you been? The party's just gettin' on here." She leaned heavily on the cue with both arms.

"Got somebody I'd like you to meet," I said.

Selena took one hand away from the cue and waved as if shooing flies.

"Well, trot 'em out, bird dog. I guess I sure as hell owe ya one."

Jed thrust Karen Mendolson out from behind his back. She stood awkwardly at the end of the bar. Selena looked her over from head to toe and then refocused on me. "So," she said.

"This is Karen Mendolson."

Selena offered a bleary hello and looked back my way.

"You're up, Lena," Waldo hollered from the snooker table.

"You ever seen Karen before?" I asked.

Selena blinked three times, attempting to focus on the girl's face.

"Never in all my days," she said.

"You sure?" I pressed. "Take another look."

"You gonna shoot or what?" Waldo wailed.

"Hold your water, Waldo," Selena shot back.

Selena stepped in closer, getting almost nose to nose. A glimmer of recognition elongated her face.

"Maybe I have," she said finally. She touched Karen's forehead. "You the one threw that funeral for old Earl, ain't ya?"

"Yes," Karen said.

Selena looked over the woman's shoulder at Jed and me.

"Miss Mendolson has a problem we thought maybe you could help her with," Jed said.

"Why not?" Selena said affably. "Hell, all of a sudden, everybody wants somethin' from old Selena. Kenny wants a new truss. That crazy old Ralph wants me to buy him a friggin' hospital bed, for chrissakes. Frank wants one of those Everest mountain sleepin' bags. Ain't no end to it at all. People think this shit grow on trees." She refocused on Karen Mendolson. "What's your problem, Missy?"

she said with a smile.

Karen told her. Selena knit her brow several times during the story, but remained silent.

"And you just give it all away?" she asked incredulously when Karen fell silent. She looked to me for confirmation and got it.

"Hell, girlie, you might even be dumber than old Lucky dog here."

Karen jammed her hands back into her pockets and started to turn away. Selena stopped her. "You play snooker?" she inquired.

"Some," Karen said tentatively.

Selena handed her the cue. "Let's see what you can do," she said.

"Wadda you think?" I asked Jed as the women crossed the room. "They gonna make Conover for Lukkas Terry?"

Payton sidesteps it up the floor, Casell on his hip . . .

Jed pursed his lips. "Touch and go," he said. "Pretty much depends on the analysis of the syringe. If it matches the Terry sample, there's a lot better chance."

"If not?"

"He's hired Stan Rummer to defend him."

Stanley Rummer was locally renowned for being able to take a simple traffic infraction and turn it into a three-ring circus of such interminable duration that he simply wore judges and juries down. Two solid months of having their spines crushed by the benches in the King County Courthouse generally worked wonders on even the most spiteful jury. What was certain was that, whatever happened to Gregory Conover, it was likely to be well into the next millennium before it actually came to pass. Jed read my thoughts.

"With Rummer rambling on, God only knows when the estate will finally settle."

Foul on Kemp. That's his fifth. The Sonics can't afford . . .

"Where's the Goza kid?" he asked.

"Getting a tattoo."

He arched an eyebrow at me.

"On her back," I finished.

"This Space for Rent?" he inquired.

We shared a snicker. The game went to commercial. "How short is she?" I asked, nodding at Karen Mendolson.

"Still about fifty-five hundred bucks."

"If she comes up with the dough, will they prosecute?"

"Oh, they'll huff and puff, but I don't think so. Marty Kroll has got her a therapist. The kid's making all the right moves. Considering all of it. The Earl thing. What she did with the money. How she paid it all back. At most, a misdemeanor. Probably just probation."

Ralph leaned over the bar and came back with the remote. He began changing channels. The bar erupted in disapproval. He stopped on 23. Same Sonics game being telecast on Turner. Terry snatched the remote and switched it back to NBC.

Big Smooooth, from behind the arc . . .

"Maybe they ain't gettin' beat so bad on that other channel," Ralph suggested to the assembled multitude.

The bar went silent but for the rustle of eyebrows, as narrowed eyes looked from each to each. George smiled for the first time in a week and threw an arm around Ralph's shoulder. "Ralphie boy!" he said.

SLOW BURN

*According to these documents, I, Leo P. Waterman,
was the official security coordinator for Le Cuisine
Internationale. Dude.*

Anticipating disaster, a prestigious global restaurant convention hires Seattle P.I. Leo Waterman as Special Security Officer. His assignment: to monitor the movements of two adversarial steakhouse competitors whose "beef" has previously made for some nasty confrontations, and a food critic who's caught in between the warring factions.

Leo sends his band of scruffy irregulars – "the Boys" – off to shadow all three parties and report back to him. But even the simplest of plans can cascade into catastrophe. And our unconventional detective soon finds himself served up as the prime suspect in a murder . . . realizing that both his life and career are at stake.

"A hugely entertaining, over-the-top caper"
Publishers Weekly

Slow Burn, the fourth Leo Waterman novel,
will be published by Pan Books
in August 2007.

The opening scenes follow here.

1

I NEVER MEANT TO BREAK HIS THUMB. All I wanted was a ride in the elevator. The burnished brass doors were no more than ten feet away when I was gently nudged toward the right.

"Pardon me . . ." I began.

He was a big beefy kid with a flattop, smelling of scented soap and Aramis. He kept pushing, his blue blazer now locked on my elbow, his big chest bending my path steadily toward the right, toward the stairs, away from the elevators.

I planted my right foot and swung back, only to find myself nose to nose with another one. African-American, this time; otherwise, same blazer, same size, same grimace.

"What's the problem, fellas?"

"No problem," said Flattop. "You just come along with us."

I stood my ground. "What for?" I said with a smile.

He reached out and locked a big hand onto my

upper arm, squeezing like a vise, sending a dull ache all the way to my fingertips. His hard little eyes searched my face for pain. "Listen, Mr. Private Dick . . ." he sneered. "You just . . ."

I took a slide step to the right, putting Flattop between me and his partner, jerked my arm free, grabbed his thumb with one hand, his wrist with the other, and commenced introductions. Something snapped like a Popsicle stick. His mouth formed a silent circle. When I let go, he reeled backward, stumbling hard into his buddy as he danced in circles, gasping for air and staring at his hand.

"Whoa, whoa," his partner chanted.

"You want some, too?"

He reached for the inside pocket of his blazer. I froze. He flipped open a black leather case. His picture over the name Lincoln Aimes.

"Hotel security," he said quickly.

Flattop was still turning in small circles, eyes screwed shut, cradling his damaged hand, whistling "The Battle Hymn of the Republic" through his nose.

I shrugged. "All you had to do was say so, fellas."

He rolled his eyes in the direction of his partner. "Lance wanted to," he said with a sigh. "You know, he—"

His explanation was interrupted by a familiar voice rising from behind me.

"And what's this?"

Marty Conlan had put in his twenty-five years

with SPD and then gotten himself a steady job. He'd been the security chief for The Olympic Star Hotel for the better part of ten years now. Other than having an ass that was cinched up tighter than a frog's, he wasn't a half-bad guy. "These belong to you, Marty?"

He ignored me, glowering instead at the twirling Lance.

"Did he attack you?"

I don't think Lance heard the question. He was otherwise occupied, making noises like a suckling pig and hopping about like a weevil.

Conlan turned his attention to Lincoln Aimes. "Well? Did he?"

Aimes thought it over. "Not exactly," he said.

"Did you identify yourselves?"

"Not exactly," Aimes repeated.

"I thought I told you two—"

This time, Aimes interrupted. "Lance wanted to . . ." he began.

Conlan waved him off, checking the lobby, whispering now. "Jesus Christ. Take him down to the staff room. Call him a doctor. I'll be down as soon as I can."

We stood in silence as the pair made their way around us, heading down the hall in the opposite direction from which they'd been trying to move me. "All they had to do was identify themselves," I said.

"Yeah, Leo. I know. You're famous for being the kind of guy who comes along quietly." He heaved a sigh. "Come on up to the office for a few minutes, will ya? We need to talk."

I checked my watch. Five minutes to ten. "I've got a meeting at ten."

"I know," he said, turning away. "That's why we need to talk."

I followed him up the carpeted stairs to the mezzanine and then around to the security office. Security consisted of two rooms. The first was filled with a U-shaped bank of TV monitors which nearly covered the room from floor to ceiling. Maybe a dozen in all. The cameras covering the entrances were left on all the time. The others, which monitored selective areas of the hotel, could be used on demand.

Another kid in a blue blazer stared at the screens as we entered the room. He had a wide mouth, large liquid eyes and absolutely no neck. His blue-and-red-striped tie seemed to be pulled tight, just beneath his ears. He looked like Stimpy. He started to open his mouth, but closed it with a click when he saw me.

Marty paused to speak. "Call Frank Cooney," he said. "Tell him we need him down here for the week."

"Frank's off this week, Mr. Conlan. He and the missus are gonna—"

Marty cut him off. "Tell him it's an emergency." He threw me a glance. "Tell him Lance had an accident and is going to be laid up for a while."

Stimpy still hadn't moved. A mouth breather. I pictured him red with a blue nose and inwardly smiled.

"Call him," Conlan bellowed.

As the kid dove for the phone, Conlan pushed his hands deep into his pockets and kicked open the door at the back of the room. I followed him through, into his office.

Marty made his way around to the back side of the polished oak table that served as his desk and wearily plopped himself down into his black leather chair. "Have a seat," he said.

I stood in the center of the room and checked my watch. Two minutes to. "I have an appointment upstairs," I said.

"Room sixteen hundred."

"If you say so."

The smile evaporated. "What is it with you, Leo? Always the hard guy. Always making a pain in the ass of yourself."

"Color me with a crabby crayon, Marty, but I don't like being strong-armed by amateurs. You know what I mean? It's not good for my image. So either get to the point, or I'll be on my way."

He quickly stood and pointed a manicured finger at me.

"Listen, Leo, I don't have to let you in here at all. You know that, don't you? This is private property. I can have you removed."

"You'll need a lot better help."

A film fell over his eyes. "The corporation won't

pay for it," he blurted. "By the time I get 'em house-trained, they're outta here. The suits just don't get it. You can make as much in a frigging Burger King as they pay these kids. All they do is bust my ass about the high turnover."

I gestured at the well-appointed office, with its plush carpet, gilded mirror, real wood paneling and awesome collection of framed photographs and certificates.

"Beats the hell out of a squad room," I offered.

"Some days," he said. "Other days . . ."

I seemed to have found a sore spot.

"They're bouncers with Brylcreem," he lamented.

I was tempted to point out that it was more likely mousse and that the Brylcreem reference seriously dated him, but this didn't seem like the best time. I settled for: "I guess that's how come you're making the big bucks, Marty," an utterance which earned me only a short porcine snort.

He rolled his eyes toward the ceiling and pointed at the wall behind me. I knew what it was, but I craned my neck anyway.

There, lovingly framed and mounted on the wall, was the infamous UPI photograph of the ten lousy seconds which, much to my chagrin, seemed destined to serve as my solitary contribution to local popular culture. Marty was rolling.

"And here I am, spilling my guts to the bozo whose actions constitute the single most embarrassing moment in the history of this chain of forty-nine hotels. How's that?" he demanded of the ceiling.

In the photo, I stood, up to my knees, in the fountain at the hotel's main entrance, my hair flopped down over my right eye and plastered to my head, my pants seriously sagging. That was bad enough. It was, however, the two nearly naked hookers to whom all eyes were inevitably drawn.

"They use that frigging picture at training seminars. It's been in all the industry journals. We're a laughingstock. You know that?"

I reckoned how I might have heard such a rumor.

The irony was that I hadn't even been in the hotel that evening. I'd been on my way to meet Rebecca for a couple of quick drinks and an even quicker appearance at a mayoral fund-raiser, when my progress across the driveway was blocked by a white stretch limo which jerked to a halt inches in front of my toes. I heaved a sigh and started the four-mile hike around the rear of the car.

At first I thought somebody had popped a flashbulb inside the limo, as the interior was suddenly filled with a bright blue-green light. The violent rocking of the car and the four-part choral screaming suggested otherwise, however.

Without thinking, I grabbed for the nearest door and pulled. The blonde came out first, wearing a pair of crotchless panties, a red feather boa and a pained expression. Both the boa and her hair were on fire.

I used her own momentum to hustle her past me into the fountain pool, where she landed facedown with an audible hiss.

The little Chinese woman was another matter. Screaming in agony, she burst out through the limo door like a cannon-ball, butting me hard in the solar plexus, leaving me hiccuping for breath as she flailed wildly at herself and began tottering down the drive.

She was wearing a pale lavender corset-type thing that left her small breasts bare, a tiny matching garter belt and white shoes and stockings. All of which were on fire as she hotfooted it down the drive, her blind terror pushing her in exactly the wrong direction.

I sucked in one long breath and ran her down, lifting her from the ground with one hand and tearing at her burning clothes with the other. In the time it took to turn back and take the two steps into the pool, her flames claimed my eyebrows, and the heat of the small metal corset hooks blistered my fingers. Ten measly seconds.

A nameless UPI photographer, sent down to cover the fund-raiser, had caught the action at just the moment when I lifted the two women from the pool, one arm around each, all of us grinning for all we were worth. One big happy family.

Turned out they'd been freebasing cocaine and balling a pimp who called himself Eightball when the red velour interior of the limo, having finally reached its chemical saturation point, spontaneously burst into flame. Despite his best efforts, the driver, one Norris Payne of Tacoma, had been unable to extricate himself from his seat belt. In his thrashing about, Norris had inhaled a couple of lungfuls of the brightly colored flame and died under heavy sedation a couple of days later up at Harborview.

Eightball had eventually managed to roll himself out the far side and, with the help of several bystanders and a handy fire extinguisher, had successfully saved ninety-nine percent of his considerable epidermis. As irony would have it, however, the remaining one percent consisted of none other than his wanger, which, in a travesty of bad timing, had been experiencing liftoff at the very moment of ignition and thus took heavy lateral damage. He still calls himself Eightball. Behind his back though, they call him Brother Beef Jerky.

Marty Conlan peered over my shoulder at the photo. "Maybe if you hadn't all just seemed to be having such a hell of a good time," he mused.

"People who find themselves suddenly on fire tend to be somewhat elated when the fire goes out," I countered.

"Or if *you* hadn't been the one holding the dildo."

"I don't know where it came from, either, man. It was just floating there in the water. I thought it was an arm or something. I just instinctively picked it up. It must have been part of the ensemble."

Resigned, he flopped back into his chair. After a moment he asked, "You know who's in sixteen hundred? That's the Edwardian Suite, you know."

I decided to give him a break. "As a matter of fact, I don't, Marty." I told him how the message on my machine had merely requested my presence at ten A.M. on Sunday morning. It had assured me of a day's pay, no matter what. Said I'd have to check in at the desk, because there was no elevator button for the private floors. A special security key was required.

"Sir Geoffrey Miles," he said.

"A sir, you say? You mean like nobility?"

"I do."

"Where do I know that name from?" I asked.

"Food. He's famous in food."

Yeah, that was right, food. Sir Geoffrey Miles. The world's foremost authority on food. The Guru of Gourmands. The Bagwan of Bouillabaisse. The Ayatollah of Gorgonzola. Dude.

"In town for the big food convention?" I asked.

"Nice to see you still read the papers."

"An informed citizenry is the backbone of a free society," I said.

His nostrils suddenly flared in a manner usually reserved for sniffing long-forgotten Tupperware containers.

"They're all here," he said. "At least all the muckety-mucks. We palmed a few lesser luminaries off on the Sorrento, and the hired help is camped out down at the Sheraton, but everybody who's anybody is here."

According to the *Times*, for the next five days the best and brightest of the world food community would be holding their annual confab in beautiful downtown Seattle. The article had gone on to note that it was only following prolonged political wrangling at the highest levels that Le Cuisine Internationale had ever so reluctantly consented to the Seattle venue. Never before had the event been held outside Europe. A number of aquiline noses were seriously bent.

Marty wasn't through. "I figured, you know, these were classy people. Robin Leach. *Lifestyles of the Rich and Famous* and all that, and, you know, it's a holiday weekend, so I figured we could get by with a skeleton crew . . ." He shook his head sadly.

"No, huh?" I prodded.

"Biggest bunch of assholes I've ever encountered," he said. "Bar none. No lo contendo," he enunciated carefully.

"How come?"

"Everybody hates everybody else. These people got grudges going back thirty years. I don't watch my ass, I'm gonna have an ethnic cleansing right here on the premises. The service staff is pulling its hair out. These people complain about everything. Nothing is good enough for any of them. They fax room service ten-page instructions on how they want their lunch prepared and then send the sucker back, anyway. I've got royalty on sixteen. I've got armed camps hunkered down on fourteen. I've got—"

I interrupted his litany. "Wadda you want from me, Marty?"

He was ready. "You know, your old man and I—"

"Stop the bus," I said quickly. "Don't take me there. Just tell me what you want. I've gotta go."

My father had parlayed an early career as a labor organizer into eleven terms on the Seattle City Council. Four times he narrowly missed being elected mayor. The good people of Seattle had instinctively known that Wild Bill Waterman was not the kind of guy to be left running the store. It was bad enough that nearly every city department was headed by somebody named Waterman. As several opponents had suggested, both Wild Bill's sense of humor and his inclination for nepotism were simply too advanced for any office with wide discretionary powers. From what I hear, he knew everyone, and everyone knew him.

Everyone but me. I was left with an uncomfortable composite of myth and remembrance upon which, at times like this, nearly anyone who had so much as passed him on the street could be expected to attempt to trade.

Marty Conlan nodded his head at me and laced his fingers together. "Yeah . . . I suppose you must get sick of that shit, huh?"

"I've gotta go," I said, turning. Ten-oh-seven.

"So, Leo . . . you'll keep me informed, huh? I've got enough troubles already without trust-fund private eyes roamin' about the hallowed halls, stirring up trouble."

"What's that supposed to mean?"

"Don't get me wrong, Leo. You've always been straight with me. Far as I know, you've always been straight with everybody. I'm not saying you're not a stand-up guy. I'm just saying that if I had my drothers, I'd rather be dealing with somebody who needed the money. That's something I can relate to. You understand what I'm saying?"

What he was saying was that he, like nearly everybody else in town, was aware that my old man had left the family fortune in trust. Whatever his other failings, the old boy was a hell of a judge of character. He'd always sensed in me something less than a firm commitment to the Puritan work ethic and had wisely arranged to protect me from my own worst urges. The result was a trust fund of truly draconian complexity. For over twenty years, the trust had repelled all attempts to break it. A succession of greedy relatives, annoyed creditors and one remarkably resolute ex-wife had squandered bales of cash, only to be left on the outside looking in.

"What the fuck does that have to do with anything?"

"Hey, hey," Marty said. "Don't get upset. I didn't mean anything. It's just that you tend to act unilaterally."

"Unilaterally? I act unilaterally?"

"You're just not a good team player, Leo."

"Exactly what team would that be, Marty?"

Conlon ignored the question. "Just keep me informed. Okay, Leo? No surprises. I've got all I can handle. Okay?"

"I'll do the best I can," I lied.

He stood, placing his hands flat on the desk in front of him.

"I best get downstairs and see about Lance."

Visit **www.panmacmillan.com** to read more about all our books and to buy them. You will also find features, author interviews and news of any author events, and you can sign up for e-newsletters so that you're always first to hear about our new releases.

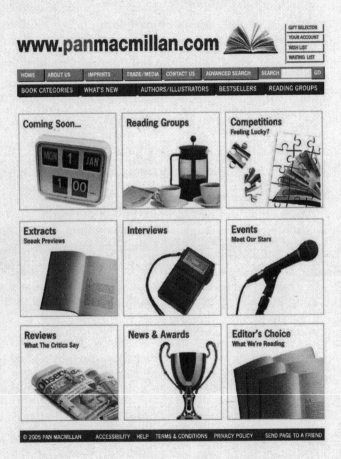

SEP 2 0 2011